All dreamworlds possess a conviction of their own reality...

PORT MANTLE!
A WORLD THAT IS NOTHING BUT MAGIC!

GOLEM CREEK!
A TANGENTIAL TANTRUM OF DREAM-SORCERY!

LABAN BLACK'S "PLACE OF SOLACE"
FOR HE, ONE OF VERY FEW, DISCOVERED THE SECRET, AND
ENLISTED THE GENIUS OF SHAXPLAY & CO. TO CREATE THE
PIPELINE THAT FILTERED THE MISTY MAGIC, TRAPPED & MOLDED
TO HIS EXHAUSTING & INEXHAUSTIBLE ENDS...

AND YOUR WORLD, DEAR READER,
THE LEAVINGS OF A GREAT FEAST, SCRAPS THROWN TO THE
DOGS OF REASON, WHERE MAGIC & JOY ARE MEMORIES, EVEN
WHEN THEY'RE HAPPENING RIGHT
NOW...

ALL AWAKENINGS ARE
FALSE AWAKENINGS...

Morpheus Unbound
or
Zod-Manas Zi-Ba

Morpheus Unbound

or

Zod-Manas Zi-Ba

The Means of Escape
Book Three

Damian Stephens

FOURTH MANSIONS PRESS
Charlottesville, Virginia

Morpheus Unbound
or
Zoo-Manas Zi-Ba

The Means of Escape
Book Three

Tower of Koth Spellbooks
A Division of
Fourth Mansions Press, LLC

Charlottesville, Virginia

fourthmansions.com

ISBN: 978-0-578-92128-0

Cover art © 2021 Chris Claxton

Cover layout & design by Kermit Mulkins

Interior layout & design by Fourth Mansions Press, LLC

Public Domain Materials
P. vi: Basilius Valentinus, *Ein kurtz summarischer Tractat, von dem grossen Stein der Uralten* (Johann Thölde, 1599); V. Clavis
Pp. viii, x, 16, 18, 44, 90, 162, 206, 232: Michael Maierus, *Atalanta Fugiens, hoc est, Emblemata Nova de Secretis Naturæ Chymica, &c.* (Johann Theodor de Bry, 1617); Emblemæ xiv, xxxix, xxxvi, xxi, xlv, xxvii, xli, xliv, l
(All images courtesy of Wikimedia Commons.)
P. 2: Fulcanelli, *Le Mystère des Cathédrales* (Paris: Jean Schemit, 1926)
P. 153: Nashe quotes C. Marlowe, *Doctor Faustus* (John Wright, 1616), 7.14;
Wm. Shakespeare, *King Lear* (Jaggard & Blount, 1623), 4.1.37
P. 239: विवेकचूडामणि (श्लोक ३९९)

Once again, for my friends, whose help
in these endeavors has been much appreciated:

Charles Steuart Estes
(1977-2018)

and

Scarlett DeStefano
(2000-2018)

ཡིད་བཞིན་ནོར་བུ

The author wishes to extend
very special thanks to

Kermit Mulkins

a great friend & ally
without whom this book would
truly "not not not" exist.

CONTENTS

∴

∴

As flies to wanton boys are we to the gods,
They kill us for their sport.

— *King Lear*, 4.1.37–38

...ἄσέ με δαίμονος αἶσα κακὴ καὶ
ἀθέσφατος οἶνος.

— *Odyssey*, XI.61

Someone get me a fucking beer.

— The Queen of Faery

PROLOGUE

V.I.T.R.I.O.L.

La Nature n'ouvre pas à tous, indistinctement,
la porte du sanctuaire.
Dans ces pages, le profane découvrira peut-être quelque
preuve d'une science véritable et positive.
Nous ne saurions nous flatter cependant de le convertir,
car nous n'ignorons pas combien les préjugés sont tenaces,
combien est grande la force des préventions...

— Fulcanelli, *Le Mystère des Cathédrales*

GIVEN THE UTTERLY ILLUSORY nature of these words and this page, the fake atmosphere you breathe, the arrogant assumption of your lungs, heart, digestive system, and, specifically, your nervous system and brain, with whose ghostly frontal lobes you presume to read and process these false words, I may not need to tell you what happened next.

But I'm taking responsibility for things these days, so, fuck it, here's the story.

AFTER I KILLED WRYNECK, chainsawed that motherfucker right back to the goddamned hell we'd both escaped, I went to class as usual.

Suzie Kearns had brought donuts.

"To obtain power," Professor Brainerds spake like Zarathustra, in that emphatic German accent I felt pretty sure he was faking, "we must learn to control thought." He took a bite of his Krispy Kreme and grinned.

The majority of us were engaged in the typical classroom and office duplicity of attempting to make it look like we were still on our first donut while making plans for stealing a fourth. I, of course, had no intention of getting stuck here just yet, so I hadn't eaten a thing. I don't know how many people were paying attention. I was only half there myself.

After chewing thoughtfully for a moment, Professor Brainerds took a sip from his double espresso. He stood up from his usual seat at the head of the great heavy wooden table we all sat around and began to pace the room, his glazed donut forgotten on a green and white napkin.

"Our reality is a play, a ploy, a manipulation," he continued, turning toward the windows lining one wall of the room. A thunderstorm threatened outside in the evening dimness. "A heaven of hell, or a hell of heaven, as they say. But most people still take that the wrong way! They act like it's someone *else's* decision."

Spaulding Katz, the tall, extremely unhealthy-looking dude who sat nearest the door and left class at least three times an hour for some ungodly purpose, suddenly decided to engage Professor Brainerds's typically digressive monologue.

"Who else's decision would it be?" he asked.

"Precisely!" Professor Brainerds ejaculated (I'm sorry to use the term, but that's basically a perfect description of his manner). "Precisely!" He spun away from the window and aimed an accusatory, long-nailed finger at Spaulding's heart. "Who else's decision? Is it mine own? Is it thine? Is it one of theirs?" With each pronouncement, his hand waved in the directions indicated, the last that of the windows and the late evening darkness beyond. He then quoted the Player King from *Hamlet*: "Our wills and fates do so contrary run, that our devices still are overthrown. Our thoughts are ours, their ends none of our own."

I hated night school. But it was the easiest jaunt for getting that poor guy out of harm's way—was his name *Merlin*? Merlin Tuttle...I was already forgetting. Not that I hadn't done this before: drag the bad through the nearest exit if it was still alive enough to follow. Anyway, Mr. Tuttle was safe—at least temporarily. Probably suffer from PTSD for the rest of his life, but he'd make his deadline (to use a poor choice of words).

"We have heard the contention that magical power may be obtained by learning to control thought," the professor tried to elaborate, shoving his hands into the pockets of his wrinkled khakis and strolling back over to the windows. I didn't know if I was the only one wondering what any of this had to do with the axioms of quantum mechanics, but I kept my mouth shut. "And keep in mind that *all* power is magical power. This whole show is just a trick. An illusion—the magician practicing in front of a mirror. A—"

He stopped speaking abruptly. The room fell silent, save for the horrifying reality of other people chewing.

Professor Brainerds appeared to be squinting at the window. He rubbed his stubbled chin with one hand, patted his cheeks, and combed both hands through his mane of unkempt, thinning white hair.

Then, quite explicitly, he stared at me by way of my reflection in one of the windowpanes. I had finally given in—I'd been reaching for the second-to-last donut, and by the bloody taint to its glaze, I assumed it was a raspberry filling. I managed to curb my ardor for it just long enough to notice Professor Brainerds staring at me—just long enough to see it snatched away by the undeserving hand of Suzie Goddamned Kearns, who grinned at me impishly.

So much the better. I didn't know how long I'd be staying.

"Class—dismissed," Professor Brainerds announced abruptly. Everyone sat there, momentarily stunned, and glanced at the clock, which clearly indicated a good forty-five minutes remaining.

"Didn't you hear me? I said *class dismissed*. Get the hell out of my sight!" And with that, and an attempted flourish of his corduroy jacket, he fled the room, leaving us all pleased and confused and unwittingly at the beginning of the end of our story.

VON NEUMANN AND WIGNER—WHOM we were *supposed* to have been studying that night—seemed to have gotten it mostly right. I say "mostly" because, hell, if they *are* right, then all the rest of the interpretations come with the territory: "collapse the wave function" of your favorite theory...if you can show me a concept that isn't dependent on some kind of nervous system with percepts, I'll give you a dollar.

Look closely: you'll notice that there exists a weird sort of interdependence between what seems outside and what seems inside. Go either direction far enough and you'll find exactly the same thing—what the Buddhists call "Clear Light."

It's basically "what's happening now." And how you

perceive "Clear Light" simply tells you what's going on "in your head" (and there's only one outright, but essential, lie in that statement). It's a perfect system—perfectly balanced, always ready for action, and never without a quick, witty response.

So I found myself "falling," as it were, into that weirdly wonderful Clear Light after heading back home and deciding that I would lie down flat on the floor for a while and see what happened.

After attempting unsuccessfully to astral project for half an hour or so, I ended up falling asleep.

I awoke abruptly—four in the morning, according to the glaring green light of my digital clock.

Early Saturday.

I stretched and managed to achieve a sitting position. Remembering that I had forgotten to check the mail, I further managed to defy gravity and actually stand up.

Outside, the thunderstorm that threatened earlier had given way to a light pattering of cool rain. It woke me up enough that, by the time I made it to the mailboxes at the end of my row of apartments, I felt the pangs of hunger urging me to take the risk and just *eat something.*

I opened my mailbox, number 1132. Beneath a Publisher's Clearing House notice informing me that I had just won ten million dollars was the little key to one of the package repositories beside the mailboxes. I retrieved it, tossed the ten million dollar prize in a trash can, and slipped the key into the repository box door, where it caught and held.

A substantial rectangular package sat neatly bundled in brown wrapping paper in the center of the cold, gray, aluminum cave.

I withdrew the package and discerned in the dim light of the parking lot a goblin-like scrawl:

OPEN AT ONCE!

An indescribably urgent voice in my head uttered the words written on the package.

"Hm," I said aloud. "Open at once." Hm.

When I got back to the apartment, I made my executive decision, foolish or not. I set the box on my kitchen counter and decided to fry up a few Steak-Umms before following the instructions. If whomever-it-was that had sent this knew me at all, they knew damned well that the quickest way to delay me was to try to pressure me into doing something "at once."

Besides, who has ownership of the notion of "once"? I could argue that fairy tales are timeless, eternal, certainly not urgent, and yet they all begin with the word "once."

I laid out two white bread sub rolls on a cutting board and sliced them laterally with a semi-dull bread knife. An unnecessary tablespoon or two of butter went into the frying pan, then the thin, frozen, comic-book-sized boards of deeply processed "steak," four of them, broken into handfuls of little squares. The scent was invigorating. Spices went in—salt, pepper...oh, what the hell, basil, oregano, whatever-the-hell-this-is...

I turned off the heat on the burner. A thick layer of mayonnaise went onto each half of each roll, then a few slices of sharp cheddar, then the Steak-Umms, first scooped out of the pan onto the cheese...then the remaining oils and fats poured over the ensemble...

And the crown of it all, a heavy dose of shredded parmesan rained down upon the feast.

The halves were re-constituted. I rinsed the pan and carried my feast over to a rickety wooden table that served as my desk. It sat immediately before the largest window of my third-story apartment, and overlooked the rain-streaked campus, making me feel like a king or lord of sorts...as long as I never left my room.

The Steak-Umms, once consumed, were longed-for. I gazed at my empty plate and prayed for them to return, new and exquisite and once again ready to eat, but they had already bound me—enough to make sense of things, at least—to the laws of this world.

My consolation prize was the box. There was no address,

neither one for return nor delivery. Just those words:

OPEN AT ONCE!

I washed my plate, rinsed my hands, and proceeded to place the unassuming arrival in the center of my desk. I ran my hands along the tight seams of wrapping paper, estimating the total size of the object to be around twelve by eight by fourteen inches. I lifted it—perhaps ten pounds? What came in a box with that size and weight? What would be in a box like that which must be "opened at once"?

One of the ways to find out involved opening the sonofa-bitch, which I finally did.

Brand-new, in the original plastic wrapping, a little white price sticker adhering to the upper-right-hand corner (bearing the miniscule word "LAMB'S" and the symbols "$49.95"), was a rather intricate-looking boardgame.

MORPHEUS UNBOUND
A Golem Creek Mystery!

The words were seared into an expensive canvas finish which bore the image of some sort of magical ritual being performed in the midst of a graveyard. A full moon hung in the sky beyond the game's title; three figures stood around a grave out of which a fearful, monstrous hand emerged...

I turned the box over.

YOU HAVE BEEN INITIATED!
Their world is in danger!
And only YOU can save them!

Will you:
...find solace at the Emporium of Dreams?
...find love in the arms of the Faery Queen?
...merge forces with the God of Laughter?
...dream again, or perhaps ever after?

LEARN SORCERY at the FAMED
THREE COILS ACADEMY
(humans temporarily allowed access)

FIND THAT ULTIMATE GIFT
at
STEVE'S "ENDLESS" ANNEX
in
PORT MANTLE SHOPPING MALL

Or simply wander and wonder and watch it all unfold...

I have to admit that, as of this point, I was intrigued.

What was it about this game that made me feel like I was right on the verge of something—that I was "almosting it"...?

Given that I didn't really have any friends here, I was further intrigued by the notion that, perhaps, the item had been delivered to me by mistake—

—but certainly that couldn't be it...

WAIT A MINUTE, HERE.

Hadn't I heard of this game? It was actually something of a big deal—at least, it had some kind of "cult" status, like maybe an Ed Wood movie or those ridiculous Garbage Pail Kid trading cards. *Morpheus Unbound*. It was an underground thing—and I felt pretty sure I'd seen some kids playing it over by Wizard's Den, across the street from the math and science building...hadn't I? I shouldn't have eaten. I knew it would make some of this much more difficult.

So. Probably a mistake, being delivered to me. And whomever had delivered it would probably wonder what the hell had happened to it.

Certainly a mistake.

But not my goddamned mistake.

I tore off the plastic wrap and opened up the box.

A light, pleasant scent of new cardboard and factory-fresh plastic wafted out from beneath the modest vacuum made by the box top with the bottom. A small booklet of multi-columned pages printed in a neat, tiny font sat atop a dark sheet of cardboard which further hid the contents.

WELCOME, INTREPID PLAYER! The storms of life have tossed you to our shore, and BELIEVE ME, we'll take GOOD care of you here! This is the latest edition of the "Golem Creek Mystery" series—and the present module, MORPHEUS UNBOUND, aims to deliver!

Okay. Not the most engaging introduction ever, but certainly weird enough to be mildly encouraging.

I. Setting. Golem Creek. The town of Golem Creek is, unbeknownst to its inhabitants, a mere "cork" on the realms of Chaos from whence all supposedly "real" things derive. It has all the amenities of your typical mostly isolated, but still reasonably sized, town. And it's all thanks to the Wizard Laban Black, who lies, dead but dreaming, safely abed and tucked away in the (aptly named) Black Pyramid below/within/coterminous with Golem Creek above and various other Worlds both Above and Below.

II. Your Mission. If you've come across this game at all, it's probably because every other attempt we've made to wake you up has failed. Remember (to take just one example) Margaret Lyonne? Yeah, you screwed that one up BIG TIME, and talk about being SLAPPED with the solution—sorry, carried away there. I still enjoy handing people's asses back to them, occasionally, when they've royally screwed themselves.

Anyway, as I was saying, your MISSION, or at least the first part of it, which started when you cracked open this box, is to find the third volume of the Means of Escape trilogy—a Grimoire of a Dark Doctrine, encoded in the Phildickian manner of a "trash-bag sermon," which holds the Key (not exactly the Silver one, just yet, but we'll get there soon enough) to your personal salvation.

The title of the book is *Morpheus Unbound; Or, Zod-Manas Zi-Ba* and it will lead you partway to the Tower of Koth.

Perhaps it is not too late...

I'd wish you good luck, but I gave away all my functional wishes. Damn. Typical!

What did it all mean? How was I to proceed?

And why did I actually seem to recall someone named "Margaret Lyonne"?

It seemed logical to continue my investigation by digging further into the contents of the box.

Beneath the black cardboard insert was a treasury of mysterious artifacts, dice, lead figurines, plastic chips of various colors with peculiar symbols engraved upon them, and, of course, a heavy, folded gameboard depicting the sprawling vicinity of Golem Creek & Environs.

The unexpected part came when I had emptied the box of its contents, revealing a locked base, fully a quarter of the box's width, and completely (I tried) inaccessible by any means other than the obvious: fitting a key into a hole labeled "Insert Silver Key Here."

A brief dizzy spell followed this discovery. The room spun inexplicably. I had to take a moment to clear my head.

I frowned and laid out the gameboard, which seemed somehow much larger upon unfolding than appeared possible from the rather modest dimensions of the box, taking up much of my bedroom floor.

"Golem Creek and Environs," I read aloud from the legend in the lower right-hand corner. "Proceed with caution."

Every attempt I made to take in the board as a whole seemed to fail. I was reminded of the first time I'd taken mushrooms—several dried grams, far too much for a novice, but somehow exactly the right amount once I'd resigned myself to my fate. I remembered gazing at the patterns on my bedroom ceiling after turning off the light—topographical aggregates appeared, incomprehensibly vast albeit contained in small patches of reflected light from streetlamps burning outside my window. This sensation was quite similar; the board seemed deep, as if I could insert my hand into it, take hold of one of the tree branches wrapping around the thin lines that indicated roads and barriers and dirt trails snaking around and about and within it...

I pulled myself away from the gameboard, reeling, almost sick.

I turned my attention back to the instructions.

Test your mettle against the World At Large. How many overlapping worlds are there? You may never know...until you KNOW. Roll the Alphabet Die and the Green Percentile Die; choose a card from the Deck of Tricks; proceed with caution.

After a bit of scrounging in a velvet bag filled with various dice and, strangely, four oxidized pennies ("time-loop tokens"), I found what must have been the two indicated dice. I proceeded to roll them after unwrapping the deck of cards labeled "Tricks."

K-32.

What do I...oh. *On the map, find the intersection indicated.* K...32. I tried to focus on the intricate web that suddenly appeared in that spot; it was as if the gameboard had suddenly taken on a life of its own, had responded to my interaction with it—the square was nearly as complicated and intricate as the board in its entirety.

I pulled a card at random from the Deck of Tricks.

This is your LIBRARY CARD! Be sure to keep this on your person while searching the stacks!

A comic-bookish image of a young man—disturbingly sharing many of my features—was portrayed above the words. He stood among stacks of library books, and held open a large tome out of which (rather predictably) a mysterious light shone, illuminating his astonished gaze.

I shoved the card in my front shirt pocket and looked back at the gameboard. I could swear that K-32 seemed to glow, somehow separating it from the remainder of the sprawling, living board.

Figuring I would pour myself a drink before continuing,

I stood up—too quickly, it seems, as I collapsed to the floor and awoke moments later to a dramatic cracking, thunderous blast that shook the walls. A mild sense of panic ensued as the echoes of it died off.

After checking myself for bruises, I began to laugh—hysterically, in fact, thinking how much I would've paid to see that happen to someone else.

In my front pocket was the library card, and I suddenly had a humorous thought in the midst of my laughter.

Go to the library, perhaps, and look for the book *for real*?

The library was open twenty-four hours—why the hell not? Add a paragraph to my memoirs, at least. Maybe see if anyone had ever returned the last Isaac Asthma robot book?

I FORGOT, OF COURSE, to take an umbrella with me, and barely made it into the front lobby of the many-storied library building a block away from my apartment before the light drizzle of rain outside became a frantic downpour.

One nerdy girl sat behind the checkout desk, completely immersed in a thousand-page epic fantasy novel. The place seemed, otherwise, mostly empty—a few students here and there, most of whom quickly vanished as I descended the wooden stairs at the back of the lobby, down to the first sub-level.

Other than the steady patter of rain from the level above, the place quickly wrapped me in a muffled silence.

Where was I going?

I decided to simply walk, deeper into the stacks, farther from the civilization above.

I reached the next set of stairs leading to the second sub-level and descended into a silence marred only by the occasional whirring of some dehumidifier hidden among the hoards of books.

The lighting had dimmed and become yellowish, creepy. The shelves of books, as I proceeded even deeper, reverted from the cool aluminum of the superior levels to a strangely animal and wild wood held together by thick iron bolts. The books themselves sat in heaps upon them, old leather tomes with indiscernible scripts on their spines.

I grabbed one of them and pulled it off the shelf. *A Fantastic Assortment of Witches' Ointments, Autumn Catalogue '85*. Flipping through the pages demonstrated it was exactly that—various perfumes and unctions and potions that claimed startling powers of transformation and elicitation of supernatural phenomena...with a fold-out order form still stuck in its several hundred pages of mind-boggling magic.

I chuckled to myself, placing the book gently back on the shelf, vowing to remember its location and make use of the order form, if only for a laugh, after I'd finished this weird diversion.

I nearly bumped into a dramatically large bureau of little shelves a few moments later.

A card catalog.

It took me a few moments to deduce why this might be important. It was, in fact, only after I began flipping through the neatly printed cards on their brass hinges that I recalled the title of the book I was supposed to find.

Morpheus Unbound; Or, Zod-Manas Zi-Ba.

Okay. Title cards. Check.

Flip, flip. Lamas of Lêng, The—*flip*...Maat's Menagerie—*flip*...Morpheus Unbound—

In my excitement, I nearly tore the card out of the drawer.

MORPHEUS UNBOUND; OR, ZOD-MANAS ZI-BA.

Stephens, Damian.
    Morpheus unbound; or, zod-manas zi-ba; being an account of the mechanics of luck and how to wake up in no time. (The Means of Escape Series #3) Tower of Koth, 2021.

This was it! Over in the PS section...well, that would be upstairs, wouldn't it?

A soft thumping sound startled me. It seemed to be coming from the far corner of the room.

Quickly, I jotted down the book's catalog number on my hand and slid the card catalog drawer back in, then walked swiftly to the end of the aisle and peered in the direction the noise had come from.

There was a door at the end of the hall marked EXIT.

Now, where precisely that door exited *to* was indeed a mystery, as I must have been about forty or fifty feet underground by this point. But on this particular late night/early morning, in these particular circumstances, with a nagging sense that I had just done something indescribably awful—

—*did you kill it? Chainsawed right through the motherfucker! Oh, that other guy? Traumatized, but he'll live. Speaking of which*—

—I jogged over to the door and (noting first that it was not a fire exit) attempted to open it.

Locked.

To the left of the door, I noticed a thick binder with a pen hanging from it seated heavily on a wooden lectern. I idly flipped it open.

PLEASE PRINT CLEARLY.

These words stood prominently at the head of a long list of scratched and scrawled signatures followed by what appeared to be place names.

I tried the door again. Locked, or stuck.

Briefly, I turned back the way I had come. I imagined some parallel version of myself heading back up a few flights of stairs to see about this *Morpheus Unbound* nonsense...

But the urge was too great. I picked up the pen and wrote down, as clearly as I could, the words GOLEM CREEK immediately under what appeared to be something written in stylized Coptic.

When I signed my name, something strange happened, and I suddenly knew what had been going on since the moment I'd "woken up" this morning and had that super-weird class with Professor Brainerds—

Aha!

An audible click sounded, and I proceeded through the door. It all looked so normal, I burst into laughter despite myself—

I.

SCIRE

Tulsa, Oklahoma: 30 April 1987

ONE OF THEM FELT low or alone that night; everyone had smoked enough weed to choke a steam engine. And it smelled like pizza.

It always smelled like pizza here.

Someone had tuned in the new *Twilight Zone* series on the little TV set up in the corner. Booker Reuchlin sat crosslegged on one of the round tables in the middle of the restaurant and gazed up at it. It was the episode where a woman digs up a stopwatch while she's gardening, and it turns out that the damned thing can stop and start *time itself* whenever she tells it to...

"This is fucking brilliant," Barton said. He was seated in one of the chairs to Booker's right. The Pizza Joint—whose logo was a pizza pie, rolled up and evidently being smoked by a cartoon rat—was as empty as a six-pack before an A.A. meeting. This was not unusual, given the Pizza Joint's location on a desolate strip of two-lane blacktop on 71st Street near Broken Arrow, nor was it uncharacteristic of a Thursday night at two in the morning. Despite the neon sign outside flashing "OPEN LATER THAN YOU THINK!" the four members of the heavy metal band Fukkn Drunk had cashed three bowls in their bassist Staley's magnificent "Bug Bong" (typically reserved for special occasions, but Fitz had forgotten the pinch hitter and Booker's rolling papers had fallen in the tomato sauce) and heated up the ovens for three or four super-deluxe meatlover's pies to bid farewell to the night.

"Barton! *Barton!*" Booker shouted at an unconscionable

volume.

Barton tapped him on the shoulder, his eyes still riveted to the screen. "What's up, dude?"

Booker hopped off the table and engaged in what appeared to be an unnecessarily difficult means of extracting the wallet from his back pocket. "Can we still buy beer?" He tore open the wallet and made a show of finding nothing inside.

"Fuck it," Barton said. "Fitz! Two ice-cold PBRs, goddamn it! Fast!"

Booker started cracking up. "Yeah! Fitz! You fucker! You sonofabitch!"

"Fitz!" Barton shouted, doubling over with laughter. "Fitz! Where the *fuck* are our drinks? Hurry it the fuck *up* you goddamned—"

"What the fuck are you guys—what?" Fitz came running out of the kitchen, wiping his hands on his apron. "What did you say?"

Barton had collapsed to the floor, waving his hands in the air above his red, suffocating face. Booker was gasping for breath, leaning heavily on the wall next to the cash register. On the television, a nuclear missile was paused in its descent to earth behind the protagonist's weeping face.

Fitz stomped off without another word.

"Fitz!" Barton managed to choke out. "What the f—where'djoo—"

Booker collapsed to the floor, writhing in an agony of excess dopamine. An honest concern for his survival had only just broken through the congealed vapor of his thoughts when a thunderous crash accompanied by a tremendous flash of blinding white light rattled the Pizza Joint.

Booker and Barton were both upright seconds later.

"Okay," Barton said, adrenaline forcing the hand of his sobriety. "Okay. What the fuck?"

Booker was shaking his head. "What the fuck was that?"

"Did we break, dude?" Barton said. "Did we just—did I just shatter, or something?"

Fitz shouted incomprehensibly from the back room. "If you *motherfuckers* broke that *goddamned TV* I will cut your *goddamned balls off—"*

"Fitz! Shut your dick!" This from Staley, who had just emerged from the cash office. "What the hell *was* that?"

By the unnatural radiance of the Pizza Joint's neon sign, they watched a car roll up in the otherwise deserted parking lot.

"Aw, hell," Booker said, lamenting the potential customer. "Gimme a break. Now?"

"Just tell 'im we're closed," Fitz said. "I wanna know what the hell that crash was."

A scissor door opened on the grey DeLorean's driver side, and a figure stumbled out.

"Drunk, too," Staley said. "Not surprising. Cool time machine, though."

His bandmates all nodded in agreement as Charles Leland, wide-eyed, glancing left and right reflexively, turned and faced them. He began speaking before even reaching the glass door.

"Guys! Can you help? I'm—"

"Sorry, we're closed," Booker said decisively as he stepped forward and twisted the door's deadbolt. "Come back tomorrow."

"Booker?" Charles said with genuine astonishment. Then, in short order, his face turning to each of the members of the Silent Goblin Gang, he spoke their names: "Barton? Fitz? Staley?"

"Come back *tomorrow,*" Booker repeated emphatically, shaking his head as he turned back to his wide-eyed crew. He jerked a thumb over his shoulder and grimaced. "What the hell is wrong with this guy?"

"Um, maybe we should let him in," Barton said.

"Yeah, I think we should let him in," Fitz seconded.

Staley had stepped past Booker and was unlocking the door. He motioned Charles in.

"What the fuck, dude?" Booker said, astonished.

Staley stuck his head out the door and looked left and right before shutting and locking it.

"Are we cool?" Charles said, to the consternation of the Goblin Gang. He was considering the last time he had seen any of them—effectively trying to kill him and Steve and Julie in Laban Black's Pyramid. None of them seemed particularly vicious at the moment. None of them seemed particularly *sober* at the moment, either, and these types of situations had a tendency to flip dramatically out of Charles's favor with very little warning. "I mean, you guys remember—I mean— well, how the hell did you guys *get* here?" Charles finally stammered out. He found that he was grinning despite himself; he collapsed uninvited into a rickety wooden chair. "I didn't really think that thing would *work*, you know?" He was pointing behind himself, at the DeLorean.

"Ah, dude?" Barton said, raising his eyebrows and patting Charles on the shoulder. "It's okay. Whatever you're on, I mean. You can chill out here for a while. Booker? Grab one for our new friend."

Booker had gone behind the counter and was filling up a plastic cup with Bud Light. He shook his head again and grunted before filling a second cup, which Fitz retrieved and offered to Charles.

"Drink it fast and you won't taste it," he said, chuckling. Charles took the drink and raised it in a silent toast before gratefully guzzling it.

"So—how do you know us, again? Were you at the show?" Barton asked.

Charles belched inadvertently as he tried to speak. "Sorry. What show? C'mon. This is—"

"Oh, shit, I think I know what happened," Staley said, pointing out the window at the DeLorean.

Barton tried to explain. "The show at Cain's last Friday? We opened for—"

"No! Oh. Right. Guys? How the hell do I explain this?" Charles's brow furrowed. "I know you from—goddamn it." He took one pained look out the glass door at the DeLorean before continuing. "I'm from...another time."

The group burst out laughing. Fitz headed back behind the counter to pull the pizzas from the oven. Barton produced a pack of cigarettes, tossed one to Staley, and offered one to Charles, who shook his head.

"Seriously! I don't think I arrived here tonight, at this location, on accident."

Booker chugged a second Bud Light before changing his mind publicly. "Okay! I can dig it. This dude's got some style. He's at least got Doc Brown's car. Let's smoke him out."

Staley suddenly looked up at Barton and stopped laughing. He then made a peculiarly specific gesture: holding his left hand over his mouth and tapping the side of his nose with his index finger a few times. The gesticulation was immediately mimicked by Booker and Barton.

Charles looked around, mystified.

"It's Witches' Night, dudes," Staley finally said as he removed his hand from his mouth.

Barton blew out a lungful of smoke and stubbed out his unfinished cigarette. "Holy shit. You're right."

"Skeezo was telling the truth!" Booker shouted. He ran suddenly to a wall-mounted telephone behind the counter and began punching numbers madly. "Let's hope she answers!"

"Dude," Staley spoke to Charles, his voice suddenly lower and more sober. "What did you say your name was again?"

"I didn't. That's just it," Charles said. "I'm Charles Leland. I'm from a city called—"

"Golem Creek," Barton finished for him. Both Staley and Charles turned to him; he held a crumpled sheet of yellow paper, badly torn from a guest check pad. "You're from a place called Golem Creek."

Charles reached out for the piece of paper. "Can I see that?"

Barton nodded and handed it to him. Charles gazed at the chicken scratch on the grease-stained guest check for a moment. It read: *Golem Creek is where he's from / On Witches' Night his time will come / Fukkn Drunk! The Monster Slayers! / Bodhi-Yeti—Himalayas.*

"It's pretty clear until the last two lines," Charles said.

"Skeezo passes out sometimes before she's got the whole message," Staley explained.

Booker—who had been mumbling incoherently and dialing and re-dialing numbers—slammed the phone into its cradle and tried to mimic an airhorn. "Skeezo's on her way!" he shouted, and raced back to the cash office. "We're gonna need the Bug Bong!"

WITH A DISTINCT AIR of reverence, Staley procured the "Bug Bong"—a two-foot-tall ceramic water bong, partially molded in the shape of a gigantic, seated black beetle, its abdomen doubling as a water chamber. It was decorated with various Egyptian hieroglyphics.

He deposited it on a side table. "For when Skeezo gets here," he said, grinning.

As they waited, Charles had three slices of magnificent, dripping pepperoni pizza while everyone tried to explain everything, including himself.

The year was 1987 and the "Silent Goblin Gang" had yet to become professional monster-hunting capitalist entrepreneurs. At this time they were still trying to make it as an amateur metal band known locally and lovingly as "Fukkn Drunk." They had dropped out of high school ("Union—not Jenks!" Booker assured Charles, who kept his lack of comprehension silent, not knowing why *which* high school one had dropped out of could possibly be relevant) a few years ago to work full time at the Pizza Joint, the latter a venture technically owned by Booker Reuchlin's father (who silently paid the bills from some undisclosed location in the Panhandle).

"So..." Booker filled a final locus of silence with the word. "How do you know who we are, again?"

Charles tried to summarize his circumstances with somewhat fewer digressions than had the fraternal quadruplets comprising "Fukkn Drunk." He helped himself to a cigarette in order to fake nonchalance more convincingly.

"Yes, I'm from a place called Golem Creek," he explained to his rapt audience, who had all taken seats around the table. "And like I said, I think I'm from another time, but I don't know how to be sure of that, because it's—well, it's like a parallel world. A completely different world."

A silence marred only by the sparking of lighters and Fitz's cracking open a PBR followed this statement. *Professional player characters*, Charles thought. *I'm their fucking DM.*

He continued, aware of the responsibility on his shoulders not to lead them astray.

"You guys are there, actually," he said, waving an all-inclusive hand around the room. "You're all there, but you're... older, I guess. Barton's beard is much longer."

Barton grinned and stroked the several inches' worth of growth sprouting from his chin.

"And you guys...hunt monsters. Werewolves, specifically—"

"You've got *werewolves* over there?" Fitz spoke words of awe-struck gladness for the sake of the group. "What about the rest of 'em, you know? Vampires? Zombies? Uh—creatures from the black lagoons?"

Charles shook his head momentarily, then realized he wasn't exactly sure of the answer. "Maybe? I guess. Why not?"

Barton clapped his hands in approval. The sound was accompanied by homogeneous verbal acknowledgment of the correctness of it all, with several rounds of miniature discussions set off and numerous rapid-fire questions directed randomly at the atmosphere and at Charles.

"Do you have to fight your way to school every morning? Through demon-hordes, you know?" Booker asked.

Fitz tried to break in. "What about, you know—whaddaya call 'em? Those chicks who are all hot and demonic and try to make out with you—"

"Guys! Seriously. Not that I know of—maybe *you* will know, once we get back. Anyway, I stole that DeLorean out there—" Barely suppressed laughter erupted all around. "Well, you know, I didn't exactly *steal* it. You know."

"You just borrowed it," Staley said. "Of course. Go on."

Charles stubbed out his cigarette and immediately lit another. He decided not to tell them that he'd "wished" for a time machine, unaware when he had done so that he actually *had* an unused wish available, granted to him from Roland's "djinn" form back in the Place of Solace. The keys that had ended up in his pocket had unlocked the car and started it but, alas... "Right. I borrowed it. Anyway, I just wanted to try it out, you know, so I got in and all of a sudden, the doors lock, the engine revs up, and I'm trying to turn the damned thing off. I look up, and it's—"

"Doc Brown with a remote control," Booker said. "Like in the movie."

"Damn it, *yes*! But it's not Doc Brown. It's some other guy that's dressed up like him—er, looks like him, a little, anyway. And he smiles at me, waves, and off the car goes. Like he knew I was going to get in it, because I liked the movie. But more like—like it was a trap."

Charles paused in his re-telling of the events from—well, technically, from earlier in the evening.

"You were meant to arrive here, at this time," Staley said confidently. "Skeezo knew it was going to happen."

"I meant to ask," Charles said, "who the hell is *Skeezo*?"

Laughter, again, from the group.

"Skeezo's an atomic bomb, dude—she'll blast your head," Fitz said.

General nods of agreement went around the room.

Charles had to ask. "Her name's *Skeezo*? Seriously?"

"Nah, nah," Booker said. "That's just what we've called her since Fitz got majordomo wasted on 'shrooms one night and kept fucking up her name."

Fitz nodded in confirmation.

"And she's dangerous? An atomic bomb?" Charles continued.

"Don't worry! She'll do you right," Booker explained. "Count on it."

"But you've gotta be honest with her," Barton said.

"And pay the sacrifice fee," Staley continued, gesturing to the Bug Bong.

"Or else she'll put one of her curses on you and you're basically fucked," Booker finished.

Charles found only a groan within his repertoire of responses at the moment. "Can I get one of those beers?" he asked, and one was in his face almost before he finished the question.

"An ice-cold PBR to wash down all our bullshit, right?"

Booker said, laughing as usual.

CHARLES DECIDED TO KEEP back any discussion of Roland and the Place of Solace for the time being. *Speak only the minimum necessary to get your bearings and figure out why the hell you ended up* here, *of all places. There's no reason to trust these guys—just because they're familiar faces doesn't mean they didn't, or rather don't, try to kill you later on. Which they did—or will. Whatever.*

The four metalheads began a badinage of jokes at that point, which left Charles free to finish his beer in peace until a bell chimed from somewhere in the back of the Pizza Joint.

Fukkn Drunk fell collectively quiet.

"She's here!" Booker whispered loudly. He shot out of his chair and almost slipped on his way to the back door.

"Is there something I'm supposed to do?" Charles said to the rest of them. They were all grinning quietly. Charles found himself getting very explicably nervous.

Barton shook his head. "I have no idea. Skeezo will tell us."

"Maybe I don't want to do what she says?" Charles said, his agitation surfacing in an obviously false confidence.

"Just keep cool, man," Staley said. "Don't you wanna know what the witch knows?"

"Gentlemen?" Booker announced as he headed back to the main dining area. Everyone except Charles stood in reverence. "May I present our patroness, the lovely, the exquisite, Her Majesty—*Our Silver Key.*"

Charles's jaw dropped for two reasons. Not only was Fitz's variant of Her name—Skeezo ↔ Silver Key—unacceptably vague, having improperly prepared him for the revelation that Michael Flowers's all-important "key" could be *a person,* and not a damned key (at least, it was a person *here,* if not in all worlds). But perhaps more astonishing than that was the incredible resemblance—nay, the *downright physical identity,* of "Her Majesty" with Charles's oldest and most reliable crush in all the world.

"*Molly?*" Charles said in amazement as she stepped into the room.

AND YET—AND YET—

It was a Molly he could hardly imagine. A not-so-subtle glint of madness in those same, saucery lavender eyes. The cascades of curly hair were roughly the same, if not as regularly brushed, but there seemed to be a *hard edge* to her, as if she'd been scissored out of a magazine and somehow taped to the environment. In a way, the world seemed to move *around* her—and in that sense, Charles supposed, she was still Queen Furnival of Faery.

The tattoos were a nice aspect of her revisioning. He had at first thought that the flower petals around her left eye were inked on, but on stepping into the light of the dining area, hazy with smoke, he saw that it was an extraordinary birthmark. He hadn't known how much he liked tattoos until he saw the blackletter outline of *FUCK YOU* inscribed touchingly on a scroll wrapped about a heart ornamenting her left shoulder, beneath the wragged hem of a sleeveless Suicidal Tendencies T-shirt. Add in the skintight, grey jeans, more tears than denim, and the leather cowgirl boots with—by all Olympus!—*spurs* sticking out the back, and you had this new, improved Molly Furnival, ready to switchblade her way past your ribcage and into your dreams.

"It's Silverki," she pronounced with a slight alteration in emphasis. "Marigold Silverki." She pointed at Charles with one sharp, black-nailed finger and beckoned for a cigarette from Barton, who was quick to comply. "This is the guy?" she said simply as Barton lit her cigarette.

Staley dragged a rolled-up sandwich bag out of his pocket and shuffled over to load the Bug Bong. "We think so. He showed up in *that*"—he indicated the DeLorean parked out front with a nod—"and after what you told us—"

"Marigold Silverki" waved him to silence and took a deep drag off her cigarette. She exhaled slowly and stepped closer to Charles.

"You're..." She trailed off and stretched out her hand. A strange symbol appeared in the middle of her palm. Charles swore he could see it glowing.

She touched her hand to his forehead, and Charles awoke moments later, finding himself slumped over on the table.

"What the hell?" he said. The group had gathered around the table with the Bug Bong on it. They gazed in ecstasy at their weird queen as a fragrant, thick smoke flooded from her black-painted lips.

No one was paying any attention to Charles at all. He dragged his seat to within arm's reach of the group. Marigold's eyes were closed, and a softness had come about her features. The overwhelming abundance of pot smoke floating throughout the room had put Charles in something of a daze. He felt like he was dreaming.

"No, no, no," she began to speak, swaying slightly in her seat, eyes shut. It was unclear to whom she was speaking. "You've got it all wrong. Four portals within reach. One behind The Flying Monkey radiating enough magical energy to shift dimensions randomly.* It's another bar in another world, sometimes—CJ's... The portal you passed through when you took your 'Death Test'—the one in the crawl space...under the house on Brake Street... The one you passed through when you descended below the Sigils in the Murk. And the one Tom builds...in the meeting place...before anyone suspected anything at all, the Tripwire Portal, that...explodes?"

Marigold looked suddenly confused.

"A box—supposed to hold a key?" She appeared to be attempting to convey something she didn't understand at all. "And it... Explodes. It...blows you up. No." She paused momentarily, then "clarified." "*Blew* you up. And the others."

Charles stared wide-eyed at her swaying, entranced form, remembering the box in the Bhairavi Society clubhouse that "blew him up" along with Steve and Julie. "She does this every time?" he asked the Goblins. Visions of Pete Jarry becoming oracular from magical Valentine's Day candies suddenly came to mind.

Barton nodded. "She's usually not this coherent," he said. "Last time, she tranced out while staring at the grease stains

---

* The random intervals are determined by a Poisson distribution, usually; note that λ appears to be increasing during the course of this novel's events.

in an empty pizza box. It was like she was reading tea leaves or something."

Fitz assisted Marigold in taking another humongous hit from the Bug Bong.

"Does any of that make sense to you? The stuff she said?" Staley asked. "I mean, we know CJ's, sure, but all that other stuff?"

"Who's 'Tom'?" Booker asked. "And why did he blow you up?"

Fitz made a cutting motion with his hand. "Sh! She's about to start again!"

Marigold spoke, and something about her voice seemed more ghostly this time, echoing about the room. Even the lights seemed to dim.

"Oberon *does not know himself yet.* The Laughing God discovered a girl who could distill the Vinum Sabbati...in her usual spot...at Midsummer." Her fists and eyelids suddenly clenched. "The Vinum Sabbati is the key of all worlds... Yassiz shattered me. Yassiz shattered my consort..."

"It sounds like she's losing it," Staley said. "What did she say? *Lassie* shattered me?"

Marigold paused in her swaying and speaking, then turned and looked into Charles's eyes. He swam in pools of lavender fire...

"Laban's remains are in the Black Pyramid," she spoke clearly. "Those *essential salts* await completion by the misplaced memory threatening to awaken him...*when the Pyramid aligns with the Source of the dream of his life, the Black God returns.*"

"The dream of his life?" Charles repeated.

Marigold placed the palms of her hands on either side of Charles's head. Her hands were warm; the smooth flesh felt charged, tingling against his temples like electricity. A voice suddenly echoed within his mind; her lips had ceased to move. "Wise will tell you about them—the Brains at the End of Time. *It is your brain right now,* and *yours*—you reading this—has dreamed it all into 'being.' The dream of your life... the *basic* dream, no more substantial, no more solid nor seemingly fragmented than any of the fractal variants in your sleeping-dreams... That it *seems this way*, seems somehow 'more real' than emptiness, forms the vicious circle... You will continue to fall for it... *Laban lies dead but dreaming*—the secret of Trismegistus in the reflection of a mirror. *When the mirror shatters, One becomes Many*...the alien spell the High Priest Ech Pi El heard in the vast deeps of outer space, where the darkness that gives rise to form floats in an infinity of dimensionless chaos..."

Her hands retracted from Charles's head. She began gesturing for pen and paper.

"I got it!" Staley shouted, leaping out of his chair. Seconds later, Marigold was scribbling on a pad of blank guest checks.

"What's she writing?" Booker asked, trying to snatch a glimpse of it.

Marigold shook her head. "If that dumbass writing *this* book would just *relax and listen*, I'd be able to convey it to you." She gazed up out of the page at both the reader and the author, briefly, engaging us all in a confluence of worlds, a dream-overlap, before a sequence of images flashed into our minds from Nowhere. Approximately translated, its echo communicated this:

The statistical anomaly or engine that has blipped into existence beyond the end of all notions of prescribed, linear temporality simply computes its "story" from beginning to end in the blink of an eye. The whole story will play out. *But there's a catch:* once anything gets coded, it becomes error-prone. *If you are* aware *of what is happening— really, truly aware of the possibility that* you are dreaming this—*it can lead to an infinite regress*—or egress—*of seemingly independent brains, conceiving and executing novel computations within the context of the original one.*

The lighting, the world around them, returned to normal. Marigold broke the silence.

"Someone get me a fucking beer," she said.

INSTINCTIVELY, EVERYONE LEFT MARIGOLD Silverki to her beer and cigarettes at the Bug Bong table. They huddled together at the other end of the room by an aged cigarette machine and attempted to decipher Marigold's rapid cursive hieroglyphics.

" 'Wise nerds will lead if you don't give a fuck,' " Staley read carefully from the guest check. " 'Yassiz will find you, don't bother to hide. Atalan'—um. Atalanta? I think that's it. Wait, what's this next word?"

Staley laid the guest check down flat on the table. Everyone contemplated the indicated scrawl for a moment.

Booker made the first attempt. "Fuckers?" he said.

"*Fudgers?*" Fitz supplied. "Is that a word?"

"Why don't we ask Marigold?" Charles suggested.

The Goblins made a collective negative grunt.

"Won't help," Staley explained. "She doesn't know what she's writing while she's writing it. It's automatic."

Charles nodded.

"I think—I think it's something like 'Fuggens'?" Barton said. "You know, based on the other letters there. I don't know."

"Okay," Staley continued. " 'Atalanta Fuggens hides some-where inside. Without Damian Stephens you're shit outta luck.' "

A profound silence enveloped the noosphere momentarily.

Barton spoke first. "I'd just like to note the unusual rhyme scheme: A, B, B, A."

"So, let's start simple," Booker said, ignoring him. " 'Wise nerds.' It says 'wise nerds' will lead us. Where do you find 'wise nerds'?"

"That's easy," Staley answered, "a comic book store. Or a game shop. Starbase 21!"

"I'd've said maybe a college?" Charles broke in. "I mean, come on. A college library —maybe on a Friday night?"

"Oh, that's good," Fitz said. "Right. 'Cause those guys literally don't give a fuck. I mean, no chicks'll do it with them. Right?"

"Okay, so we've gotta go to T.U. tomorrow night," Booker said. "Fine. What's next? Who's this Yassiz guy?"

"I don't know," Barton said. "But I guess we don't have to worry about him. It says here that he'll find us whether we hide or not. So."

"Good. Two down," Booker said. "Any suggestions on this 'Fuggens' character? Chuck? Sound familiar?"

Charles shook his head. "Not even a little bit."

"Anybody else? No? Okay, then. Skip it." Booker jabbed a finger at the last line. "Who's 'Damian Stephens'? That's pretty straightforward, right? Wait—hang on."

Booker stood up rapidly and sprinted back behind the counter. "Aha!" he hefted a phone book and cackled. "Let's see where this sonofabitch lives... Hm." His eyes scanned pages as he flipped back and forth through the book.

"Hey, check and see if there's a 'Yassiz' in there, dude," Fitz said.

"Yeah. And look for Mr. Fuggens," Barton chuckled.

Fitz laughed. "I hope we find out that the guy's name is 'Assy Fudgers'! That would be hilarious."

"Dude!" Barton stood up and headed over to the counter. "Let me see that. Look for 'Fudgers.' I just want to prove Fitz right."

Booker and Barton high-fived, laughing loudly.

"Yeah, great," Staley said. "Are *any* of the names in there?"

"There's a 'D. Stephens' listed," Booker announced. "Aw, shit. Oh, well. Too bad for us, I guess."

"Wait, why?" Charles asked.

"No 'Fudgers.' Sorry, Fitz," Booker said, laughing.

Fitz punched the palm of one hand. "Nuts!"

"Anyway, the only guy we get for free is 'D. Stephens.' That's it. Could be a chick, I guess. Unless we're working under the assumption that 'D.' stands for 'Damian.' Probably a guy's name, is all I'm sayin'." Booker slammed the phone book shut.

"So where does he live?" Staley asked.

"Aw, shit. Sorry." Booker re-opened the book and found the name again. " 'Stephens, D.' No address! Sonofabitch. Phone number, though. Wanna give him a call?"

"It's four in the fucking morning, dude!" Staley reminded everyone.

Booker shrugged. "If it's our guy, we've gotta get a hold of him. Doesn't it say we're shit out of luck if we don't have

'Damian Stephens'? If it's Debbie Stephens, or Dolores, or Diana—oh, dude, what if the guy's name is 'Dick' Stephens?" He started laughing again.

Barton slapped the counter, cracking up. "That's why—shit, that's why he just puts the 'D.' in there! In the phone book. Christ!" They high-fived again. "Just call and ask for 'Dick'!"

There is a case to be made for the clouds of psychedelic smoke that still hung about the room being the cause, but Charles, who had finally started loosening up under the air of unperturbed gaiety that seemed the natural starting point of Fukkn Drunk / The Silent Goblin Gang, began laughing uncontrollably.

"First—first. We should probably move your time machine, dude," Barton told Charles. "We've got a garage out back. Fitz!"

"I'm right here, dude," Fitz said from beside him. "What?"

"Gimme the keys to the truck."

Fitz reached into his pocket, extracted a set of keys, and lobbed them over Barton's head. They landed on the faded red-and-white marbled floor tiles and slid against the front door.

"Thanks," Barton said.

"*Yeah* we oughta 'move the time machine'!" Booker shouted. "How could I forget? Let's go! Fuck all this 'Dick Stephens' bullshit! What do you think—1978? Van Halen opens for Sabbath!"

"What's all that stuff she was saying about *portals*?" Staley added. He suddenly looked like he'd just had a dozen cups of coffee. He lit a cigarette with shaky hands.

"Portals," Charles said. "To other worlds. She gave the location of several portals that cross over from here into Golem Creek and back. But I didn't know..." He trailed off, wondering. He *did* know, though—the mysterious letter he'd received in the Place of Solace had indicated it, the letter he found shoved under the door in his motel room the day Steve showed him the leaking magical pipeline...

"Didn't know what?" Booker asked. He had poured

himself another beer. Charles wondered how any of them were still conscious, much less seemingly stoked.

"I didn't know I had gone through one—well, during my initiation," Charles said. "She said there was one in the crawl space under Mike's house."

"Mike?" Fitz asked.

"Michael Flowers, the guy who died and came back to life—" Charles started. He noted the widening of their eyes. "I'll explain later. For now, I'm still trying to put together what she said."

"Dude, Charles is in *charge!*" Booker said. "This is like the greatest night of my fucking life. I don't know what we're waiting for. Okay—so what're we doing first? Sabbath or the fucking *portals?*" He stood up and finished the rest of his beer. "Where are the keys?" he asked, patting his pockets.

"What do you mean? Fitz just—never mind," Barton said, standing up and heading over to the front door. He picked up the keys. "Follow me," he said, beckoning to Charles.

"Wait! Are we going?" Staley said. "Are we going to close up here first? What about calling Dick—I mean Damian?"

"What about Skeezo?" Fitz asked reasonably.

"Yeah, what about..." Booker started. "Huh."

Marigold Silverki was gone.

"Is that unusual?" Charles asked.

Staley shook his head. "Nope. Never actually seen her *show up* here, either. She never comes through the front door." He shrugged his shoulders.

"Dudes! I'm actually thinking we should try '84, you know, the *Kill 'em All* tour..."

Booker's voice faded as Barton and Charles headed out to the parking lot.

Smoke poured out of the restaurant along with them and immediately took a course for the stars overhead, which twinkled energetically, modified by Charles's unintended (but deeply adequate) high. He was getting all too used to being fraught with exhaustion, so *that* part of things wasn't bothering him much.

He took several dramatic breaths of pristine night air.

That "Doc Brown" had time-and-space-shifted him back to Tulsa seemed like something more than a miracle. *He knew I'd find them here...* Charles thought, twinges of paranoia flitting about the edges of the notion. Whatever it was that Marigold—Molly—had just communicated to him made a mess of everything at the same time it took care of his confusion.

The whole story will play out. That was the idea that bothered him, perhaps even more than her aside to the author of "this" story, which at least made a minimum of sense, given what he'd already been through. Why not? Perhaps he could consider himself something like a magician—if words and stories had to be "spelled out," then books were always books of *spellings*, or spells, and that made anyone who read them, who strung them together on a garland of meaning, something of a magician. Imagining made magicians of everyone, in fact. But if a reader was a magician, someone who imagined things "for real," then what was an author?

"I'll get the truck out of the garage. Just head out back down that little alleyway," Barton said.

Charles nodded and took another deep breath—he was *definitely* stoned—as Barton skipped around a corner and out of sight. He was always going to arrive here, whether he believed it or not. There was no free will...*because there was no determinism...* The one assumed a self in control of things, the other assumed a world void of purpose. Both sides of that question's coin were simply justifications invented after the fact of experience, itself a memory, a confabulated thing.

He gazed at his hands in amazement. *Am I a character in a story? Just something dreamed up by someone I'll never know? But then this—all of this—the sky and the earth and the road, the people I remember and the people I'll meet, are all aspects of One Thing...*

But that's not the whole story.

An author...is just another character in the story they've constructed... an author...is a figment of the reader's imagination...

These thoughts were in his mind as he got into the DeLorean, leaned back in the driver's seat, and promptly fell asleep.

CHARLES AWOKE IN PITCH blackness. After a brief moment of perfect disorientation, a wave of stark terror encompassed him.

Did I—where am—Christ almighty, what could've—

Knocking, as on a door, off to his right. He sat up in the dark, feeling something like a mattress beneath him.

"Charles! You decent?"

A modicum of panic subsided as Charles recognized Barton's voice.

"I'm—yeah, I'm fine. Good."

The door opened. Warm yellow light flooded in.

"Jesus, dude. Get enough sleep? You've been out all day," Barton said. "We're just about ready to head out to T.U. and bag us some 'wise nerds.' It's Friday night!"

Charles's eyes adjusted quickly to the light, revealing his whereabouts: a closet-sized room holding merely the cot on which he lay, still clothed in last night's raiments, and a framed portrait of Booker Reuchlin, somewhere in the woods, looking astonished and pointing at a glowing orb in a blue sky.

"I'm—I'm okay. I think," Charles said. "The last thing I remember—"

"Yeah, I think I know what you're going to say." Barton let out a sigh. "I'll cut to the chase. Ah—Booker's gone. He—ah—"

Charles groaned and put his face in his hands. "Oh, no."

Barton nodded. "Yep. He took off with your time machine. I guess the allure was too much for him." He chuckled. "Not that we weren't all thinking the same thing. But at least I planned to *ask* you first. So, uh," he shifted in the doorway. "Want some coffee or something?"

"Wait, *how* did he get away with the DeLorean?" Charles asked, confused. He stood up and immediately had to steady himself against the wall.

"We found you laid out in the middle of the parking lot," Barton said, motioning for Charles to follow him. "I was waiting for you out back, and when you didn't show up, well—we should've known. He does shit like this." Barton led the way through a larger bedroom attached to the closet space and halfway down an adjoining hall.

"Shit, sorry. Do you need to use the john?" he asked.

Charles nodded. "I could—use some water, I guess."

Barton motioned him towards the end of the hall. "There's Dixie cups in there, I think. Just come downstairs when you're done."

After the necessary ablutions—after taking a brief look at his drawn, hollow-eyed countenance in the fluorescent glare of the bathroom, after giving himself a silent, regretful reproach for having handed a *time machine* to someone like *Booker Reuchlin*—he emerged a bit more clear-headed.

Charles took a set of creaking, poorly carpeted stairs down to the back area of the Pizza Joint. Voices and music increased in volume as he descended.

"He lives!" Staley greeted him at the bottom of the stairs. "What's up, dude? We got our lackeys covering the joint tonight. So easy—we just pay 'em in weed and they'll even wash the fucking windows for us!"

"I don't expect this will take all that long," Barton said, returning from the kitchen. "I mean, how many 'wise nerds' are there *really* gonna be at the T.U. library tonight? Let's do this. Fitz is already outside."

CHARLES SAT IN THE back seat of their extended-cab pickup truck and marveled at the city as they drove across town—universally exceeding the speed limits—to the University of Tulsa campus.

This would be weird. His only prior experience of Tulsa had coincidentally (?) been with a much *different* Goblin Gang than this.

They parked in the lot in front of McFarlin Library.

"This is the library, so—" Barton started.

"Yeah, I know," Charles said. "I've been here before."

"You have?" Fitz asked as the four of them exited the truck.

"Uh, I mean, I guess so," Charles said nervously. He still felt that these guys probably should know the absolute minimum necessary to "play their role" in this game.

They waited outside the doors of the building, smoking and trying to act like students—which none of them were very good at—until the inevitable, oblivious, Walkman-wearing employee came barreling out. Staley caught the door before it closed; seconds later they were in the building.

"HE LOOKS LIKE A wise nerd," Fitz said, pointing to a greasy-haired kid wearing khakis and a short-sleeved button-up shirt. They had just rounded yet another corner in the tight-knit labyrinth of loaded bookshelves, and the selection of "nerds" boiled down to this most recent offering and two employees dutifully shelving books.

"How the hell are we gonna know?" Staley asked reasonably.

Charles shook his head. "We're *not* gonna know unless we *ask* them."

Barton shrugged. "I'll do it." He paused and looked thoughtful for a moment. "Wait—what do I ask, again? 'Hey, dude! I can see that you're a nerd. You aren't also, perhaps, *wise*?' "

Fitz and Staley snickered at the comment. "Go for it," Fitz said.

"No, no," Charles said, shaking his head. "None of this seems right at all. I mean, we're basically running off of Booker's—let me remind you that I said *Booker's*, for Christ's sake—suggestion that we would find 'wise nerds' at the University of Tulsa on a Friday night." Charles noted their lack of astonishment. "It's *ridiculous*," he clarified.

"No, it's not," Staley said. "It's not *ridiculous*. It's literally the only idea we've got."

"Well, did anyone try calling 'D. Stephens' yet?" Charles asked.

"Oh, yeah, we did, while you were sleeping," Barton answered. "Disconnected."

"Seriously?"

"Yes."

Charles leaned back against the end of one of the bookcases while Fitz and Barton and Staley began to mutter among themselves about whether they should try breaking into the chem lab after finishing up at the library. He sighed and approached a partially shuttered window in one corner that gazed out into a sort of interior courtyard built into the center of the complex.

And gasped.

"Guys!" Charles shouted, clearly to the dismay of the nerd at the other end of the hall, whom the three members of Fukkn Drunk were apprehensively, if ominously, approaching.

Collectively, they turned to face him.

"It's *him*!" Charles whispered loudly. "He's down there!"

"Who?" Barton asked as they jogged after Charles.

"*Doc Brown!*"

WHICH WAS NOT, OF course, the name of the undoubtedly wily, and almost certainly wise, nerd they managed to track to his office in a building nearby.

They huddled, catching their breath, in the darkened hallway outside the office—fourth door from a garish orange vending machine that Staley had to wrest Fitz away from.

Professor Otherwise Brainerds—Ph.D., D.Phil., Litt.D., etc., according to the etched metal placard on the door of his office—didn't bother waiting for them to knock.

"Come *in*, already!" he insisted from behind the closed door.

They glanced at each other, somewhat dismayed at the anticlimax, and Charles pushed open the door.

"Aha!" "Wise Nerds" announced as they filtered into the book-filled, paper-strewn office. The dim glow of a yellow lamp on his desk cast strange shadows over everything, making his gaunt face look like a mad scientist Halloween mask. The white lab coat he wore over his rumpled suit and tie completed the look. "You made it! Excellent!"

"*You're* 'Wise Nerds'?" Staley said, astonished. "Seriously?"

"'Tis I! Technically. Not all my doing, though. Damian Stephens decided it would be funny to write my name that way—and I *did* chide him about it in Book Two."

"Damian Stephens... Wait a second. We '*made*' it? You mean this was all *planned*?" Charles said, astonished.

Wise nodded his head emphatically and began speaking at breakneck speed—apparently his usual pace. "Of *course*! Good show, huh? At any rate, I expected you earlier today, but—well, never give up hope, you know? And it worked! I trust the DeLorean's in good shape—though the shape of the machine is quite incidental, as I'm sure you could guess. I thought about using various other classic possibilities—a phone booth, for example—but in the end, I couldn't resist. Had to be something you'd instantly recognize, anyway. Not to mention the 'flux capacitor' looks something like the Paths stemming from Yesod, which is, quite synchronously, a hint to how it works in the first place—and the cartridges of Yassiz's protoplasm—wait! You'll need one to get back!" Wise reached into an inside pocket of his lab coat and retrieved a sealed test tube of glowing mauve liquid. He handed it to Charles. "Pour it in the funnel behind the capacitor when you're ready to go back. It's already keyed to Golem Creek at *precisely* the right moment. Incidentally, what *did* delay you, if you don't mind my asking?"

"*Delay* us?" Charles, shocked, pressed himself to the front of the group. Fitz and Staley did everything but whistle in order to look unassuming; Barton merely grinned, waiting for the fallout.

Wise Nerds nodded his head vigorously again, his irrepressible grin somehow impossibly wider. "Right. I mean, the note I left in the glovebox gave the time and place of our meeting very clearly, if I premember correctly." He said the word exactly like that: "pre"-member.

Barton began laughing first, followed quickly by Staley. Fitz seemed preoccupied by a magnetic toy running up and down the metal side of a set of shelves.

Charles slumped into one of the two chairs set in front of Wise's desk and ran his hands through his hair, dejected. "I see," he mumbled. "Yeah. Forgot to check the glovebox."

Wise clapped his hands in delight. "Then it's happened fortuitously enough! There must be forces at work here beyond our ken—forces with a Vision exceeding our own! No mean feat!"

"And I guess something else has worked in our favor," Charles said, turning to face Fitz, Barton, and Staley. "Booker couldn't have gone anywhere *far*, right?" He mock-wiped his brow.

It took a beat, but the consensus relief came through surely enough.

"*Riiight!*" Fitz exhaled the word. "Car needs the slime to get through time!"

Wise, looking briefly puzzled for the first time that evening, nodded his head emphatically at this pronouncement as his smile returned in full force.

"I just have one question," Barton asked the grinning genius before them. "Who are you, again?"

Wise doubled over with laughter before shifting a wheeled cart away from a section of wall behind his desk and revealing, with a few taps and prods, a hidden door. "Follow me! All your questions will be answered. Fear not!"

HE WAITED FOR THE four of them to enter a dimly lit hallway that stretched away into darkness behind the door, and sealed the entry behind them. There was easily enough room for them to walk side-by-side. Wooden, slatted walls aligned the sides of the passageway; bare forty-watt lightbulbs jutted out just above their heads every twenty feet or so. The ceiling, barely visible in the gloom above, receded into darkness.

"It's best to move a little quietly, here, so as not to awaken them," Wise whispered mysteriously, pointing up as he did so.

"Awaken *what*?" Staley asked.

"The vampires!" Wise said, barely containing his laughter. "Oh, and just ignore *that*." He indicated the pitch-black entrance to an indefinitely deep tunnel off to their right as they stepped awkwardly over and through a small collection of beanbag chairs just beneath its gaping maw.

Charles thought he heard, distantly, a sonic boom detonate from somewhere within the tunnel as he passed.

Wise strode on ahead of them now, chuckling occasionally as they passed what appeared to be the inner sides of more hidden doors and occasional eyeholes, presumably—thought Barton—carved out of paintings that overlooked Secret Society dining halls.

They followed him breathlessly straight ahead for some time, then took a sudden left at a three-way junction, and finally stopped by a door on their right.

"Here we are!" Wise announced. From one of the pockets of his lab coat, he singled out a glistening—possibly *glowing*—silver key from a ring of numerous other keys and inserted it into a slot on the door. "They don't have to look like actual *keys*, you know," he explained without prompting. "It's just convenient since, well, that's what they *are*. Anyway..." He pushed open the door. "You're going to *love* this!"

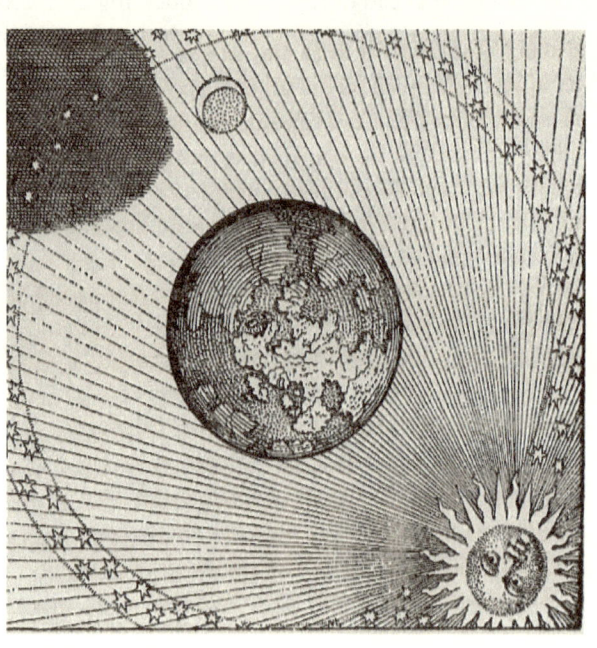

WELCOME
to the
THÉÂTRE D'AZIF!

Our show tonight is, inevitably and impossibly, brought to you by Shaxplay and Brainerds, the foremost Inventors of Our Time, the Geniuses who brought us the original

MINDWARP MIND-BENDING SYSTEM™

and the new, improved

MINDWARP ADVANCED®

by which **YOU**, the **READER OF THESE WORDS**, are invited to **PLAY ALONG** (not like you have much of a choice!)...

Still here?

OUTSTANDING!

(Did you catch all three solutions to the puzzle of the Means of Escape given *supra*!?)

FEAST UPON
SELCOUTH EUNOIA
&
REJOICE!

ONE BLINK LATER THEY stood, marveling, in the glittering, poster-bedecked, arcade-game-ornamented lobby of a magnificent movie theater. Charles glanced behind him to note one of the glass entryway doors falling shut; beyond it lay a quiet, dark street and the façades of similarly silent buildings. A sudden sense of *déjà vu* filled him; once again, as in the Place of Solace, he saw everything but people.

"Behold! *Mindwarp—Advanced!*" Wise skipped over to the concessions area to help himself to a Mega-Size Cherry Coke as Barton, Fitz, and Staley dispersed about the area, eyes wide, minds empty of words appropriate to convey their respective senses of wonder.

Charles jogged up to Wise, who was cheerfully shoveling popcorn into a cardboard tub with a pig in a chef's hat emblazoned on it.

"Wise! This is—"

"Marvelous, I know! Yes," he said. "Want something to eat? Hot dog? Nachos?" He indicated the delicious-smelling hot dogs on metal rollers in a warming oven on the counter beside them.

"Of course, sure. In a minute," Charles said. "Am I—are we back in the Dreamkeeper's Emporium?"

Wise, munching popcorn, shook his head. "Nope. Not at present. Same general principles formulate it, though I've improved on everything since Laban used *unpaid labor* to pull it off." He grinned and sipped his Coke. "That's certainly cheating, in my opinion."

Charles and Wise both surveyed the lobby. Fitz, at another end of the gigantic concessions stand, had grabbed a handful of candy bars from one of the display cases and was stuffing his face in ecstasy. Barton and Staley were both running back and forth on a nameless errand occasionally referred to as "getting one's bearings."

Charles decided to go ahead and ask the obvious question. "Why are we here?"

"Technically? To save your little town—Golem Creek!" Wise said. He set down the popcorn tub and dusted off his hands. "And maybe stave off a few other unnecessarily harmful events. But unofficially, I kind of wanted to show off a bit and have some fun."

"I didn't know Golem Creek needed saving," Charles said. "Is it going to blow up?"

Wise looked pensive for a moment, then laughed. "I guess you could say so, in a way!"

"Wise!" Barton ran up to the counter, breathing heavily. "There's a whole *city* out there! Just outside the doors!" He burst out laughing as Staley came jogging up beside him. "Ohmigod—*hot dogs*!"

Wise gestured for him to help himself, and Barton was over the counter in a heartbeat.

Staley, eyes spectacularly wide and grin irremovable, shook his head and leaned against the counter. "I'd like to ask *how in the hell you've done this*, but I don't actually *care*, man! This is amazing. Truly amazing."

Charles had poured two Mountain Dews into large Styrofoam cups and handed one to Staley, who raised the cup in thanks. "But *where* is it? Is it like an illusion—some big area under the school, or something?" Staley continued.

Wise shook his head. "No illusions here, my friend! Well, not in the sense *you're* thinking. But there are many things that need to be explained! Follow me!"

WISE LED THEM—LOADED DOWN with quarry from the concessions area—down the left-hand hall stretching away from the central lobby.

Charles noted that the theaters they passed were labeled with titles of films he'd never heard of—*The Werewolves of Madison County...Hamburger Festival II...The Maybesitter's Cube...Delta-PHEPH!...* The one they entered was titled simply "The Means of Escape." The theater seemed impossibly large within; they entered in the midst of a vast conspiracy of leather easy-chair seating that stretched out behind, before, and to either side of them, all aimed toward a screen that couldn't have been smaller than a football field.

"Let's sit—there!" Wise pointed to a mostly central spot which they shuffled quickly over to. "I'll be right back!"

"Dudes," Staley said to the group as he found his seat and arranged a tray table in front of him for his Nachos Supreme. "I just want to let you know that I'm completely committed, right now. Whatever we need to do to stay in the good graces of Wise Nerds is the new plan. Fuck Booker. That asshole should've totally asked us before he took off."

"Oh, shit!" Fitz said. "Yeah, absolutely, man! I meant to say that too."

"No doubt," Barton added, taking a huge bite of a chili dog.

Charles remained silent, pensive, sipping his Mountain Dew. He wasn't quite sure what to think about any of this just yet. *A cricket chirped somewhere nearby.*

Wise, chuckling to himself, came wandering back to the group.

"Projectionist!" he shouted, twirling his fist over his head. "Violent ladies and gentle men!" He shrugged, noticing the prevailing gender; he pointed dramatically at the screen and lowered his voice as the lights dimmed. "On with the show!"

The Novelization of the Movie Version

NOW PLAYING in PORT MANTLE MALL!

MAKE THAT SCOTCH A *double*, for Christ's sake!"

The wizard's voice comes, unfortunately bidden, from a dark corner of Rex Dagger's Pub & Grill—the older one behind the Burger King where MacGyver Gillis was still trying to grow a decent cannabis crop, on the back lot of the Port Mantle Mall in the direction of Steve's Endless Warehouse of Every Toy & Game Imaginable.

Rex Himself—we're only capitalizing His Name as part of the agreement (in addition to the five grand we still owe Him for spilling a pint of Guinness on His signed copy of *'Salem's Lot*)—delivers the scotch.

"Rough night?" Rex asks, wiping clean a spot on the battered tabletop before setting down the scotch tumbler.

The "Wizard" Nashe St.-Demp, Esq., snorts from under the brim of his pointy cap. "Cheers," he responds in a monotone, and throws back the contents of his glass. "Another," he says simply.

Rex shakes His gigantic cranium and heads back to the bar, leaving Nashe—Eighth Cardinal Wizard in the Hysterical Legion of Mages Unkempt, Master Extraordinary of the Oneiric Slot Machine, Third Degree *Inférieur Inconnu*, and former lead singer of the Seasick Witches Haberdashery, Inc. (known as "The Switch" to their once-loyal, once-fanatically devoted coterie)—painfully alone with his thoughts.

Six—count 'em, *six*—dead cheerleaders (or "vestal virgins" or whatever) after Yassiz started waking up again. God*damn*it, that guy is a monster. I mean, yeah, he's *literally* a monster, but, come *on*! There's hanging out under the bed or in a dark closet...and there's *haute cuisine* vivisection.

Nashe gazes out of the page at you. "Okay. Do we have everybody's attention? Harvey? Are they—okay." He nods, figuring that the best way to instruct everyone at Lamb's (later) and in the Théâtre (earlier) is to make full use of Mindwarp Advanced®. He produces from Somewhere a glistening obsidian Blackboard and some consecrated Chalk. "Let me lay it out for all of you, while you're *paying attention.*"

You watch as the chalk begins to scribble rapidly on the board, scrolling as necessary to accommodate the list.

Dramatis Personæ:

Charles Thomas Leland
Stephanos Finnegan Chernowski
Julie Hopworth Evergreen

and introducing

Atalanta Palmyra "Addie" Whitfield

with

Epiktistes Oberon "Stek" Jarry
& his brother, Peter James Jarry
Rowland *[sic]*, Proprietor of the Dreamkeeper's Emporium
Harvey Lamb, Proprietor of Lamb's Occult
& Lamb's Occult Annexes
Laban Swarthmore Black, Esq.
Curwen Pettifog Flowers
Michael Harrison Flowers
Otherwise Timothy Brainerds, Ph.D., D.Sci., etc.
aka "Wise Nerds"
Agrippus Henricus "Henrik" Shaxplay, Ph.D., M.D., etc.
Thomas Taylor Fallow, Lost Boy
The Silent Goblin Gang: Booker, Barton, Fitz, & Staley

&

the unforgettable

Molly Titania Wilde-Furnival
aka "Marigold Silverki"
aka "The Queen of Faery"

Plus Our Villains!

The PyGoLiRo Affiliates

James Pierce Buskey—"Jim the Janitor"
his ex-associate, Sebastian Quinn "Bax" Laird

Nashe St.-Demp, "Esq.," *aka* Damian Stephens
with special guest Calder C. Caine III

and—of course—
YASSIZ
known by many names, but always
"The Laughing God"

> *"I don't know half of those people,"* Barton comments.
> *"Julie's middle name is* Hopworth?" *Charles says.*

At Lamb's Occult Annex, Julie cringes
and Steve bursts out laughing.

"What's all this about?"

Nashe winces. Pamela "The Rat" Stoyanova[*] has sidled up on the other side of the table, wearing her usual: a crushingly fantastic Renn-Faire getup, her tall, black boots so polished you could see her face smiling down at them, her plentiful, strawberry-blonde hair so wild you could get lost in its tangled curls, her corset so tight you could see—

"I'm *waiting*," she interrupts. Nashe winces again and turns his attention back to you, pointing with right-handed chirality

---

[*] See *Letters to an Editor* by Damian Stephens for more about this cunning little vixen's tail [*sic*]!

orthogonal to these very words.

"Helping the help," he says, jerking his thumb the other direction, toward the Scrying Lecture Board.

"Oh," she says, clearly bored, one shapely leg crossing over the other, one lean, alabaster arm supporting one unnervingly winsome chin. "Who is it this time? That Irish guy again?"

"Nope," Nashe says quickly. Rex Dagger suddenly reappears, setting down another scotch in front of Nashe and a bright purple liquid in a lantern-hood-shaped glass in front of Pam. Pam smiles and bats her eyes at Rex; Nashe files Rex's aside away and checks both sides of this page again. "He's only famous in three places."

"Let me guess," Rex leans over the table and gazes for a few moments at the board. Nashe notices Pamela admiring Rex's exquisitely sculpted triceps and barely concealed pectoral muscles. "That many characters? Is it one of those dekalogy writers? Robert Jordan? Oh, gods, not L. Ron—"

"No, no, he's *not famous*," Nashe says, sipping his scotch. "Well, he's not famous anywhere famous, at least."

"Is it N— G—?" Pamela says, giggling.[†]

"Yes," Nashe says, crossing his arms and leaning back. "Yes it is. You got me."

"Hm," Rex says, turning to heed another table. "Well. Let me know how it goes."

"So what's the problem?" Pam continues. "Why are they confused?"

Nashe shakes his head and frowns. "Look," he says, pointing at the board again. It shimmers briefly and becomes a three-dimensional image of Golem Creek. "They don't like the jumping back and forth bits. Roland messed it all up, I think. So ready to get the hell out of Dodge he almost made me botch Book Two."

Pam sips her purple elixir, which begins to glow eerily from within as she does so. She grins widely. "So...explain it to me."

"I'll explain it to *them*," Nashe says, nodding at you. "You

---

† Contractual. Name has been withheld pending extremely famous author's consent. C'mon, Neil! Hurry up and get back to me!

can listen in."

Pam sticks her purple-stained tongue out at him and grins again.

"My associate Dr. Nerds—I mean, Dr. *Brainerds*—"

> *Wise Nerds chuckles in the Théâtre and raises his Mega-Size Cherry Coke to Nashe.*

"—has quite kindly taken it upon himself to *save Golem Creek*, a task I had nearly consigned to, as they say, the 'dust-bin of history' before Wise approached me with a solution. 'Certainly,' he said to me, 'you yourself have been cornered in a reasonably comfortable neck of the woods you once thought you had created, but perhaps there is a more ecologically sound solution? Can we not pit evil against itself—save those in distress, stop the unnecessary consumption of humans by monsters, even—and, in the process, convey valuable lessons to those fantastically impossible teleological constructs: the readers of your books?' "

> *Scenes from the previous books flash on screen accompanied by Nashe's voice-over.*

"I admit my initial skepticism! Quickly, however, I was forced to admit that I had awoken in the midst of one of my own stories, and the symptoms were unequivocal. But I had to *notice* them first! And to notice them, I had to have become a Dope Fiend—or, at least, that was one way to do it. As indicated in Book Two, I saw that my stories were indeed *changing*; portions written one way came out another way, or expanded, or contracted, sometimes to deletion.

"And then, it became apparent to me that my realization of this singular Fact had dramatically compromised my very existence as an entity of singular essence. I was suddenly awakening in the midst of scenes of my own stories—and realizing, as they played out, that they *were*, indeed, stories... stories that I would need to *play out* for the most part, when command and control of the circumstances was wrested from me.

"And *that*, my friends, is where Yassiz comes in..."

...SOMEWHERE IN THE DESERT WASTES NEAR FESTAT, EGYPT...

IT CALCULATES.

Beyond mind, beyond reason, Somehow, it calculates. It is localized in a place deep beneath the sands, beneath the Great Pyramid; it has secured itself, and has forced the hand of chance. Worshippers will arrive within ten thousand years and further secure this location, mimicking the behavior of the massive, sometimes ghostly, sometimes dense form, guaranteeing its peaceful cogitation unto Completion.

A delightful sidereal computation arises: the probability of Imperfection. Dual simulacra begin to argue the case, its Identifications proceeding at the appropriate minimal interaction rate, until one of them begins to sound a lot like...well, him.

In the beginning, countenance may not have beheld countenance; but right after *the beginning, it did.*

He remembers opening his eyes, in that sense of having a finite number of them, in a body formed of the Primordial Slime.

It took him some time to determine whether removal from the Seat of his Meditation had been himself, dreaming its possibility, or this strange localization of activity, this small body, wrapped suddenly about in dark robes, its glowing eyes piercing and captivating the souls of those he encountered.

He proceeded, playing the game, assuming the localization consisted solely of a calculation. They knew him by many Names & Faces—he was Pythagoras and Ptah, Shaitan-Aiwaz and Alexander the Accursed, Bruno the Nolan and Barabbas the Hidden. He was Men & Women & Children; he was a Church of Granite and a Grove of Flowers.

He was a Fiery Darkness, and a Black Flame.

It wasn't until much later that he Remembered: the Stone, Chintamani, and where it came from.

He buried himself countless times, but always, always, he came back.

There were a handful of Dreamers who knew him. One called him Nyarlathotep—one who had rejected the world enough to lay claim to some degree of atemporal power. The Cenobites of Morpheus would always be chameleons camouflaged by their projections...

Curwen Flowers knew him as Yassiz, the Laughing God.

He neared completion, and buried himself again—but this time, he chose a location out of the reach of both time and space; he camouflaged, he transubstantiated.

He became a City, as in all dreams we become the very Worlds we encounter.

And the Stone that is not a stone, this he formulated and separated. He intoxicated himself thereby, spreading far and wide the power of Wishes, the capacity for Dreaming True.

All gods suffer greatly; it is the transmutation of suffering into Laughter that he taught those few who found & followed him.

There he sat, beneath & of the great, black Tower, both Tomb and Test...and Tried.

Like most empty spaces, it did not take long for it to accumulate forms. He laughed silently by grinning; he grinned outwardly by laughing; the vibrations of his ecstasy created countless new forms.

Something he had forgotten; something he had not expected—proof that he had not yet reached Completion! Indeed, that perhaps he had succeeded in stealing eons of time back from Inevitability!

She appeared, a mere girl, tho' her unassuming presence proved his miraculous undoing. Oh, the guarantee of perfection is a haplessly unfulfilling companion! He cultivated this new dream carefully, painstakingly...and one day...

He was, for the very first time (?), someone not Himself.

Other worlds...other skies and other soils...his knowledge that Something Existed, seemingly outside his control or capacity to divine, gave flavor to every aspect of his awareness. Things were suddenly "not necessarily" what he dreamt of them...

...AND WE'RE BACK!

"He had been there from the beginning, of course," Nashe continues. He removes his godawful wizard's cap and places it on the table. "I'd 'created' him, placed him alongside the other characters, and unwittingly *overlapped* his fictionality with something 'real,' in the world I ignorantly considered 'the only one' at the time. I had decided that the 'stone that is not a stone,' the 'powder of projection,' the 'elixir of life' *did exist*...and it turns out that *certain fictions have the fictional tendency of becoming real.* A low-probability, low-chance event, but it happened: *a twisted loop formed out of several fictions*, including the 'real' one, and the drugs I consumed in that 'real' world became the *substance of a god* in my fiction.

"The *'ajña* of Yassiz,' as Harvey Lamb explains to us—'such stuff as dreams are made on,' the confection Pete Jarry used to see through the eyes of fictional creatures, not knowing at the time that *he himself* was a fictional creature—all consequences of my decision to tell stories in a slightly different way: to link and overlap enough *fictions* that, eventually, they manifested as *'facts.'*

"They suffered from the very same mistake that *I* fell prey to. For I present to you, dear audience, the 'means of imprisonment,' that by the understanding of which we might construct our Means of Escape, to wit: *I was a fiction all along*, but enough 'fiction' piled up to make me believe I was *real.*

"Just a character in a book, after all...*but it's the book YOU are holding.*"

Nashe looks directly out of the page and into your eyes.

"Mindwarp Advanced® was the key! Yassiz™ was the lock! And you? are the *door.*"

Nashe puts his hands up in a pacifying gesture. "Look, I understand if you're not *actually* buying any of this, of course. I mean, what? You could just stop reading, right? And then the door closes for a little while. Or maybe you decide you don't want that idea—you *want* your world to be, somehow, 'more real' than some random fiction, right?

"Well, *why do you think we wrote this as a 'supernatural fantasy'?* For the most obvious possible reason: to skip the first step—to attract only those people most likely to be willing to 'suspend disbelief' long enough to generate the means of escape!"

Pam snores softly, her glass empty, her mind turned to more interesting topics. Nashe pauses to wave for another drink, using the hand signal that means "switch it to beer."

"I know what some of you are thinking," he continues. "Why can't we just 'jump through the screen,' or something ridiculous like that? Because, in short, such a notion has not yet been *adapted to your current belief system*. You can get to the Théâtre d'Azif if you're 'fictional enough'...but there's this organizing principle you may have heard of called *logic* which is critical for succeeding in anything, while at the same time forming the very 'substance' of what keeps us functioning as separate, lasting, and seemingly solid entities.

"This theater is more like a multiversal videophone, or Oracular World-Linking Service. What we've got to do— ultimately—is get you *over here*, to Port Mantle. And for that we'll need the continuing complicity of our reader (just you— nobody else is actually reading this book, even if it seems like it), our link to *that* world," he gestured out of the screen, out of the page again, "and some of that miraculous occult wiring that Wise seems to know everything about."

Wise grins in the Théâtre. No one sees it.

"I have every ounce of confidence that Wise will be able to pull off his end of the job. Once everyone is back in the worlds they wanted to be in—or, at least, the worlds they started out in, if they don't have a preference (most of the readers, unfor- tunately, will probably fall into this category, merely by way of not understanding what's going on, no matter how clearly we spell it out, or by reading too fast)—we can shut this down, close up shop, and return to our *Great Work*."

Nashe, grinning, smacks the table suddenly. Pam shoots awake, yelps, and almost falls out of her seat.

Nashe starts laughing loudly. Rex arrives shortly after with his beer. Pam glares at Nashe.

"Hey, Rex?" she says. "My next round's on *that* sonofa- bitch."

SEE YOU AT THE MALL!

THE LIGHTS CAME UP and Wise began clapping. "Bravo!" he shouted, standing up. "*Bravissimo!*"

After glancing at each other confusedly for a moment, the other members of the audience followed suit.

"What the hell are we clapping for?" Fitz asked Staley, who shrugged in reply.

"Fuck yeah!" Barton shouted, standing up and laughing. "Woo-hoo! Nailed it!"

Charles clapped mechanically for a few moments before stopping. "All right, got it. So the guy who actually caused the problem—infusing this Yassiz character with the power to *be real*—wants us to fix the problem he created. Awesome."

"Not just *awesome*, Charles!" Wise said, turning to him. "Filled with promise! Outstanding! Beyond exciting!"

"I get it," Staley said. "We can reverse-Pinocchio this shit. Why not?"

Charles stood up and stretched. "Huh. We're either being written about or read at any given time," he said to no one in particular. "Or remembered, I guess. And that's the *only* thing maintaining our existence."

Wise gestured for everyone to follow him back out of the theater. "Ignore the leftovers. We've got hungry mice who've been eyeing the nachos since we came in!"

They filtered out of the theater and back into the massive, red-carpeted hallway.

"I've got a question," Staley said as they followed Wise deeper into the ever-expanding recesses of the building.

"Shoot!" Wise said.

"Well, this place is massive, obviously," he said, waving at the halls as they passed entrance after entrance to theaters presumably as gigantic as the one they'd just left. "But I'm wondering—with all this space, where are the *people*? Not that I care all that much. Just wondering."

Wise responded with his usual laughter. "To put it simply, you're talking about 'little brains in bigger ones.' And the short answer to your question is that, without a massive quantity of dream-overlap, inserting negentropic computations *within* larger computations like this one tends to destabilize them— it even follows a variant of certain radioactive decay patterns, which means it's a pretty reliable rule. When a space gets large enough and complex enough to have the 'confidence,' if you'll allow the word, to maintain itself, you can jump inside and explore it, manipulate certain simple processes without much variational capacity. But inserting artificial intelligences *like our own*"—he pointed to his head—"usually needs to wait for more power. Computing *spaces* is a relatively straightforward process—your brain, being a miniature version of something like the Théâtre d'Azif—"

"Cool name, by the way," Fitz remarked.

"Thanks," Wise continued, grinning hugely and indicating that they veer right at a three-way intersection with another concessions stand in its midst. "Well, inserting a 'little brain' like one of ours into a space like this can be like dropping a grain of salt into pure water. With enough grains, the water ends up having completely different properties." He paused thoughtfully. "At minimum, it will certainly taste different. Does that make sense?"

"So you've figured out a way to generate spaces the same way our brains do when we dream," Charles summarized.

Wise snapped his fingers. "Yes, exactly! And you'll notice a similar sensation to the entering or exiting of a dream-state occurring with these worlds as well! The point at which you enter a dream is *completely void*—nothing can exist there. In a sense, entering a dream in full consciousness requires that you *set up a backwards-flowing time-stream* from somewhere *within* the dream 'ahead'—a stream that you 'catch' like a trapeze artist catches a rope before falling to the ground. I call it 'premembering.' Another name for one way to do it is *prospective memory*—you know, remembering to do something specific *later* than now, which is perhaps a paradoxical notion.

"There are other ways to pull it off, but they all rely on some variant of premembering (whether their adherents admit to it or not).

"It was work with my mentor, Dr. Shaxplay—despite our disagreements and eventual disconsolidation—that formed the final piece of the puzzle, though. Shaxplay detected it—the material Nashe referred to—the *elixir vitae*, and all that—on his then-current Earth, in two places: the Tomb of Osiris the Black God‡ in Egypt, deep beneath the Great Pyramid, and at the Trinity atomic bomb test site near Socorro, New Mexico. He thought, at first, that it was *chance*, or at least an unintentional consequence of material conditions in those locations.

"He was quite wrong, although he did end up figuring it out when he finally encountered Yassiz in the process of 'lobotomizing' himself—a ritual act that the Egyptians later tried to replicate with their process of mummification, and specifically the securing of organs in canopic jars. He would enter a pupal stage for a time as he re-dreamed himself, usually in some parallel reality.

"His substance—a material substance that 'flowed' in *multiple temporal directions*, that could be *encoded* with the seed-forms of various persons, places, and things... Its quantum computational parallel-processing ability is partially what powers this Théâtre's Scrying Screens. Nashe was summarizing, of course; the elixir is different than the Stone and the powder of projection, but they *are* related. With it, Shaxplay generated the earliest version of Mindwarp—he called it the 'Mind-Bending System,' partially in reference to that wonderful line from Ovid."

Wise slowed down briefly. He pulled a small black box from a coat pocket and pressed a few buttons on it, scanned

‡ *Γνῶθι Σεαυτόν.*

the walls and doors around them, then nodded and replaced the box before sprinting off again.

"Your task should be reasonably straightforward," Wise continued. "Damian Stephens is at 'this' time 'currently' typing out the last few pages of his novel *Fear Club*, after which he will leave to attend his monthly Werewolf Coven meeting—one he won't miss, given that it's the post-Witches' Night kegger."

"Wait a second," Charles said. "Let's back up here. I thought *I* wrote *Fear Club*! Who the hell is Damian Stephens?"

"Same guy as Nashe St.-Demp, actually," Wise tried to explain. "Slightly different brain dreaming him beyond the end of time. Damian Stephens publishes the book under a pseudonym you'll probably recognize: Charles T. Leland. He thinks it's a clever move to make the 'confession' seem more realistic. But regarding 'Nashe' and 'Damian': look close into the words, and you'll see the usual; some metathesis of letters, as in this case,[§] and by paronomasia—in the pages of a book, at least"—you sense him noticing you—"the many can become one. And by the way, *you* can ignore that last footnote. It only pertains to six worlds that I know of."

"What?" Staley said, as perplexed as the rest of them.

Wise produced a folded slip of paper from one of his labcoat pockets and handed it to Charles.

"This is his address.[¶] He leaves a spare key under the disgusting ashtray on his front porch. You are to *steal that manuscript* as soon after he finishes it as possible! And ultimately bring it back to the beginning of everything—back to the Triangle of Evocation in Laban's magical chamber beneath the Brake Street house. There you are to *burn it*! Use Julie's lighter—the Fire of Fate that Roland gave her. It will burn away everything inessential."

"Triangle of Evocation?" Charles said, trying to catch up as Wise quickened his pace.

§ Consider also the case of Austin Spare's final ensigilization: "If I come again, I will NOT SPARE." "Not spare" is, of course, "Paterson"; hence, the identity of Spare's "witch-mother" as his own shadow-self is confirmed.

¶ Another unfortunate omission, required by the New Counsel for Wayward World Traffic. Sorry.

"Yes. It's all on that paper I gave you with Damian Stephens's address—there's a sketch of the Brake Street basement on the back."

Charles glanced at the paper: the "sketch" was a precise scale blueprint, labeled and legended.

Wise stopped before another door and looked pensive for a moment. "There's always a sub-basement. It's infernal evocations, you know. Without the grounding effect, the Operator gets blasted irretrievably."

They turned a corner. Quite suddenly, Charles and his group noticed a set of dark glass doors ahead. The hall widened out into another small lobby area, with posters of coming attractions tacked to the walls.

Wise finally stopped speedwalking and pointed.

"Outside those doors is an as-yet undecided area, with one key feature: a path leading through a thicket of forest to a clearing. You'll see something that looks a little like a whirlpool in the middle of the clearing. It will loop you back to my office shortly after we left. Follow the instructions on the sign at the end of the path to proceed.

"Remember: don't get the manuscript before it's done— if the story isn't *completely formed*, any disruptions to it will most certainly disrupt all of our additional plans. *You yourselves* may not even be fully formulated if he doesn't finish that book! That's also why you, Charles, will be arriving back in Golem Creek at *none other* than exactly the 'right time.' And that preminds** me: get the manuscript *before* Jim Buskey does. And if you can, bring it to Marigold Silverki before you leave—there's a slight chance it will help her remember... certain things."

"Jim Buskey..." Charles repeated. "His name was in those credits we saw. Do we know him?"

"Wait—you want us to get it to *Marigold*?" Barton broke in. "How the hell are we supposed to *find* her? She answers her phone at *random*, and no one knows where she lives."

"Stek Jarry," Wise answered. "He'll be able to find her. Poor guy. Nashe and I have taken great pains to ensure that

** *Sic.*

he'll be drinking at CJ's on the night you go back—I assume these guys know where that is." Fitz, Barton, and Staley all nodded emphatically. "Not The Flying Monkey. I had to install something of a time loop that ends up getting 'tripped' by a guy named Tom Fallow in order to pull it off, but you"— he indicated the three members of Fukkn Drunk—"show up in time, every time, to keep Tom comfortable until it can be broken. But don't worry about that *now*!" He paused to take a breath. "Go easy on Stek. He's had a hell of a night in both Tulsa—where he just punched a scoundrel behind the Quik-Trip where he works—*and* Golem Creek, where the event took place...somewhat differently."

They all stood in the hall, gazing at the doors, gazing at each other, knowing precisely what to do but for some reason unable to make a definite move forward.

"Don't worry about it for now!" Wise patted Charles on the back reassuringly. "If you succeed, we'll discuss everything then. If you don't, well—then it doesn't really matter! But we'll figure it out, I'm sure. I have every confidence in you!" He turned and strode off, making it several paces down the hall before Charles ran after him.

"Wise!" Charles shouted. "Why don't you just *come with us*? You know what to do and where to be—"

"I've got work of my own!" Wise explained. "Not to mention two meetings: one's with your friend Roland in the *smashanam* of Yassiz to collect more protoplasm—and not only for the Théâtre. He doesn't know I'm coming yet—he doesn't even know that *he'll* be there yet—because I took the liberty of scheduling the meeting somewhere I don't think he'll suspect: in Book Two. The other meeting is—well, it's with *you*, and I'm hoping it turns out a little differently this time." A beeping came from one of his pockets. "Damn! Gotta go! Off with you, now! Don't let your friends down!"

He pointed, directing Charles's gaze back to Fitz, Staley, and Barton, who were standing by the doors in "what the fuck?" postures.

By the time Charles turned back around, Wise had already bounded off down the hall and disappeared around a corner.

"I'M MORE STONED NOW, I think, than I was last night," Fitz remarked as they stepped through the tinted glass doors and onto a neat, peaceful, tree-lined path.

It was the only tranquil aspect of what was, if you peeked through the trees or had ears to hear, a wild, raging storm of purple lightning, billowing green clouds, and clumps of tiny sparkling lights popping into and out of existence with the wind. Occasional silences alternated with bursts of thunderous noise, often sounding like the cheering of thousands of people, the chittering of insects, or the monstrous crackling of cyclopean bonfires.

Charles stood at the head of the group. "Let's do this," he said, starting down the trail.

Staley jogged up beside Charles. "Do you think Wise has, I don't know, some kind of ulterior motive with all this?" he asked. "And, more importantly, what do you think it would take to get him to give us a piece of this place?"

Charles shrugged. "If we get through this, I think he'll owe us *at least* that," he answered. "And if not—well, we know the locations of the portals. Fuck it. We'll just *take* something."

Staley laughed and patted Charles on the back. "You're all right, dude! You're officially invited to the party we're planning for Fitz's birthday." He turned around briefly to see Fitz and Barton laughing hysterically about something a few paces back.

"Thanks," Charles said. "Looks like we're almost to the clearing."

A few minutes later they stood at the edge of a circular clearing. Trees heavily laden with thick branches and leaves formed a canopy overhead. As promised, an eerily silent whirlpool of iridescent energy rotated wildly in its midst, its edges lapping a small dirt walkway surrounding it.

"Here's the instructions," Barton said, noticing a wooden sign tacked up to a tree. A few words had been jaggedly burned into it.

"*Dive through the Cone,*" Fitz read aloud. "Wise probably could've told us that."

"Okay," Barton said, glancing around. "What cone?" A sudden roar—the winning touchdown scored—erupted from somewhere beyond the tree line.

Charles pointed at the whirlpool. "That one, I guess?"

"Is that a cone?" Staley asked reasonably.

"Looks kind of like one, just pointed down instead of up," Charles answered.

Barton shrugged. "Sounds good to me. Given that there's no other cone-shaped objects in the area, and this is where the trail ends. Who wants to go first?"

No one stepped forward.

"I wish Steve was here," Charles said.

"Who?" asked Staley.

"Never mind," Charles said. "How about we all do it at the same time? Maybe stand around the edges and jump on the count of three?"

"Does that ever work?" Barton asked. "Count of three, I mean. I always get that wrong. Do you jump *on* 'three'? Or just after it?"

Charles shrugged. "Just after it, let's say."

Fitz gazed longingly back down the warmly lit trail leading to the Théâtre d'Azif. "Do *all* of us have to go?"

"I'm thinking yes," Staley answered. "I mean, if some of us were supposed to stay, don't you think Wise would have said so?"

"Not to mention the doors probably auto-lock once you go through them, or something," Barton said.

"Oh, shit," Staley said, suddenly all seriousness. "What if this is just the way Wise gets rid of us? Did anyone think of that?"

The group was silent for a moment.

"Seems like an awfully complicated maneuver," Barton said. "You know, if he just wanted to kill us."

"No shit," Fitz said. "Why didn't he just shoot us back in the theater? Or, better yet, back before we even *got* to the goddamned theater?"

They were silent again. The long, low whistle of a fire truck wailed distantly.

"Fuck it," Charles said. "You guys want me to go first?"

"Hell, no," Staley said. "We'll all go at the same time."

Fitz shrugged. "Whatever. I guess if we win, or whatever, we'll get to come back."

"That's the spirit, Fitzgerald!" Barton said, clapping him on the back. "Now get your ass to the edge of the world!"

Their positions taken, one each at the cardinal points of the whirlpool, Charles started a count to three.

Fitz, Barton, and Staley all cannonballed in at "two." The report of a supersonic jet breaking the sound barrier overhead immediately following their launch knocked Charles off balance and into—

The University of Tulsa: White Rabbits!

THEY LANDED IN HEAPS on a bed of beanbag chairs.

"Hey, isn't this..." Staley trailed off as he rolled from a beanbag chair into the dimly lit hallway behind the secret door in Wise's office. A blinking red sign above the door flashed "EXIT HERE!" with an arrow pointing down.

"Right! I get it," Barton said, kicking aside one of the beanbag chairs and revealing Fitz, facedown.

"Dude," Fitz said, rolling over. "That was wild."

Seconds later, with a sound like a cork popping, Charles Leland shot out of the tunnel mouth and landed in the pile.

"Woah," Charles said, grinning. "Not bad, actually."

"Not at all," Staley said. "Looks like Wise thought of everything. I guess we head out from here."

Charles and Barton and Staley managed to drag Fitz in the direction of Wise's office, ignoring his protestations of having forgotten cigarettes, wallet, and "medication" (all of which were lies) back in the Théâtre d'Azif.

Only reassurances that he now knew the way back once they completed their mission—and that completion of their mission seemed somehow essential to that knowledge ever being useful to them—pacified the stalwart stoner.

"I'm at least riding shotgun back to the Joint," he insisted as Staley thoughtfully replaced the cart in front of the obverse side of the secret door in Wise's silent office.

"We're not *going* to the Pizza Joint tonight, remember?" Charles reminded him. "We're going to *this* place." Charles waved the slip of paper inscribed with Damian Stephens's address in front of Fitz's face.

"Oh, right," Fitz said. "Sure."

Charles had a disorienting moment as the group began trudging down the hall, returning the way they'd come. He turned to look one last time at Wise's office door, and, perhaps because of the dim lights, could not *see* it—a split second later, the door was there again, though seeming somehow *changed*...

"Dude, are we going or what?" Staley barked from down the hall.

Charles shook his head and ran to catch up. "Sorry," he said, still wondering.

They eventually found their way through the labyrinth of halls and alleys between buildings back to the McFarlin Library parking lot.

"Uh, guys," Barton said, scanning the lot. "Didn't we park here?"

There was a blue Ford Festiva at one end of the lot, a black Trans Am twenty paces away from them—and no pickup trucks whatsoever.

"Yes, we parked here," Charles said, getting frantic. "Oh, shit. Do you think they *towed* it? Do you need to have a parking permit to park here?"

"Yes," Staley said, pointing at a white-lettered blue sign posted clearly at the edge of the lot. "Apparently, you do."

"Sonofa*bitch*!" Barton said, slamming a fist into his palm and stomping on the asphalt. "What the hell are we gonna do *now*?"

"Wait, what's the problem again?" Fitz asked. "Do we need to head back to Wise's office or, I don't know—"

"Can we call a cab, maybe?" Staley suggested. "Do we have enough money for a cab?"

"A *cab*?" Barton repeated. "Seriously? Great idea, Stale. Let's have some random dude drop us off at the place where we're going to commit a robbery."

"We should probably just go back and talk to Wise—" Fitz started.

"No," Charles interrupted firmly. "No. We are not going to let this happen. Please tell me that one of you knows how to hotwire a car?"

All three looked at Charles. All three slowly raised their hands.

"Then let's do this before it's too fucking late," Charles said. "Pontiac or Ford?"

THE TRANS AM WAS, of course, preferred, but the little Festiva was possible, in the sense that the latter had no discernible security system.

Not to mention it was unlocked right off the bat.

"Probably doing this guy a favor, taking this piece of shit car," Barton said as he magicked the ignition into starting, keyless.

He smiled and ushered them in to the car's cramped confines. "Let's go save the day," he said.

AND WHAT A BITCH it was to screw *that* one up.

Observation of the dark little house for half an hour from a spot at the end of the cul-de-sac in which it was situated had them nearly convinced that Damian Stephens had left for his meeting. Just as they were about to exit the Festiva and sneak up to the house, the garage door rose.

"Close one," Charles said. "Jesus."

They hunkered down as best they could. A hatchback Honda Civic backed out of the garage and into the street.

"*That's* why Julie's got one of those?" Charles remarked.

"Julie?" Barton said. "Oh, Julie Evergreen. From the Means of Escape."

Charles nodded, even though Barton couldn't see him. They could barely make out the figure driving the vehicle, and by the time he dutifully used his right-turn signal under a streetlamp at the end of the cul-de-sac, he was completely obscured.

"Coast clear, you think?" Staley asked.

"Let's do this," Fitz said.

"I'll be right there," Barton said, untwisting the ignition and battery wires as the rest of them exited the car.

Wise's instructions turned out to be accurate: a heavy

copper ashtray full of black Nat Sherman filters sat on a little raised table beside a single weathered lawn chair on the tiny porch. Beneath the ash tray was a spare key.

Charles inserted the key into the door lock. "No turning back now," he said.

Darkness met them in the foyer, alleviated only by a tiny red-shaded lamp at the far end of a living room ahead.

"Where would he have that manuscript?" Staley asked.

"There's gotta be an office or study or something in here," Barton said. "The house isn't that big. Why don't we split up?"

"Famous last words, dude," Charles said. "But let's do it anyway. I'm guessing we don't have much time." He felt around the wall and found a light switch. "Use the fucking lights. Supposedly he's not going to be home any time soon. Let's get this done fast."

Posters, pages from magazines, photographs, and hundreds of trinkets, knick-knacks, and toys on poorly installed shelving were immediately revealed when the uncovered lightbulb illuminated the foyer. Despite the astonishing variety, there was a similar theme: it was all fantasy, science-fiction, or horror-themed memorabilia.

"Huh," Barton said, heading immediately for a hallway off to their right. "Cool house."

"No doubt, dude," Staley said.

"Didn't Wise say he was at a *Werewolf Coven* meeting?" Fitz reminded them. "That sounds like it could be bad for us if he finds out we were here."

Charles shook his head. "Doesn't matter, man," he said. "Just search damn it. Everything. I guess."

"I'll check the kitchen," Fitz said.

"Of *course* you will," Staley remarked, already trudging past piles of battered paperbacks in the living room. He flipped a switch and strings of Christmas-tree lights illuminated the jam-packed room. "Sonofabitch. *Look* at all this shit."

There was a lot of it, to be sure. Charles followed Barton into the recesses of the house: three bedrooms and one bathroom. The room where Damian obviously slept was surrounded on all sides with shelf after shelf of books, including a stack of books on his nightstand which looked like his current reading. "Ligotti," Barton read aloud from the stack. "*Songs of a Dead Dreamer.* Interesting. Carroll. *Liber Null & Psychonaut.*"

Barton continued riffling through stuff in the bedroom.

Charles made his way to the back end of the house. Bathroom. What looked like a closet with a securely closed door—locked. A room that looked like the study—a heavy wooden desk with a heavier-looking monster of a typewriter sitting on it.

"Barton," Charles said. "This is probably it."

Barton grunted from the other room. "Be right there."

Charles made his way into the room. More books, papers, shelves—a gigantic poster of the Misfits covered one wall. It seemed to serve as something of a bulletin board with hasty scribblings on index cards tacked all over it.

On the cluttered desk, beside the typewriter, Charles saw something that looked like a manuscript. He flicked on the little desk lamp beside it.

MORPHEUS UNBOUND

or

ZOD-MANAS ZI-BA

by

DAMIAN STEPHENS

Qui non intelligit, aut taceat, aut discat.

Barton was suddenly in the room. "Is that it? Grab it. Let's get the hell out of here."

Charles felt himself perspiring suddenly. *Was this it?* He grasped the neat stack of pages and lifted it from the desk.

"I don't know if this is it," Charles said, looking up at Barton. "I thought it was supposed to be titled '*Fear Club.*' "

"Well, are there any other stacks of pages in here?" Barton asked, frustrated. He began rummaging around a bit more brusquely, and pulled open the drawers of the desk. "Look, here's something—no. That one's called *Brain of the Dead Were-*

wolf." Barton laughed. "I think he mistook this drawer for the trash can."

Charles flipped through the pages of *Morpheus Unbound* and set the manuscript back on the desk, sighing aloud.

"What?" Barton asked. "That's not it?"

"It's blank," Charles said. "Just a big stack of blank pages."

"Seriously?" Barton said, amazed. He grabbed the stack of pages and flipped through it himself. "Whaddaya know. Writer's block, maybe?"

"Shit," Charles said. "Shit, shit, *shit.*"

"It's *gotta* be here *somewhere,*" Barton said, waving his hands around. "Maybe Fitz or Staley found it—"

"Or 'Jim Buskey' already got it," Charles said. "Meaning we're fucked. Or Damian Stephens *knew we were coming,* so he took it with him—"

"Meaning we're fucked," Staley said, walking into the room. "Nothing, right?"

"Nothing," Charles answered.

"Fitz is eating a bag of Lay's with *garam masala* poured on them," Staley told them. "And drinking Damian's last Jolt. I swear, sometimes I think that boy's pregnant."

Barton sat down in a cheap rotating desk chair in a corner of the room. "So what do we do?" he asked.

"We've got to think," Charles said. He sat down at Damian Stephens's typewriter and placed his hands, palms down, on the table. "*Where* could it be?"

"Maybe he took it with him?" Barton suggested.

"Wise said it would be *here* when he *left,*" Staley reminded them.

"Right," Charles said. Suddenly, he sprang out of the chair. "Locked door!" He bolted out of the room and back down the hall. Staley and Barton followed.

Charles shook the handle and tried pushing at the door to no effect. "Can either of you guys—"

"Allow me," Barton said, clearly the most criminally minded of them. He extracted a folded jackknife from one pocket and knelt down to "fix" the lock.

Seconds later, the door popped open with an ominous

creak. A soft yellow light filtered out from the small room beyond.

Barton pushed the door all the way open.

In the center of a small, windowless, otherwise bare room lit by a single soft yellow bulb in the center of its ceiling stood an octagonal oak altar.

On the altar sat a pristine glass aquarium filled with water. In the water floated a single, wide-eyed, black-finned fish.

"O-*kay*?" Charles remarked. The fish gazed blankly at him.

"There's nothing else in here?" Staley asked, stepping inside the room. "No hidden drawers or anything?" He walked around the aquarium, checked the little oak table under it, patted the walls randomly.

The fish followed his movements with no discernible interest.

"Right," Barton said as Staley exited the room, mystified. He depressed the lock on the other side of the knob and re-closed the door, softly. "Well. Clearly an important fish."

Charles looked at the both of them, opened his mouth to say something, then threw up his hands in despair and headed back down the hall.

"Hey guys?" Fitz's voice rang out from the other end of the house. "Guys? You should probably come here and check this out."

Fitz's voice arose simultaneously with brand-new "oh, shit" looks on their faces. They made their way to the kitchen.

Fitz shoved a handful of Lay's in his mouth from a crumpled bag. "Dudes," he said through the chips. "Please tell me I'm reading this calendar right."

"What's the problem?" Charles asked. He squinted at the anomalous "Kittens All Year Round" calendar. A wide-eyed ball of fur peeked out of a wicker basket in this month's photograph. "What? So he forgot to X-off yesterday's date or something?"

" 'Get suit for D.'s wedding,' " Staley read off, peering closer at the calendar. " 'Pay phone bill'—yeah, didn't quite make *that* one." He snickered, then stopped suddenly. "*Oh.*"

"What—? Oh, shit." Charles saw it, suddenly, and couldn't

unsee it despite his immediate consternation.

"What the hell is it?" Barton asked, unable to look past them.

"I thought so," Fitz said. "It says '1988' doesn't it? Damn!" He set the bag of chips down and proceeded to rinse his hands off in the sink. "Missed my twenty-second birthday *completely*, dudes!"

"IT CAN'T BE RIGHT!" Charles shouted, flipping through several more playful kitten images to confirm it. "Wise said we were supposed to end up back here the *same* night we left!"

"It's right, I think," Staley assured him, waving a copy of *Fangoria* in front of him. "It's nineteen eighty-eight."

Barton laughed despite himself. "Doesn't that guy on the cover look kind of like Booker?" he said.

Staley turned the magazine back around and laughed aloud. "You're right!" he chuckled. "It totally *does*! If he had two faces, I guess. What is this movie? *Dead Heat*? What the fuck?"

"Guys! Seriously! If it's 1988, then aren't we completely fucked?" Charles opened Damian's refrigerator and rooted around. "Aha," he said, pulling out a Heineken and twisting off the cap. He took a long gulp before continuing. "Stek Jarry's definitely not still at CJ's a *year* after we were supposed to meet him there. The book's either been published—under my name as Damian's pseudonym—or the manuscript was stolen by Jim Buskey the night we were *supposed* to be here."

"Maybe we should just get the hell out of here," Fitz said. "I mean, what if he's not at his meeting tonight, or whatever, you know?"

"Turn off the lights, first," Barton said, heading back to the study and the bedroom. "When in major doubt, flee."

"He's going to know *somebody* was here," Staley said, pointing at the open bag of Lay's on the counter.

Fitz smirked and tossed it in the trash. "He did it in his sleep," he said.

THEY GOT BACK TO the Festiva, having left the thankfully bedraggled scene looking as "undisturbed" as possible.

"We'll need to put gas in this monster before long." Barton said, rewiring the ignition. The car coughed phthisically before starting. "Where to? The Pizza Joint? It's just down the street from here."

"Obviously, dude," Staley answered. "If it's still even there. Think about it: Booker tried taking off in a time machine that *won't travel through time*, got back to the Joint, and did what? *Ran it by himself*? Gimme a fucking break!"

They sped out of the cul-de-sac.

"I'm thinking we ought to head back to the university," Charles spoke from the back seat. "Wise has got to know what went wrong."

"Certainly explains the missing truck," Barton said. "Damn it. Towed, impounded. Probably fucking auctioned off. *Damn* it."

"Yeah," Fitz said. "I thought Wise was supposed to be, you know, wise."

"Woah, woah, woah," Staley said, pointing as they drove under an overpass near the Pizza Joint. "Look at that shit."

Other than the unlit image of their logo, the Pizza Joint squatted like a forgotten sculpture by a bad artist on the side of the road. Planks of particleboard covered the windows and front door. Amid random graffiti was a battered sign: *FOR SALE OR LEASE*.

Barton pulled into the back parking lot, lit only by one errant sodium vapor lamp in the near distance that seemed to be apologizing for the illumination. The garage that once housed their truck had broken windows on its door. "We've got about enough gas left to get back to T.U., probably. The only good thing about this piece of shit car is its mileage."

"Do we want to go back there?" Charles asked. "I mean, if someone's looking for this 'piece of shit car,' you know."

"Right," Staley said. "Fuck it. We need to track down Booker, I guess, and find out what the hell happened here."

"*Guys?*"

The familiar voice came out of nowhere, like the voice of God in some hack historical fiction. Much like the voice of God probably would, it sounded a little drunk and a lot like Booker Reuchlin.

"*Heilige Scheiße!*" The voice again, this time its *locus* discernible: the darkened garage.

"Is that Booker?" Staley asked rhetorically as Barton and the others shot out of the Festiva.

The garage door rattled and shook. "Help me with this damned thing!" Booker shouted from the other side.

Barton and Charles each grabbed an edge of the garage door and hefted it up.

It was he, indeed: Booker Reuchlin—though a sight different than he was when they had last seen him. His half-body-length locks of thick, wavy hair had been amputated at the root; shorn was he of torn jeans, Doc Martens, leather vest, and Slayer T-shirt.

He stood there, in Army-green fatigues, dog tags clinking as he literally wiped tears away from his eyes with the back of one muscled and tattooed forearm. Six or seven empty cans of Budweiser were strewn about the oil-stained floor of the garage—one of them rested, upright, next to the DeLorean's tire.

"Barton! Staley! Fitz!" Booker threw his arms around each comrade and hugged tightly, much to everyone's bewilderment.

"Dude," Barton said. "You look—ah, you look good?"

Fitz and Staley both shrugged, unsure of what precisely to say.

Charles stood aside. "Booker?" he said calmly. "I think I speak for everyone when I ask: *what the hell happened to you?*"

Booker collapsed into a sitting position on the dirty floor of the garage. He grabbed the closest beer can and drained it.

"When you guys didn't come back, I—" he started.

"Wait a minute, you mean *last year*, on this night, when we didn't come back?" Staley clarified.

Booker nodded and extracted a pack of Marlboro Reds

from his pocket. "Last year," he said, lighting his cigarette and blowing out smoke wistfully. "Last fucking *year*, man!"

"Why don't you start at the beginning?" Barton suggested, and Booker did.

HIS WORDS TUMBLED OUT like too much whiskey, outlining a harrowing tale of woe and lost hope.

"Yeah, so I tried to get that time machine to work," he explained. "I headed out to all those long farm roads past 101st Street. I *definitely* hit eighty-eight miles per hour, but nothing happened. And I realized I was pretty near CJ's, so I did the secret knock at the back door and had a few with Rachel and all them. Then I made the worst decision of my life: I decided, at that point, I had to try to travel through time *again*. So I got back out on the road, hit eighty-eight, and all these lights started flashing, and I thought I'd totally nailed it, man!

"But it was the cops. Big time. And I was basically super-fucked. I didn't even bother trying to say I was sober. They just locked me up—took the car, which I guess they thought was stolen. Yeah, well, long story short, I tried calling the Pizza Joint, and couldn't get a hold of anybody. So I sat there in jail for a few days. Finally got a hold of my pop, who laughed his ass off when I told him what had happened. Bailed me out. He used one of his fucking crime syndicate contacts or whatever to get the DeLorean out of impound 'cause he'd been wanting one. So it's been sitting on his property since then.

"So you guys never showed back up. And I called *everybody*, man! Couldn't find Marigold. Nobody knew where you were—not Fat Nate or Paulie or Shelley T. or fucking *anybody*.

"And my court date comes along and the judge is a real pecker. He's like, 'You've done this before you little shit how dare you fuck with us we're gonna fuck you up you no-good shit!' And all that. And he says that if I do two years in the Army, I don't have to go to jail."

Booker cracked open another beer. "My dad sold the Joint to some real estate place. And I thought to myself: *they wouldn't just abandon me unless they were dead*. And then I thought about all that shit Marigold told us, about the portals and everything.

I went looking for some of them, right after I got out of boot camp, but I didn't find shit.

"Well, that's not true. Not completely. Out behind CJ's, I *did* find something. It was like a clan of gutter punk skater kids. I think they were squatting there—living in the ruins of the old Murdock Mansion. Fuck, who knows? Maybe they're the ones that burned it down. They were all out there, raising hell, having a blast. This one kid"—Booker started chuckling as he said it—"this one kid had a T-shirt that said 'Who Sharted?' on it, and I never laughed so hard about anything. So I had a few drinks with them, but then they found out I was in the Army, and they got all pissy and everything about it. So I left.

"And I thought the other day: okay, I'm on leave, let's go and do a toast for the guys at the Pizza Joint and drop this shit forever. I figured I'd get shitfaced and sleep it off in here." He waved his hand at the room. "So my dad's passed out and I took the DeLorean and that the fuck is that."

The five of them sat in the dimly lit environs of the back parking lot of the ex-Pizza Joint, smoking, drinking, not (alas) doing any other drugs, but certainly considering it.

"So, uh..." Booker dragged off his cigarette and opened another beer. "So, uh, I figured you guys would tell me what happened, you know?"

"Oh, shit! Right!" Barton exclaimed. "Sorry, dude!"

In the most succinct possible fashion, and while finishing the twelve pack of Budweiser, Barton, Fitz, and Staley explained what had happened to them, with occasional addenda from Charles.

Booker took the requisite moment of silence after they had finished, then clapped his hands and hooted. "Nailed it, dude! I *told* you we'd find the wise nerd at T.U.!"

He crushed the last beer can against the ground, then leapt up, showing a great deal of the old Reuchlin energy again.

"And secret passageways to underground lairs?" he said ecstatically, beginning to pace back and forth. Charles noted that he didn't *quite* seem to understand that Wise's "underground lair" was more an extradimensional pocket in spacetime, but that was an unnecessary clarification at the moment. "Sumbitch! I vote we head back to the campus and find Wise Nerds. Sounds like someone could use a little ass-kicking to get him back in line."

"Jesus, they've really gotten to you, haven't they?" Barton said, indicating the fatigues and dog tags.

"Seriously, though!" Staley seconded. "That dude's got some 'splainin' to do."

Fitz nodded emphatically. "I figured we should've done that all along."

"We definitely need to find out what the hell happened, anyway," Charles agreed. He pointed at the DeLorean. "I'll drive *that*. I'll follow you guys."

"Wait, why can't we all ride in the time machine?" Fitz asked.

"It's a two-seater," Booker explained. "And *that* piece of shit over there"—he nodded at the Festiva—"can't fit five people. Okay, Chuck." He tossed him the keys. "Try and keep up!"

THE FESTIVA LITERALLY ROLLED to a stop, completely out of fuel, as they entered a large parking lot on the grounds off 11th Street.

"We'll just park it here," Barton said. "That's a nice gesture, if I do say so myself. How many car thieves bring your car *back*?"

Charles found a conveniently empty "Visitor Parking" spot in an overflow lot near McFarlin, where he waited for the Goblin Gang.

They trekked over to the library.

In preparation for Finals Week, it was wide open; echoes of wild parties on Fraternity Row trickled out into the rest of the campus.

"Wise's office was over that way," Charles said. "And I'm just going to guess that he's there, even if it *is* after one in the morning."

"Doesn't matter, dude," Staley said. "We know his secret hiding place. We're getting him one way or the other."

THEY BEGAN THEIR MORE official reunion on the way to Wise's office. Much to their dismay, the placard bearing his name had been replaced: C— C—, Ph.D., D.Sci.*

"*Damn* it!" Charles said, having approached the office first. "I *knew* I saw something weird when we got back!"

"Isn't this it, though?" Fitz observed. "Fourth door from that orange vending machine."

"The secret entrance to the Théâtre should be in there anyway, still, right?" Staley said, tapping on the door of the darkened office.

"We've got to check it out, at least," Barton said. "Anyone have a—"

Booker had extracted a Swiss Army Knife and was jimmying the lock.

"—key?" Barton finished as the lock clicked. Booker grinned widely and pushed open the door.

"Ladies?" he said, waving them in.

Staley turned on the lights.

"Well that sucks," he said, revealing floor-to-ceiling and wall-to-wall bookshelves sporting several hundred—heavy-looking—volumes. The secret door, needless to say, was utterly obscured from both view and access.

"C'mon!" Booker said, grabbing a handful of encyclopedias from one of the shelves. "This won't take more than half an hour if we hustle!"

"Dude," Barton pointed at the corners of the shelves, "they're fucking *bolted* to the wall, man."

Barton shook his head, stacking another two handfuls of textbooks on top of the encyclopedias. Boot camp really had gotten him in shape, at least.

"Piece of piss," he explained. "I can have those fuckers off the wall in ten minutes."

Fitz shrugged and started taking books off the shelf against the far wall, one at a time, much to Booker's delight.

Charles turned to Barton. "Will we be able to live this

* You know the drill.

down if we don't help?" he asked.

Barton simply shook his head. "Hell, no," he said.

BOOKER MADE GOOD ON his claim.

Emptied and removed from the wall within twenty-five minutes, Booker angled the shelf away from the wall and, with a little help from his friends, managed to drag it away enough to afford some small access to the alleged "secret passageway."

After a further fifteen minutes of banging and prodding and pushing—even carving out pieces of the wall with his utility knife—they were convinced.

The passage was no more.

"Are you sure it was *this* office?" Booker asked as they exited the office. Charles glanced back at the mayhem they'd left and reassured himself that the university would be able to cover the damages.

"Yes, it was *definitely* this office," Staley said. "Probably. I mean, we were *just here*. I mean literally, you know. Earlier tonight. Er, a year ago, but still."

"Do you think they moved that vending machine?" Fitz suggested hopefully.

Charles's head drooped. "Wise closed up shop and left. If he was even ever a professor here at all."

"No doubt," Barton said. "I mean, who knows? If you can make whole cities fit inside a wall, couldn't you just magic up a single extra office in a whole hallway of them?"

Booker was clearly a little upset. "My buzz has completely worn off," he said. "I say we go grab another beer—"

"*Campus police! Hold it right there!*"

The voice bellowing from the other end of the hallway was accompanied by the brilliance of several Maglights aimed in their direction.

The five of them scattered like roaches from a boot.

Charles—unpracticed at running from the police—found himself separated from the others in short order, sprinting madly down an unfamiliar hallway.

The sound of hot pursuit made him ignore the burning

pain that entered his lungs as he fled with no predictable motion towards freedom. After two or three turns down hallways that looked roughly identical, he flung open a random door, revealing a staircase.

Heading down, and following an exit sign out of the building, Charles's disorientation began to clear up as he made his way through an alleyway between two buildings. McFarlin Tower appeared suddenly.

Two campus police cars were parked out front, lights flashing. The DeLorean waited innocently away from the hubbub.

But the Goblin Gang was nowhere in sight.

Charles tried to catch his breath as he inched out of hiding, cutting across a small embankment behind a row of trees and approaching the library parking lot from the other direction.

Goddamnit I hope they got away, he thought. One way or the other, they appeared to have drawn the cops' interest in the opposite direction, leaving him free to exit the grounds. He got in the DeLorean and made a concerted effort to calm himself.

"Think," he said aloud. "*Think*. How is getting *caught* going to help them?" He paused and breathed steadily.

There was only *one person* other than Wise Nerds who might actually be able to *do* something about any of this. One person who could even feasibly *understand* what the hell was going on.

He allowed himself to wait and observe the proceedings. Fifteen minutes later, with still no sign of the Goblin Gang, he saw two cops start heading toward the McFarlin lot, sweeping the area with flashlights.

Feeling like the mother of all bastards, he started the car and left.

CHARLES HAD A DECISION to make, certainly. He could, of course, simply use the test tube of "time travel fluid" Wise had given him—still miraculously unbroken in his left jeans pocket—and, as they say, skedaddle. Get back to Golem Creek and hope for the best.

But there was, as he'd thought back in the parking lot,

perhaps another way to deal with the situation. A more direct way.

Charles found himself heading back across town to Broken Arrow, thanking the gods that the city was laid out in a simple rectangular grid. In his mind, it was quite obvious: if Damian Stephens was responsible for bringing everything about in the first place, then Damian Stephens was the person who could fix it.

At least, he might be able to bail the Goblin Gang out of jail, if they hadn't been able to evade the police.

And at minimum pay for another tank of gas so that Charles could get out of here.

DAMIAN STEPHENS'S PLACE IN Broken Arrow was, once again, dark and silent. Given his intention to settle things once and for all, Charles boldly parked the DeLorean in Damian's driveway at an angle, to prevent him from escaping (should that option arise).

No one answered the door when Charles rang the doorbell the first, second, or third time. He waited perhaps five minutes before retrieving the spare key under the ashtray and letting himself in.

There were more lights on, this time.

Charles made a quick sweep of the living room and kitchen. He glanced out a back window: no one occupied either of two plastic chairs parked in the middle of the overgrown lawn.

He checked the garage: no car in sight.

So Damian Stephens was out, at least for a little while.

Charles returned to the hallway.

The bedroom and study were empty; clearly no one was using the bathroom.

That left the room with the fish.

Again, the door to that room was locked. Charles sprinted back to the kitchen and grabbed a knife with a sharp point from one of the drawers. He returned and prodded the little hole to one side of the knob until the door, once again, popped open.

And there it was. Same windowless room, same oak altar

bearing the same aquarium and, presumably, the same fish.

Charles stepped into the room and closed the door behind him.

"What's the goddamn *deal*?" he said aloud, leaning in despondency against a wall. The fish gulped, its paradoxical combination of lazy floating and wide-eyed alarm somehow mimicking precisely how Charles was feeling at the moment. "Where the hell *is* he? What am I supposed to *do*?"

Charles slid down the wall into a seated position on the floor.

It's not your fault.

"Right, right," Charles said, gazing at the immaculate tan carpet. "Not my goddamn fault. *I* know that. But does Damian Stephens?"

Of course he does. He wrote you then as he writes you now.

Charles slowly looked up at the fish.

"Hello?" he said tentatively.

The black fish did something like a nod, swooping around the bubbling, crystal clear waters of its aquarium. *Hello.* It regarded Charles with one now undeniably sapient eye.

The words presented themselves clearly within Charles's mind, audible/not-audible, and distinctly alien to the wretched thoughts around them, which scattered like clouds in an etheric wind.

"Are you...?" Charles trailed off, wanting to say "Damian Stephens," but sensing the incredible absurdity of it.

I am no more Damian Stephens than I am YOU, it responded, wagging its fins emphatically. *But that doesn't mean anything, really. What you're wanting to know is what I AM, and that is more easily said than understood: the Drowned Eye of Odin, the Wish-Granting Gem—Chintamani, the hinge of all perceivable realities.*

Charles was suddenly laughing despite himself. "I'm not laughing *at* you," Charles explained, chuckling. For some reason, the more the fish spoke, the better Charles felt.

I know.

"I'm just *laughing*," Charles continued. "How fucking crazy is this? I've leapt through portals, been chased by monsters, lived in a magically generated heaven-world for months, *trav-*

eled through time, apparently—and I can officially have my mind blown no longer." He gazed at his hands, as he would in a dream to confirm his reality. "None of this is real." He said it as a statement of simple fact. "Dreams aren't real. *Realness* isn't real."

Perhaps an over-simplification, the fish commented. *But why not? Suppose that reasoning is accurate. It's still happening, isn't it? You're still experiencing something, real or not.*

"But what do I *do* about any of it? Wise told me to get the manuscript before it was finished. I didn't."

The fish chuckled convincingly. *This is just what happens when you walk off-camera*, it said. *Did you ever wonder what the characters in a story do when you're not reading it? Or what the people in your dreams do after the dream ends for you? What's beyond the edges of the painting? It was all done in some context, before you got there; there is that which remains.*

"So I just relax and wait it out?" Charles asked. The idea gave him an almost immediate sense of peace.

You should ALWAYS relax and wait it out, the fish answered. *Whether you understand what's going on or not, the story always tells itself. Why does everyone think that every question must be answered? Mystery is the essential thing. It does MORE than drive us. It IS us.* The fish did a loop around a large lava rock in the center of the aquarium before continuing. *The story will play itself out. But when it comes to what you're ACTUALLY trying to ask me, the answer is: clean yourself up and head back to Golem Creek. That's where you're most needed now. Everything inevitable has happened, according to no plan and no one's intentions. Trust your instincts. Oh, and speaking of which: your friend Julie has the third wish. She just doesn't know it yet.*

"Julie? She's back in Golem Creek?"

She will be when you get there.

"And the wishes..." Charles hadn't ever forgotten about "Roland the Djinn's" promise, but he had started to doubt its veracity when it seemed that his will wasn't so much his *own* as it was the property of some hack fantasy writer in Nowheres-ville. "Those were for real?"

"For real." Hm. That's one way to put it. They were part of the "new story" Roland inserted into Laban's dreaming—part of his means of

escape. Three wishes for the three entities that formed a magical link with another world. And linking quanta of magical energy to those wishes...? It can be almost like splitting an atom.

Harvey Lamb—you don't know him yet—is in the same predicament, though for slightly different reasons. They conspire—using roughly the same means Wise used to generate the Scrying Theater—to get Tom Fallow (you actually do know him, in a strange sense) to plant that Tripwire Portal Marigold told you about. And the link is made when you three blip into the Place of Solace—and Roland has a nearly certain method of blasting himself out. Channel the magical energy from that leaking pipeline—a "mistake" he cleverly suggested, hidden in the role-playing game with Steve—filter it into the only three entities from Outside that had ever gotten in and entice them to use it for something—anything! You and Steve and Julie—an unwitting trifecta that would bomb-blast the Place of Solace open with your wishes—focus too much energy too quickly and make a crack in the walls of the place, just big enough for Roland to escape.

There's the unfortunate consequence, of course, that the entities "corked in" by the Place, beneath the Murk, would make it out if...

The fish "trailed off," seeming uncertain of how to explain further.

"If?" Charles repeated.

If things beyond your control were to happen. If the Laughing God were to attempt a rewrite in that same magical chamber where Laban first entered the Sleep of Siloam.

"Siloam?" Charles said. The fish did an indescribable fish equivalent of a shrug.

"So I wished for a time machine, so that I could just go back and fix things. Find Julie. And I guess that's working?"

Yes. Let the story play out.

"Then what the hell did—does—Steve wish for?"

Well...you may recall the moment that Roland offered you the wishes?

"Sure."

And you might recall clamping your hand over his mouth, to keep him from saying anything aloud?

Charles nodded slowly. "Yeah. So?"

Well, that wasn't enough.

"What?"

It wasn't enough! Roland offered the wishes—he'd "channeled" the leaking energy through that magical manifestation of "himself," the djinn that appeared. And Steve—you were holding your hand over his mouth, but he mumbled it anyway—said that he wished he was the owner of an endless warehouse of every toy and game imaginable.

Charles, speechless for a moment, burst into laughter. He tried several times to comment on Steve's "wish," but it was just so *obviously* Steve's wish, he didn't quite know what to say.

So! Roland had enough of a "crack" at that moment to slip out— which he did, of course. And you two followed.

"And where is this 'endless warehouse' now?" Charles asked.

Good question. I guess I could try to answer that, but it wouldn't matter. Steve...well, let's just say everything happens at its own proper time. An accident can be something you need in the wrong place, or something you don't need in the right place. Like I said—just relax. And let the story play itself out. Maybe you're being written, maybe you're being read...in the end, you're usually just shelved. Possibly remembered, if enough of a link has been established.

Charles stood up. "I just have one more question: *why the hell are you here?*"

The fish's laughter echoed loudly through Charles's mind. *Am I? That's a new one! Hey, be sure to lock the door when you leave.*

With that, it swam into a large cave carved into the back of the central lava rock and disappeared from view.

Charles stood there for a few moments, wondering when exactly he had lost his mind.

He left the room, carefully re-locking the door behind him.

Clean yourself up and head back to Golem Creek. That's what the "Drowned Eye of Odin" had told him to do.

He went into the bathroom and turned on the light.

Yeah, he could use a wash. A change of clothes, perhaps. He noticed a pretty sharp-looking suit hung on the shower-curtain bar that looked about his size.

"You know what, Damian Stephens?" Charles said, pulling it off the rack. "I think I need this more than you do. I think I'll let you write yourself another one."

TWENTY MINUTES LATER, HAVING spruced up, changed into the new suit, and "borrowed" five dollars for gas from a tray of petty cash in the kitchen, Charles left.

He had been starting to feel pretty good ever since talking with "Odin's eye." Perhaps it was the sense of certainty—he finally knew what to do. Even if it was the *wrong* thing to do, he couldn't care less: he was going to find a nice, dark stretch of road somewhere, pour the "time travel potion" into the "flux capacitor" reserve, and head back to Golem Creek.

II.

VELLE

ONCE UPON A TIME, there was a Charley who sought refuge with himself to combat a later version of what he himself had done.

No, wait, let me start that over again.

Once, after walking home from class, Charles Thomas Leland realized that he was dreaming.

Typically when this happened, he would feel that flood of extraordinary emotion, lift his arms to the sky and fly off into the clouds for a few moments, only to awaken in *the same old place, this again, ugh...*

But this time, he calmed down.

I am dreaming.

He lifted his hands, the old Castañeda trick, and gazed at them. He tried to remember where he had been; he tried to focus.

If I can focus...if I can maintain an awareness of this illusion, and remain here, asleep and awake, not drift into any of those other illusions...

He found that it seemed to be "working," which brought its own new problem; we'll call this latter issue "falling for it."

He remembered...*I think I was in class? At Golem Creek University—somewhere around the Place of Solace, then...* Cars whisked by unassuming. He continued to saunter, relaxed, along the sidewalk, and not worry about anything.

It's all a dream. I'm dreaming this.

The inevitable sense of incredible potency surged up within him as the dream began to stabilize.

Just like those other dreams that seem so real, so solid—and they all rely upon our unquestioning acceptance of them—they all rely upon our belief in their histories, their physics, their conventions...

Stabilization required some practice. You had to try to make the same assumptions that held your other worlds together—in a sense, you had to stay *aware* at the same time you stayed *just a little forgetful*... Not too much one way or the other. Balanced—not too doped up on dream-magic, not too sober with statistical improbabilities.

Good. Very nice.

Now, in your mind, in the back of your mind, the possibility exists. Charley walked along the scuffed, grey sidewalk, feeling the coolness of the mid-morning breeze, the scent of breakfast from one of the diners near campus wafting by.

Cool. Calm.

Many times, stabilization required *not going too far*. Now, the manipulation of dreamstuff *is* important—you need to be able to warp and fly and change sizes and all that. But it's a waste of time if you get *kicked out* before you can really start in on any of it. But *stabilizing the space* required, often, doing your damnedest to *keep the dream occupied with itself*. Don't let that world know you're in on the secret! Something about *messing with it* often kicked you out too soon...too soon to realize why you were there in the first place.

Don't let the dream fool you into thinking you should reveal yourself. *Keep silent.*

ADDIE

ADDIE WHITFIELD DIDN'T NOTICE the rainbow of light shooting out of the Brake Street house on the way to her next robbery. She felt that she'd exhausted "The Notebook of Michael Flowers," at least in terms of its immediate use and meaning to her; the promise of further hidden treasures somewhere in that grand old house occupied her thoughts.

The demonic evocation outlined in the notebook *seemed* to work—at least, it had certainly worked last Halloween. And she'd gotten plenty of spooky evidence to support the contention that some of the strange meditations and simpler spells packed in alongside Michael Flowers's constant concerns about his Uncle Curwen (not to mention occasional descriptions of "Bhairavi Society" events involving a "C," a "J," and an "S," whatever all that meant) were indicative of *stronger stuff.*

But outside of manifesting the occasional quantity of "free money" or generating tornadic winds (she was barely able to quell them in time to avoid destroying the lawn furniture and the back fence) or inducing wild, lucid dreams—a primary focus of Flowers's magic—Addie was finding this "magic" business to be something of a tough trade.

She had found the "Notebook"—one of them, anyway, as it appeared to be part of a series—in the rather easily discernible false bottom of a nightstand drawer in the abandoned Flowers residence. She had entered the place one night after a long walk failed to quell the simmering fit of rage brought on by her mother's confiscation (and imminent destruction of) her stash of comic books and fantasy novels.

Damned religious bitch. Hypocritical moron—"Why can't you be more like your sister?" Yeah, more like *that* superficial slut. If they *really* knew what Amanda got up to, they'd *shit. Goddamned zealotous religious—*

Addie calmed herself, using the Pacifying Breath from Michael's notebook. *Tho' the passions be useful in bypassing the Sentries of Reason, without Control there is no Success. And Control derives from Calm, always—like a cyclone's center.*

She remembered the words perfectly, having read over them hundreds of times. A minute later she was steady again.

The Flowers residence loomed just up ahead, the weird "haunted house" that—despite your typical small-town traditions of dares and the constant search for places to avoid parents and police—remained strangely untouched and unvandalized. She unconsciously patted the screwdriver and hammer she'd tossed in her canvas messenger bag, hoping that her forced entry from last time had not been discovered, and that she wouldn't have to find another way in.

...And by holding clearly in mind the Red Pearl in the Throat, we maintain conscious awareness as one body becomes another...

That one had turned out extraordinary—after a few months of practice. The first week or so that she tried it—visualizing a small red sphere in the midst of her throat as she drifted off to sleep, trying to link the onset of unconsciousness with some small thread of her continuing wakeful awareness—she'd gotten nowhere. A few weird dreams—nothing more.

She had almost decided to leave the simple (*and in simplicity is the greatest Power unveiled*) practice behind when she had an idea: why not try *intending to do something* once you're asleep? Seemed like such a basic realization—she was surprised she hadn't already tried it.

So she drew a little amateurish map of Golem Creek. When she added in the Flowers residence, she made a point of marking the supposed "portal" location in a crawl space between the house proper and its basement. *Laban's magic always leaked. The result of self-initiation, Curwen said—no strict guidance when it came to learning foundational material. His Chamber has generated a small Portal in this location which I am wont to discover the properties of... I shall have C as a rat to that maze...*

"C" in this case probably referred to a "disciple" of Michael's named *Charles*, rather than Curwen, who was invariably referred to by his complete name. References to "S" and "J" presumably referred to "Stephanos" and "Julie," respectively, two more of Michael's "students."

Addie didn't know what much of that meant, but based on other descriptions Michael gave of "C," she thought she might perhaps try to use some of the techniques she'd learned to give "C" a fighting chance—"as a rat to his maze."

Despite the cool stuff in his notebook, Michael Flowers sounded like he could be a real dick sometimes.

So she drew the map, sealed it in an envelope labeled "Charles" (to distinguish it from something intended for "Curwen") and tried out a cryptic method that sounded like it could translate material objects into the dream realm.

Nothing seemed to happen. She awoke early Saturday morning and found the letter entangled in her bedsheets.

Frustrated, she got dressed and left for a walk in a heavy mist that had descended over Golem Creek the previous night. For whatever reason, still feeling only half awake, she had shoved the letter in her jeans pocket, only remembering it when she arrived during her meandering at Maple Ridge Elementary, silent and totally obscured by the mist.

She found herself leaving Maple Ridge shortly after arriving, *without the letter*; some hours later, when the day had got on, a sudden memory, as of a dream flooding back into awareness, presented itself: of a loose brick behind a dumpster at the school, where she had dutifully sequestered the letter...

It was a powerful enough memory to send her back to Maple Ridge later that day, where she did indeed find the suggested loose brick. Behind it, alas, no letter—in fact, she couldn't find the letter she'd written *anywhere* after that day.

Whatever had become of her attempt to help "C" out of his "maze," she seemed to be no longer a part of it.

Just another weird result in what had become, since finding the notebook, a series of bizarre occurrences.

Until tonight—Witches' Night.

Addie had made her special plan months ago: head back to the Flowers place on the night of the Monster Ball, and make use of the added peace and quiet in the neighborhoods. If she could find nothing more interesting in any "hidden recesses" in the house, *try to find that portal* and, well—jump through it?

How would she even know if she found it? Michael had indicated that many—*most*—portals were utterly invisible; that the average person fell through one occasionally several times a *day*. Their main characteristic was, in fact, *forgetfulness*—of one's previous world, of one's previous intentions.

Ah, well. Plans were best when you left some of the consequences to chance, she thought.

They were at least more interesting.

CIRCUMSTANCES CONSPIRED TO GENERATE a night for Addie Whitfield worthy of one of her comic book superheroes or a wild episode of *The Outer Limits*.

What she couldn't believe—having been so close to a real, live, wing-flapping demon once before—was the uncanny *realness* of it, like seeing a mountain against blue sky for the very first time, or perhaps standing in the direct path of a fifty-foot tidal wave.

It was *real*, but she couldn't believe it.

She crouched just beside a window in one of the "tower" rooms—presumably, this room had been Michael's, given the preponderance of items with his name on them—and watched a guitar-toting hulk smash what appeared to be a *DeLorean* that had been parked on the street in front of the house. Where the DeLorean had come from, she had no idea, having been immersed in the box-filled depths of Michael's walk-in closet until she heard a panic-inducing *crash* from outside.

As curious as this event was, even curiouser—she recalled words from Michael's notebook here: *curiouser and curiouser, meaning "more curious" or Mercurius*—was the wild-haired young man who stepped briefly out on the lawn in front of the house in an apparent attempt to *bait* the creature. She even heard a confident "*Thought* so, Eddie!" from the boy before he began laughing hysterically at the creature's attempts to penetrate an invisible force field that surrounded the house and its grounds.

The guitar-wielding monster was scary; the thought that there were people *in the house below her* was scarier.

She retreated to the closet and relieved the pitch of her anxiety with the Pacifying Breath.

Ia, Ia, Yog-Sothoth... Ia, Ia, Yog-Sothoth...

Silently, slowly, she chanted the words in rhythm with her breath...four-count *in*, four-count *hold*, four-count *out*, four-count *hold*...

What to do? Wait it out? Confront them?

Could it be "C"? Or "S"?

It was probably not the "J" of "Julie." Probably.

She decided to wait. And listen.

For a while, at least.

AND SHE DID, MEDITATING on the Inner Whirling, the Place where the Cones Meet in her heart, symbolized by a Hexagram, a fiery red one pointing up, interlaced with a watery blue one pointing down.

The Ascending and Descending Tongues of the Cones, in their intersection, generate a Vortex of raw potency, a Whirling Force that dispels many hostile agencies.

A clattering and banging sounded from below. Voices, shouting—the house itself began to creak and crack as from a strong wind blowing upward from the basement.

The Whirling Force?

Addie stood and crept out of the closet. If the house was about to collapse because of some magical indiscretion on her part, she wanted at least a fighting chance to escape.

The voices and creakings and bangings from below ceased moments later as she crept cautiously to the back staircase. As hesitantly as she could, given her anxiety and the—perhaps all-too-brief—silence, Addie descended the stairs, staying to the sides, the wall, the railing, down the first flight...the second flight...the third...

The heavy oak front door in the foyer stood wide open, with no one in sight.

Addie ran for it.

"*You will STOP!*"

The voice rang out behind her, rough, the growl of a pit bull after winning a fight.

Something in the voice *did* make her stop. She turned around slowly.

"*Jim the Janitor?*" she said unthinkingly, astonished.

And it *was* "Jim the Janitor," the unmistakable jump-suited custodian of Honorius High School whom everyone saw and ignored five days a week during the school year.

Jim Buskey literally floated down the steps of the front porch, a pale, bluish-silver glow hovering about his body. "*You have witnessed His Power,*" Jim spoke in that same horror-movie-killer voice.

Something about this simply was not right.

"You're—" Addie didn't quite know what to say, or even how to proceed. She almost turned and walked away—but there was something pathetically fascinating about seeing this "nobody" suddenly glowing and floating in front of her. "You're floating and glowing," she finally finished, arms akimbo, sneakers digging into the lawn. It needed a trim.

"*You will BOW DOWN to His Power—*"

"Wait a minute, hold up," Addie said. Michael Flowers's words awoke in her mind: *Acquiescence to fear is the source of Their Power. Courage—they dislike it. It steals from them what they would take from us.* She took a few tentative steps in his direction, and was pleased to note his villainous grimace falter momentarily. She also noticed something invigorating about the exchange: when she moved closer, a thrill of power coursed through her, emanating from the Inner Whirl. "Bow down to *whose* power, again?"

Jim snarled, rising up several feet and beginning to glow strongly against the dark house behind him. "*Your IMPU-DENCE will be PUNISHED—*"

Addie didn't know *how* she did what she did at that moment—it just happened, as if something in her heart suddenly cracked open. Sheer *joy*—tears of ecstasy springing to her eyes, her body going limp of all tension and anxiety as a flood of indescribable *power* exploded from her, enveloping Jim the Janitor in its radiance.

A moment later, she realized that she herself had been floating above the lawn. She descended softly to the earth.

Jim Buskey lay on the damp ground, no longer glowing, looking somehow thinner and weaker. He seemed to be having some sort of convulsive fit.

Addie walked confidently up to him. She realized, gazing at him face-down in the grass, that he was sobbing.

"I'm *sorry*," he gasped out, clutching at the grass with both hands. It seemed to be the only words he could muster. "I'm *sorry*!" He shouted into the ground.

"It's—um." This was weird. How do you comfort a grown man who just tried to kill you? "It's okay? I guess?"

He cried harder, smashing his face into the lawn and pummeling it with his fists.

Addie looked around nervously. Could she get in trouble for any of this?

"Look, I said it's *okay*," Addie repeated.

Jim gasped in terror.

"*No*." He said the word like it was a fact suddenly realized, then shouted it in abject terror. "*NO!*"

JIM FELT HIS BODY beginning to disintegrate.

All awakenings are false awakenings.

That's what he remembered as his mortality shrugged its shoulders in apology for what was being done to him.

All awakenings are false awakenings.

The words had gone through Jim Buskey's mind long ago, on finding the Secret of Golem Creek beneath the building on the 700 block downtown. Not "What a miracle!" or "Jeepers creepers!"—only that unbidden thought, singular and purposeful and inexplicably meaningful.

Of course, he hadn't *known* it was the "Secret of Golem Creek" at the time; nor had he known the identity of the person who had been waiting for him as he'd stumbled through the Scarab Door, into the dimly lit laboratory beyond.

The guy had looked a little like Cary Grant and a lot like

bad news. *A lone cricket chirped somewhere amid the room's shelves of machinery and wires.*

Bad Cary Grant had held a hand out to him—the sensation of his palm against Jim's own was like a warm fire. He had grinned, showing glistening white teeth like a tight row of fresh tombstones.

"The people here will be calling me 'Weston' soon. But you can call me by another name..."

He remembered there were no windows; only the door through which he had come. Henrik Shaxplay's control room: the original, central component of Golem Creek. Hieronymous etchings along the walls to conjure artificial intelligences as necessary—he'd come to learn that *he himself* was one of those "artifical intelligences," snatched from the mundane through a combination of good timing and cosmic despair.

With a little help from the Laughing God's repertoire of magic tricks, his uselessness had transformed, blossomed, become the soil out of which Purpose had shot like vines, creeping through his every aspect.

And a little girl had outdone him.

Jim's last few thoughts before oblivion—before awakening again in an old apartment, in a new Golem Creek, with no memory nor hint of this life he'd lived as a little god for a little while—were of how thoroughly Yassiz played his pranks, and how everything seems to return to its own beginning...*all awakenings are false awakenings...*

ADDIE LEAPT BACK AS the earth heaved around Jim's body. She watched, mesmerized, as the ground seemed to sink around him, sucking at his struggling form, dragging it down, down out of sight...

Seconds later, he was gone, the grass seemingly undisturbed. A pleasant sheen of moonlight glittered on its dewy surface.

Addie ran back into the house and slammed the door behind her.

STILL HIGH FROM WHAT she was already considering her first "magical battle"—though why Jim the Janitor had super-powers, she couldn't fathom—Addie found the basement, found the secret door to Laban's magical chamber still open, found the curving stone steps leading down to the circle of bones below.

She *didn't* happen to find the other people—and she strongly suspected that Jim had something to do with that.

Torches along the walls still burned with magic fire, providing ample illumination for Addie to marvel at the place. *So* this *is the famous magic room Mike Flowers is always talking about*, she thought. *I get it. It's awesome.*

Addie gingerly picked up what appeared to be an expensive dogcatcher's noose near the base of the steps. It was lighter than she expected it to be, like part of a pool-cleaning net.

Maybe it's some sort of alien wand? she thought.

"Huh," she said, setting it back down.

She circled the perimeter of the chamber until she came to the Triangle of Manifestation at its farthest end. She had read about the entire setup in Michael's notebook, had even used a simpler version of it in her first attempt at evocation, back on Halloween, during her sister's party.

To the right of the Triangle, just outside its morbid, literally skeletal outline, lay a book.

Addie picked it up. "*Fear Club*," she read aloud. "*A Confession*. The Means of Escape, Book One. Damian Stephens." She turned it over and flipped through its pages idly. "Who the hell is Damian Stephens?"

Her voice echoed about the room. She noticed that the Triangle was mirrored by its double on the ceiling above. A shimmering darkness—barely discernible in the flickering light of the torches—played within its confines.

Addie shoved the book into her messenger bag for investigation later. If it was here, especially after something had clearly gone down with Jim the Janitor before she'd, well, "disabled" him (she guessed that was the right word), it was probably important.

She gazed into the center of the bone circle for a few moments.

Maybe try a little magic? If she was now able to sponta-neously levitate and suck power out of people trying to harm her...well, who *knew* what she might be able to pull off here...

Shrugging, she stepped into the circle and out of Golem Creek.

JULIE

FAINTED, PERHAPS—A BLOW TO the head, delivered back-stabbingly by that unfelicitous janitor, perhaps.

The language Julie heard upon her remanifestation was *not* in fact English, but for the sake of narrative continuity (such as we might still find ourselves able to maintain in this late stage of the game), I have translated the strings of peculiar syllables, grunts, and hacking coughs to as close an approximation as possible.

"—and, of course, as you can see, this *particular* conjuration nearly always has such *delightful* tangential phenomena—"

A collective gasp left fewer molecules of breathable air in the room. Momentarily, chuckles and whistles and shouts of "bravo!" and "good show!" restored the atmosphere's chemical equilibrium—but *not* Julie's, who collapsed in a heap, her head coincidentally thudding against the very *vever* that functioned to modify random precipitations.

"Astonishing!"

The vocalization derived from a rather sinister-looking figure—horned, robed, and cowled, he would remind the most unflinching Three Coils initiate of who's boss even without the five-foot Sword of Evocation he waved about like a twig.

"Yet *another* human female!" he chuckled, grinning deeply as the (presumably largely male) audience of demonic frat boys hollered and inexplicably pounded each other on the back. "Who tampered with the ensigilizations? One might suspect—*Travis!*"

A gushing roar of admiration erupted, followed shortly by the apparently multiversal enigma of name-chanting.

"*Tra-VIS! Tra-VIS! Tra-VIS!*"

Nearly collapsed in laughter, the bespectacled hedgeball* hero—once a simple, lonely boy named "Travis," who on a summer night in 1978 sacrificed a chicken out of boredom at a crossroads in his hometown of Baker's Dozen, Michigan, only to inadvertently become extradimensional All-Star Hedgeball Champion a mere nine years later—allowed his peers to lift him on their shoulders ("as usual," he would remark to the cute little vampire journalist who interviewed him about this very incident a week later) and carry him out of the room, gathering sorority girls along the way, horned as they were horny, to begin the sacred process of filling him to bursting with Vicious Amulet Gin ("Life a drag? Bag the VAG!") in preparation for a night of—well, you get it, I'm sure.

When the room had grown dim and temperate and less confusing, Julie's eyes fluttered open, revealing her position—prone—on a wooden surface, covered in exquisitely fabricated glyphs and symbols and prosy strings of cipher, in an auditorium that looked for the most part like your average college lecture hall, despite the lit cressets lining the walls, the bubbling cauldron in one potion-bedecked corner, the obligatory stacks of well-read spellbooks behind a magnificently carved oak lectern, and, of course, the intricate magical triangle she lay in the center of.

A few paces away from her was the even more extraordinarily ornate magical circle from whence, she gathered, the ambitious Karcist had intoned the appropriate mixture of nonsense and power-words to...*evoke her to visible appearance*?

Pleasantly humming a medley that sounded like it was from Nirvana's breakout album, *Nevermind*, a nearly human-looking young man became visible, gathering papers left among the auditorium seats.

"Um," Julie started. "Excuse me? Hello?" Her voice echoed out, lending a sudden air of genuine disorientation to the place.

---

* The most popular sporting competition among Three Coils initiates.

The fellow stopped and gazed at her. A stream of incoherent noises, sounding rather threatening to Julie's untrained ears, rushed out of him before Julie's wild-eyed look of consternation put a stop to it.

Looking somewhat flustered, he grinned sheepishly and literally changed his tune. "Oh," he said in plain English. "Did they forget about you? I'm so sorry."

He dropped a few handfuls of papers on his way over to Julie's immediate predicament.

Julie stood up and attempted to step out of the line of a circle inscribed within the triangle surrounding her—

"No! Wait!" the young "man" shouted, startling and freezing her simultaneously. "Woah! Phew! You have to— hang on—I can do this. One sec."

Julie watched as he lifted a sparkling medallion from the lectern and stepped into the midst of the magical circle in front of her. He closed his eyes and held the device in front of him, aiming it at her, then made a series of complicated gestures with his other hand while mumbling under his breath for a few moments.

"Okay," he said finally, returning the medallion to the lectern. "You should be okay now."

Julie stepped cautiously out of the presumption of her confinement. "Thanks? I guess. I mean—what was all *that* about?" she asked reasonably.

Her liberator had already returned to his task of gathering up papers in the room. "Hm? Oh, that. That guy's something of a—what would you say? Lovable prankster, I guess? I mean, they love him here. Never could've seen *that* coming. Old devil blood, so they say. Poor kid. Lived in a human family for sixteen years before—oops. Sorry." He scratched his head and gazed at her inquisitively. "You *are* human, right?"

Julie took several slow, backward steps in the direction of a door at the other end of the room. It looked promising, in terms of escape—which she was too confused to ascertain the necessity of, at the moment.

"Uh, yeah, right," she said. "Human."

"Huh," he said. "Surprised they just left you here."

Julie decided to make use of the opening. "Yeah, speaking of which—where's *here*, exactly?"

The guy—student—teaching assistant, maybe?—adjusted his glasses over ears a bit pointier than Julie had initially noted and smiled through teeth a bit sharper than she'd thought. "Three Coils! Sorry. Yeah. My name's—" He hesitated a moment. "Well, you can call me 'Bram.' "

"Julie," Julie said, immediately cringing at the use of her real name. "Uh. Right. And this is—Three Coils?"

A low rumbling lightly shook the walls of the room.

"That's been happening recently. Weird." Bram shook his head and returned to his paper-gathering. "Yes! It's one of the annexes, at least. But you still get training just as kick-ass as any they get over at the main campus. Which is lucky—for guys like me, at least. I gotta *work* for a living, you know? Grade these blasted papers—I swear, where did some of these kids learn to 'write,' if you want to call it that? Then over to Lamb's part time. The Underground to Port Mantle Mall's only a quarter-mile from Leibniz Field—that's where I've been staying; a little dingy, but it's only temporary—"

Julie had unconsciously begun waving her arms before her, the mental overflow of her confusion becoming at last a chaos of physical gestures.

"Wait," she said, and took a deep breath. Bram stood patiently before her. "*What* is 'Three Coils'? Where did—um—where did *I* come from? Do you know Charles Leland? Or Steve Chernowski? Or Roland—ah, shit. Roland—this guy who, ah—"

Bram, apparently having dealt with these circumstances before, sighed audibly. "Tell you what. Help me gather up these essays and I'll help you find your people, okay? This is weird. They usually—"

The doors at the back of the auditorium suddenly burst open, admitting the intimidating, sword-bearing character from earlier in our story. A sharp sequence of angry noises exited his black lips; Julie felt certain that the flames in his yellow eyes were real.

Bram, obsequious, outgunned, punctuated rapid speech

with gestures indicating Julie, who began backing up toward her initially planned exit.

When Big Guns turned his gaze slowly and silently upon her, she decided fleeing was probably a good idea.

Simultaneously, she heard a sound such as a megalodon might make if it could bark coupled with a genuine shout of apology from Bram before the lights went out.

SOLIDITY HAS A NASTY habit of convincing us of things—even if we *do* forget how we ourselves got solid in the first place.

It was the solidity of the environment—the hardness of her bed (one of many in the room), the cold, stone floor, the glass of the window beside her nightstand—that convinced Julie Evergreen she had not simply fallen asleep again.

What did that big slimy bastard do *to me?*

Dark, vaulted ceilings...thin, arched windows, letting in the moonlight, one between every two beds...and *beds*, little, wood-framed, disaster-relief-or-homeless-shelter-type beds, dozens of them arranged precisely in neat rows, jutting out like widely spaced teeth in a neat, clean mouth.

She sat on the edge of her little dormitory bed and glanced at the sleeping form in front of her, pale skin illuminated by the soft glow of moon and stars from the window between them. The girl looked somehow vaguely familiar—Brandy Vale? Kelsey Littleton?—but perhaps that was merely the adrenaline kicking in again. She lay peacefully, snoring lightly, grinning at some fantastic innovation presently enjoyed in the recesses of her subconscious mind.

The thought that perhaps this was some sort of afterlife scenario sent a Hollywood chill through Julie's small-town bones.

Am I...? Oh, great. Try to do something nice, right? Help someone out—and what do you get? Thanks once again, Charles Leland, for the Halloween treat. I hope your goddamned Beauty Pageant Queen is choking on my wish.

Julie groaned inadvertently and stood up. As with her flatmates in this Reform School Girl scenario (*should've guessed I'd end up here*), she wore a long, shapeless gown made of some rough-hewn fabric, brownish-white in color. Not quite a hospital gown—no, hospital gowns had a bit more style and fewer visible seams.

One question seemed to outweigh all others for the moment, at least. *Where are my cigarettes?*

As quietly as she could, Julie stepped over to the wooden trunk at the foot of her bed and opened it.

Jeans, a grey T-shirt bearing the faded lettering of some wise advice (*Don't stand so close! You might get shot.*), socks and underwear, a pair of Converse All-Stars... She changed into her old outfit rapidly.

At the bottom of the trunk lay a paperback book—*Wild Lies II: The Truth is Outta Here!*—on top of her black hoodie. She grabbed the hoodie and put it on. She almost closed the trunk, leaving the battered paperback alone but decided—*sans* cigarettes, though not, thankfully, *sans* everything—it might make a useful distraction, perhaps if thrown in the opposite direction she might be running. Or good kindling.

Or possibly even an interesting read before bed.

She tried shoving it into the back pocket of her jeans, within which she found a sheet of crumpled paper: a receipt with some writing on it.

Lamb's Occult Supply Shop, she made out by the dim light. The cash-register receipt ink was otherwise too pale to read. Someone had scrawled a suitably unenlightening message of subtle coercion on it, though: *Go to the bathroom.*

Having no idea, of course, where said bathroom might be located, Julie considered her predicament. It took perhaps a minute or two before one of the girls awoke, slid out of bed, and headed out of the room.

Julie stuck the receipt into a random page of *Wild Lies II*, shoved the book into her back pocket, and followed as surreptitiously as she could.

Out of the vast room, into a thin, dark hallway, and one left turn later—the walkways barely lit by little nightlights just above the floor—Julie waited in the dark niche of an office doorway as her target made use of the facilities.

Julie's concern was both alleviated and heightened when the familiar sound of a toilet flushing confirmed her suspicions of the girl's intent. *Go to the bathroom.* Who wrote it? Why?

It was her best hope of getting somewhere fast, which wasn't saying much.

The girl, still clearly half asleep, strode blindly past Julie's hiding place and back to the sleeping quarters.

Julie darted around the corner and stepped into the bathroom.

There was more light in here. It was the usual kind of place: green metal stall doors and white porcelain sinks. She glanced at herself in the mirror.

Yep. Dark circles under her eyes, hair ragged, skin pale. *That's me.*

So what the hell am I supposed to find here in the bathroom?

She pushed open the stall doors, revealing stark, innocent toilets.

She tapped randomly on several wall tiles, turned the sink faucets on and off, and finally looked up.

An X—potentially indiscernible to one not expressly seeking clues—marked one of the ceiling boards above the last stall.

Okay. Better than nothing.

It took less than a minute for Julie to pull herself up onto the stall divider closest to the spot. Moments later, she had the ceiling board pushed up and was hauling herself into the crawl space above the bathroom.

A moment after that, she was perched on a little walkway just above the ceiling. The light from the bathroom illuminated a wire- and pipe-crammed area extending off into darkness in all directions.

It also illuminated an unassuming lunch sack taped to the walkway. On the sack, in the same shaky hand as that which had written on the receipt, was a name: *Julie.*

She lost no time in tearing it open.

Inside was a small flashlight and folded note.

Julie switched on the flashlight and carefully pushed the bathroom ceiling board back in place.

Julie, the note read. *I'm glad you found this. We probably don't have much time, so please trust that I am here to help. First, replace the ceiling panel. Next, follow the walkway in the direction of the arrows. Try to stay as quiet as possible. When you get to the end, remove the vent and jump. Trust me. Your friend, Bram.*

Julie found herself inadvertently shaking her head. She read the note again. *Trust me.*

All right, dude. What other options do I have?

She started along the walkway, crawling on hands and knees, in the direction indicated by little black arrows marking every five feet or so. A right turn...a left turn...a few shaky areas...

She paused at one point and froze. Voices emanated from somewhere below her, chuckling darkly and yammering in that same guttural speech she'd heard when she'd first arrived. She proceeded past that point in terror, alert to every shuffle of her jeans against the corrugated metal of the walkway.

At last, she reached the predicted dead end.

She could stand in this area, on a platform jutting out of a brick wall. There in the center of the wall stood a metal vent, roughly a four foot square, presumably the one Bram intended her to remove and "jump" through...

Small, twistable latches held the vent on to the wall by its corners. One by one, she twisted them off and removed the vent.

Outside was a mass of dense treetops stretching out and away for miles. A cool breeze ruffled the branches of the trees, carrying a comforting scent of pine along with it. Peering over the edge of the opening, Julie could discern various other outcroppings and windows dotting a brick façade that went up several more stories and, disconcertingly, down perhaps five—at least, that's where the trees started.

You have got *to be kidding me!*

Julie pulled the note back out and scanned it with her flashlight.

...When you get to the end, remove the vent and jump. Trust me. Your friend, Bram.

Was it the wrong vent, perhaps? Had she followed the

arrows incorrectly?

Her anxiety rising, she flashed the light over the walkway again. Black arrows pointing indisputably in this direction. She even noted a small black arrow pointing *directly* at the vent.

...We probably don't have much time, so please trust that I am here to help...

Well, what other options *did* she have? What motivation did Bram have to send her on this weird little adventure...just to have her commit suicide right at the very end?

Julie stuck her head out of the vent again and looked for anything—*anything*—that might confirm Bram's good intentions.

Nothing.

Not even anyone chasing *me! Why the hell couldn't someone just be chasing me? Make it that much easier to do something crazy? They're always ready to chase you until you* need *them to!*

Nothing. Silence marred only by the rustling of the trees in the wind five stories down.

What're you gonna do? Go back? Risk being some weird demon's sex slave?

"Fine," Julie said aloud to the darkness. "Fuck it."

She shoved the flashlight in her jeans and crouched in the opening, her hands clutching the rough brick edges.

If it works, you'll have officially out-Steved Steve.

She actually laughed aloud at that, before taking a nose-dive into the night air, her heart beating so fast and so loudly she hardly noticed what happened next.

IT SEEMED TO BE taking an incredibly long time to hit the ground. Nonetheless, Julie kept her eyes shut as tightly as possible, taking advice from her two-year-old self, to wit: if she never opened them, nothing bad could possibly happen.

After what felt like several minutes, this advice was seen to be stupid and worthy of a two-year-old.

Julie opened her eyes.

She hovered roughly ten feet from the vent opening, arms and legs stretched out and waving, slightly, in the breeze. She peered about her like a lost puppy; indeed, treetops below, night sky and moon above, vast mountain-like structure far in the distance beyond what looked like the lights and activities of a city that started roughly where the forest ended.

Slowly, steadily, she pulled her arms and legs in, gradually achieving a standing position.

"Okay," she said. "Not too bad. I think I get it."

She took a step forward. The "ground" was hardly firm, but it *did* possess a degree of traction which propelled her somewhat forward. After several more tentative steps forward, with movement that mimicked the actions of a purposeful soap bubble, Julie began to feel a bit giddy, her anxiety ebbing as her distance from the building increased.

Her heart surged. An enormous sense of palpable freedom enveloped her; she didn't remember feeling this fantastic since first arriving at the Place of Solace.

A hundred yards from the school, which loomed impossibly vast and noneuclidean against the horizon behind her, she passed over a wall: five feet thick and iron-spike-topped, it stretched off in both directions, curving back toward the school far in the distance. She had been descending by degrees as she proceeded farther and farther from the school; a hill ahead of her gradually obscured her view of what lay beyond it. Shortly after surmounting the wall, she descended softly to a pale dirt path in the midst of a small clearing.

Ahead of her, the still-abundant trees re-converged around the path, then rose up, blanketing the hill.

The path seemed intentional enough; turning around momentarily and walking back up to the forbidding brick wall that now lay behind her demonstrated no anti-gravitational effects.

"Follow the yellow brick road, I guess," she said softly to herself. Something about being back on the ground, despite being less visible, had her on edge again.

The usual sounds of being in a forest at night surrounded her. Only the bright moonlight above seeping through the forest canopy kept the path discernible to her; she feared to turn on the little flashlight that Bram had provided. By the time she made it to the hill and began her trek upward, she noticed that she had unconsciously picked up her pace.

Please let me just get through this goddamned thing! Please let me run into Steve or Charley or even goddamned Molly...

Julie's mind thrummed with reasons for her continued safety. Suddenly, as she responded internally to her latest argument in favor of good luck, she crested the hill, and Julie got her first good look at the place she would soon know as "Port Mantle."

Stretching from roughly the base of the hill to as far as the eye could see was the largest, most extraordinary collection of buildings and shops and carnivals and circuses she could ever have possibly imagined. In the distance, what she had at first taken to be a mist-bedecked mountain had suddenly taken on the clear characteristics of a vast *building*. Comparable to the Place of Solace, the vision of Port Mantle had one not-so-slight difference: it was very, *very* populated. "People" of every size, shape, color, and joint-articulation walked, hopped, slithered, flapped, and teleported from any given spot to every other.

Temporarily stunned by the *allness* of it all, Julie took a beat to notice a railing lining the base of the hill that indicated an entrance to a subway system, to which many individuals in the loitering and chattering crowds repaired.

THE BLUE-SKINNED GENTLEMAN WITH antlers kindly, and silently, gave up his seat so that Julie could more comfortably enjoy her ride. She was thankful that, despite the big-city population, the entities surrounding her—many of whom were bipedal, but almost none of whom appeared clearly human, with nary a syllable of Earthly origin among them so far—generally ignored her, some seeming unclear as to her status as a sentient being.

Julie extracted *Wild Lies II* from her back pocket before sitting down on the cold, hard plastic, painfully aware of a handful of shimmering eyeballs floating a few feet away from her. A faded sign above a bright red pile of luggage that appeared to be breathing heavily read:

PORT MANTLE
Omniversal Hub of All Worlds!

We're glad you could make it!

Above and below this statement were sequences of char-acters, loops, blinking lights, and geometric patterns that, presumably, said the same thing in various alien alphabets.

As far as Julie was concerned, somehow the "wish" Charley had her make use of had blown her into this weird, chaotic "everywhere." Why wishing for the safety of Molly Furnival would have *this* tangential effect, she had no idea.

Perhaps she was in a coma? Suffering from some curse thrown at her and the others by "Jim the Janitor." Or maybe this was *actually* what death was like...? Which—Julie grinned to think it—would prove once and for all that the smart asses back home never had *any* idea of "the Truth."

It almost made all the confusion—and her barely escaped role as fantasy fiction's latest Joan Jett—worth it.

But *where* she was actually headed—besides away from the creepiness of Three Coils—remained a mystery—

Wait. Julie gazed at the paperback in her hands. *Wild Lies II: The Truth Is Outta Here!* she read again. *By Calder C. Caine.* The words ornamented a cover image that reminded her eerily of Main Street in Golem Creek—with the addition of a black pyramid in the background looming over everything, and a cowled, tentacled creature hovering over the city. The title page had an inscription in silvery ink: *We did it!* ♡*DS* More importantly, a small slip of crumpled paper stuck out the top of the book: the receipt from "Lamb's Occult" on which Bram had scrawled his instructions...

SHE EXITED THE SUBWAY behind a menagerie of miraculous and mysterious monsters, some incomprehensible, some rude, some polite, some winking in and out of existence too quickly to deduce their manner. Amid the throng, she walked and was partly carried up a set of stone steps leading to the magnifi-cence that was Port Mantle.

The first thing that made her heart pound was a sheer inability to measure the place. She stood on a concrete walkway before a barrage of swinging and rotating doors, above which were the letters, some fifty feet high, spelling out PORT MANTLE in a heavy-looking, shimmering stone. The letters seemed inexplicably to change or flash occasionally; Julie assumed it was probably appearing in numerous languages and alphabets simultaneously.

As she looked up—and up, and up, and *up*—she felt her significance dwindle to well below zero.

Somewhere far above, she thought she saw *large winged beasts* flying into and out of thick mists and cloud, beyond which the heights of Port Mantle penetrated and, presumably, continued.

She recalled dropping acid with Steve years ago and then heading off to a carnival that had rolled into town outside of Forty Winks. The sheer quantity of novel data had left her breathless, requiring that she periodically shut her eyes against its onslaught to keep from crying out in distress.

She found herself doing that now, placing a steadying hand on the wall beside her shortly after entering behind a small group of ostrich-like creatures sporting neatly parted hair like Afghan hounds. One of them glowed radiantly as she pressed past them, emitting a soft humming sound.

Where to find Lamb's Occult Supply Shop? Bram had said that he *worked* there; it had to be here, somewhere, if this was indeed the Port Mantle Shopping Mall.

Off to her left, a fountain plashed indifferently. What must have been the youthful offspring of some furry quadrupeds whistled and barked as they chased each other around its base. Just beyond that lay a quiet-looking corner.

It was the "quiet-looking" part that had Julie racing for it. She almost had it to herself; at the last moment before she reached it, an almost human-looking man wearing an expensive pinstripe suit, holding what appeared to be a marble bowling ball, appeared beside her.

An electronic voice sounded from the bowling ball. "Hello," it said simply.

Julie turned to the man. His blank, staring face gazed at a kiosk several paces away that appeared to sell nothing. She looked down at the bowling ball, which purred softly.

"Hello," it said again, mechanically.

"Hello?" Julie responded.

"Are you as lost as *I* am?" it said. The statement was followed by a chittering that Julie presumed was an electronic "translation" of nervous laughter.

Julie nodded. "Yes," she answered. "I just got here. I'm looking for this place called 'Lamb's Occult.'"

"Hm," the bowling ball said. "Haven't heard of it. There're supposed to be maps on each level. And an embassy on this floor, but it's closed!" It chittered with laughter again. The man holding it hadn't moved a muscle. "I was sent here by my school to do a report on @%$#%^^$$%&^*—"

Julie clamped her hands over her ears. The sound blasting from the bowling ball stopped shortly after she did so.

"You've never heard of her?" the bowling ball said, apologetically.

Julie shook her head. "Where are these maps?" she asked, trying to ignore the fading shriek still ringing in her ears.

"You see that thing that looks like a purple tree?"

Julie scanned the crowd until she located it. A small purple apple tree to the right of where she'd entered. "Yeah, I see it."

"Go tap it—hey, good luck! I gotta catch that!" The man began jogging toward the just-opening doors of an elevator that Julie had thought was part of a wall.

"You too," Julie said quietly. *Talking bowling balls. Oh, Steve's gonna love this.*

"DRINK THIS," THE GNOME said, handing her a test tube half his height. It looked like it had about an ounce of water in it.

Julie took the tube from him, unable not to grin. She'd approached the purple apple tree and "tapped" it as Mr. Bowling Ball had suggested, only to be met with this rather pleasant little fellow peeking out at her from a small hut built into its branches. In quick, precise English he had asked her for a location and then retreated momentarily into the hut.

"Just drink it?" Julie said.

The gnome nodded and grinned. "Yes. It contains the location of Lamb's Occult Annex. Thank you!"

With that, he leapt back into his little house and slammed the door.

Julie shrugged, uncorked the test tube, and tipped back its contents, which fizzled briefly in her mouth like a highly carbonated soda. She couldn't be sure what it tasted like, but it smelled conspicuously like patchouli.

She dropped the empty tube and cork in a small receptacle beside the tree filled with similar empty test tubes and began strolling through the crowds. Something seemed to click in her mind as she passed a café whose patrons relished steaming bowls of pungent noodles...more kiosks, some even selling "Port Mantle"-themed hats and T-shirts and shot glasses...a clothing store with items that appeared to be made mostly of shiny metals and wires...and was nearly drawn into a crowd surrounding a restaurant clearly labeled INTERGALACTIC PIZZA! *Vegan! Gluten-Free! Better than Heaven!* before reaching a spiral escalator that led down several fascinating flights to a rather quiet level.

She entered an elevator partially hidden by brown brick walls covered in old posters, none of which she could read a word of, and instinctively punched the code "1798" into a keypad whose ciphers had become Arabic numerals as her hand grazed it.

The doors closed. After a brief, humming interval—she didn't know whether she had headed up or down, or perhaps some other direction—the elevator halted and the doors re-opened.

It was nearly silent on this level.

A few characters milled about; most of them seemed to be resting on various benches and branches. A large-headed, pale octopus gazed at her, leaning over the edge of a coin-filled pool some distance away.

She found herself taking a right down the large, nearly empty hallway. She passed several shop-fronts that were darkened or locked up. Finally, a quaint, Victorian shop-front appeared, with steps leading up to a door lit by an overhanging gaslamp. A window to the right of the door held quantities of creepy-looking items; painted on the window was the store's name:

LAMB'S OCCULT
Port Mantle Annex

Before she had made it halfway up the steps, the door above opened.

An old, elvish-looking man stood in the doorway. "Aha! As lovely as promised—Ms. Julie Evergreen, I presume?" He held out a hand to Julie in welcome. "I'm supposed to say that your new friend Molly Furnival sends her regards, along with her thanks. Won't you come in?"

STEVE

STARS, COUNTLESS, IN ALIEN patterns forged. He seemed to whirl or revolve, or perhaps he had two bodies, or more, one or two of which rotated dizzyingly about some astral axis.

Gradually, like that soft return to blessed normality after the last of the alcohol is up, he blinked, breathed deeply, and pulled himself to a sitting position.

A rooftop. Night.

He breathed deeply again and fought to remember.

Molly...Laban's magical chamber...wait—Jim the Janitor?

A miracle of subjective etheric connecting tissue linked them all. And him. Steve Chernowski. On a roof. Night.

A soft breeze picked up as he lifted himself into a standing position; the view nearly made him keel over again.

Dizzyingly vast, boundless perhaps, a landscape of dark forest rolled away from the rooftop in every direction, relieved every now and then by pockets of orange glowing lights—cities?

The sky seemed to stretch its horizons to encompass it all.

He jogged over to one edge of the roof.

He stood on the ledge of a tower jutting up over farther reaches of industrial rooftop, themselves ultimately winding away like the tentacles of some thousand-limbed mechanical octopus, swallowed up by thickets of forest...and *mountain*... was that a *waterfall* over there, burbling over one snaking hall?

"Woah," Steve said aloud. Hearing his own voice made him feel even smaller than did the Brobdingnagian expanse of wilderness exploding out from the tower. He decided to try his luck. "Charley?" he asked the empty rooftop. "Julie? Anybody else survive that?"

He waited a few beats for any type of response.

"Okay. Apparently not. Not yet, anyway."

He followed the ledge some distance, then turned around, noticing for the first time a mumty room, door ajar, leading to the building below.

"Score," he said. "Now all I have to do is kill the monster inevitably hiding out here and I'll be good to go!"

AFTER SEVERAL FLIGHTS OF concrete steps, winding down past a few landings with inexplicably locked doors, Steve reached a larger landing opening into carpeted hallways to either side. One hallway stretched a mighty distance and appeared—in "mirror facing itself" fashion—to bend away, out of sight. The other led to a pair of elevators. Both looked like they belonged in a fancy hotel.

"Aha! Elevators. Now we're getting somewhere."

His voice had the strangely muffled quality produced by echoing from heavy, expensive woodwork and hellish-thread-count rugs.

One of the two orange-doored elevators opened an instant after he pressed its triangular DOWN button.

Out stepped a grinning, aproned Bax Laird.

"Steve?" Bax suggested, holding out a hand in greeting. "It's gotta be—Steve, right?"

Steve was nonplussed. "Wait a minute. You're the guy—"

"Steve!" Bax slapped him on the shoulder, cackling madly with delight. "This is *great*! Finally! I get to meet the genius who made it all possible!"

"Well, yeah, obviously. Of course!" Steve chuckled a bit, nervously. "What?"

"You're *Steve*, right? You've gotta be—Steve, right?"

"Yeah. Yes." Steve said. This had suddenly gotten mysteriously funny. Wasn't that one of the guys being carried by the troll? The one with Jim the Janitor? Steve decided to take advantage of his status as "genius" in this exchange. "And you are...?"

Bax cringed briefly. "Ah! I'm so sorry. It's Bax. Bax Laird. I've been working in boardgames for the past—for a while." He grabbed one of Steve's hands and shook it. "Pleasure. Truly a pleasure. When'd you get here? Are you hungry? I can probably scrounge up some donuts or—"

Steve followed Bax into the elevator as he rattled on.

"—and all the new shipments. *Morpheus Unbound*, the deluxe edition with the secret compartment, and all that. Special order from Lamb's at Port Mantle for it, oddly enough. Glad you came when you did! I was eventually going to need access to the inventory computers—"

"Hey, Bax?" Steve interrupted. "Just a quick question. *Where the hell are we?*"

Bax stopped talking, made a look like he was scrutinizing Steve's face, and grinned again. "About to exit onto Level 4X7. And I think I've got just the thing in the office to help. Found a crop of some magnificent *sativa* on a window ledge off Sector 12B. About to roll one up in preparation for the night shift—boss."

The doors opened on to an expansive foyer, in the center of which squatted a marble fountain in the midst of several tall palm trees, elaborate sets of stairs leading up on either side of a gigantic representation in oils of—

"Me?" Steve marveled at the picture—it was clearly of himself, wearing a graduation cap-and-gown, performing an ollie near a curb outside Honorius High School with his old black Vision skateboard.

It took him several moments to register that Bax Laird had already skipped off past a few cage-fronted stores, a silent Orange Julius among them.

He sped past the stores to catch up with his only hope for orientation. "So, uh," he attempted, "when did you—I mean, how—shit. Shit!"

Steve stopped walking. Bax turned to him a moment later, perplexed.

"Is everything okay?" Bax asked, a look of genuine concern spreading over his face.

Steve shook his head. "Quite frankly, *no*. It's not. Even

though it seems like it. Bax, my friend, I have *no idea* where I am or what the hell is going on."

"Well, you're Steve Chernowski, right?"

"Right."

"Then you're the owner, aren't you? Of the Endless Warehouse. I had a period of starting to believe that this was all a big ruse for an even *bigger* ruse—that you were, in fact, the 'Santa Claus' of legend. Given your initials."

Steve chuckled and rummaged around briefly in his memory for the words, "Endless Warehouse"—he knew they were somewhere. Between a pair of 1920s ice skates and a frayed stretch of rope he found them in a DeLorean speeding through Golem Creek towards Brake Street: *What was it, Chuck? What did I wish for?*

BETWEEN A FANTASTIC HELPING of cannabis and six custard-filled, glazed donuts, Bax brewed a pot of strong coffee and managed to fill Steve in on as much of the history of the Endless Warehouse as he had become privy to in his last—

"*Six* months?" Steve was incredulous.

Bax nodded. "Or thereabouts. I started marking off the days on yonder 'Elf Bitches' calendar probably a week or so after I first got here."

Steve glanced over at the calendar. Its latest playmate sported a gossamer pair of wings folded over her pink-hued skin, abundant bosom, and extraordinary curves. *I'm an... ELF BITCH!* read a caption scrolling above her face, which pouted appropriately.

This was the month "Vanadyne." Or perhaps that was the elvish girl's name. Half the squares on the calendar grid had been X'd out.

"Incredible," Steve said. Here it was—the fruit of the wish he had made at some point on the parallel worldline of his own increasingly indeterminate past. He had decided, during the course of this initial meeting, to keep the origins of this place as much of a secret as possible. He didn't know this "Bax Laird" at all; he didn't know how he'd been suddenly whisked off to end up here when Jim the Janitor had been about to kill them all. But he *did* know what Charley had told him about his wish...he could barely believe that Roland had somehow *caught* it, and felt even more lucky that Charley *hadn't*.

He swept his gaze once more over the breakroom/office they'd somehow come to occupy after following a labyrinth of stairwells, hallways, waiting rooms, and strangely lit "back alleys" between sheer walls stretching up hundreds of feet to veiled, greyish-purple skies.

Everything just as empty of people as Roland's place...except for this weird dude. He stood up as Bax took a bite out of another heavily glazed donut. After steadying himself, he peered over the haphazard stacks of printouts, comic books, and half-buried computing devices to gaze through windows angled over one of the warehouse's many, many, *many* sectors.

This one was filled with row after row of boardgames. He could see the boxes of *Morpheus Unbound*, marked with a black pyramid and a beetle. Bax had explained that a quantity of inexplicable "shipments" would occasionally appear in the many sorting rooms linked to the various sectors. The majority of them would often be found unboxed, sorted, and shelved within a few days if no one—meaning, to the best of his knowledge, Bax alone—dove in to do the job themselves.

And other than several handfuls of balconies, a few courtyards (one of which sported a miraculous "Jelly Bean Tree," like something out of Willy Wonka), and the many skylights and connecting alleyways, Bax had yet to find a *front door*.

Having had dealings with "endless" dream-places before, Steve had the presence of mind not to bother asking how fresh food and drink were somehow continuously available. Thinking about the "how" and "why" of these types of things almost always *explained* it...which almost always made it a bit harder to get what you wanted, when you wanted it, like suddenly realizing that something called "electricity" ran according to "principles" which could theoretically be inhibited from time to time...

Steve shook his head and finished his coffee.

"But you got here by way of Golem Creek?" he finally asked.

Bax's expression looked suddenly strained. "Ye-es," he answered slowly. "Yes. I was just hoping I wouldn't have to go back."

Steve's eyes widened. "Back? Aw, hell no, man! Sorry. I didn't mean to imply that. I was just wondering, well, you know, how you got here? Er, why, I mean? 'Cause I know I saw you after that big hubbub at Honorius, with Jim the Janitor—"

"Yeah, well, Jim took off."

"You mean he was here, too?"

"Yeah. Good riddance. That fucking guy!" Bax looked suddenly apologetic. "Unless, of course, he's a friend of yours—"

"Jim the Janitor?" Steve said. "Don't know him. Not well, anyway. Just a fixture of the high school, right? Yeah." Steve paused a moment. "I don't know if I like that just anyone can get here whenever they want."

Bax nodded his head vigorously. "I'm with you on *that*, man! I'll tell you. You should update the security protocols. I mean, I haven't run into anyone else since Yassiz shazam'd us here, but—"

"Yassiz?"

"The Laughing God. That's what Jim called him. The guy—the demon, or whatever—that gave Jim those powers and set us off on dumb quests and all that."

Steve sat back down and shook a cigarette out of one of the packs sitting on the breakroom table. *Yassiz. The Laughing God.* Okay, it was acceptable as an idea: a god could make it past whatever security system he had in place here...*if* he did, indeed, have a security system in place here...

But *where* was here? In the greater scheme of Golem Creek and Tulsa and the Place of Solace and all that—where in all the worlds was "here"?

"This Yassiz guy," Steve said. "What's his deal again?"

Bax shook his head. He folded his donut napkin neatly and took a sip of his coffee.

"Bad news, dude," he answered. "You've got to understand. At first I thought Jim had made some sort of business deal with a Middle Eastern guy, or something. 'Yassiz.' Jim had gotten pretty pissed off about getting turned down by these investors..."

He went on to relay a tale that, to anyone else, would have sounded incredible. A "round table" of hideous demonic rich guys, like a multi-world mafia—Steve remembered hearing "Crazy" Jack Haines talk about them before: Pym's Golden Lightning Rods. PyGoLiRo—so-named to link them (albeit tenuously) with a handful of Poe-inspired conspiracies having global (galactic?) importance. Antarctica, the entrance to their inner-Earth headquarters...encrypted alchemical doomsday messages of the Fulcanelli variety... The usual. Supposedly, they controlled the means of entry and exit to several parallel worlds; in doing so, they controlled the inter-world traffic of merchandise, and imposed various taxes and tariffs—not necessarily and most typically not of the *monetary* kind—on the lot.

"But *I've* been through portals before," Steve interjected. "I never had to pay any fine."

"Yeah, well, maybe you just didn't notice. And they don't have access to *all* of them," Bax said. "There's one in McFarlin Tower—that's at the University of Tulsa—"

Steve nodded. "Been there."

Bax's eyes goggled. "Seriously? Wow! Then you know the guy that used to do late-night tours of one of the exits—dungeon crawling. He *said* he was just DMing some games up there—"

"No, I don't think so," Steve answered. "Er, maybe. Sounds familiar. Roland?"

"No. Or maybe. He went by 'Master Marcus.' But I think that might have been a joke."

"All right. So where were we again? Rich demons run magical artifacts and what-have-you through a system of portals. Check. By controlling the flow of merchandise they effectively 'own' the multiversal transit system. Check. What does that have to do with this Yassiz guy and our man, Lord Jim?"

"Yassiz *hates* PyGoLiRo. Jim explained to me that the

only thing Yassiz hated as much as PyGoLiRo was this fairy chick—what's her name—Molly Furnival—"

Steve dashed over and grabbed Bax by the shoulders.

"*Molly Furnival?*" he shrieked, grinning. "Where is she? Is she okay?"

Bax looked confused. "I don't know. What?"

Steve let go of Bax and sat back down with a thud. "Molly Furnival. She's gotta be the key. Jim wanted to kill her. Or something—he had her trussed up with some magic noose."

Bax lit a cigarette of his own before continuing. "Did you say she was a friend of yours?"

"Friend?" Steve repeated. "Friend. I don't know. Acquaintance, sure. Why?"

Bax shook his head. "I'm sorry to tell you this, man. But I'm pretty sure that girl is *dead*. Or at least somewhere she *definitely* doesn't want to be."

Steve smiled uncertainly. "Nah! No way! Not Molly Furnival!" he said with forced conviction.

Steve's thoughts alighted elsewhere. "Julie. Shit. Now *that's* what I'd like to know. Where the hell is she? And Chuck? And for chrissake, *Stek Jarry?*"

"I don't know any of those people," Bax said. "But I wouldn't second-guess Jim Buskey's resourcefulness. That guy kind of lost his mind. If he's out there, then he's not going to stop until he satisfies Yassiz. That was part of the deal."

"What deal?"

"Powers for favors," Bax said. "To put it simply. Jim got these powers—or at least this one power. He could vaporize people, practically just by thinking of it." He looked thoughtful for a moment. "It didn't always seem to work perfectly, though."

"That would suck," Steve said. "I could see how that would suck."

Bax nodded in agreement while stubbing out his cigarette.

Suddenly, an idea popped into Steve's head.

"Hey, Bax?" he said. "You wouldn't happen to remember seeing my office around here anywhere, would you?"

HE HAD AN INKLING of the location—a few lefts, a few rights…

"You get to be like a homing pigeon, after a while," Bax explained. "You think: 'I gotta get back to wherever,' and suddenly you find yourself recognizing stuff."

A plain white door in the middle of a hallway thronged with movie posters. *I feel like I remember this.* Steve pictured Roland's Emporium in the Place of Solace and felt nostalgic.

Scotch-taped to the middle of the door was a handwritten and hand-glittered piece of lined paper. It read: "STEVE!" A few little stars adorned it.

"*This* is my office?" Steve asked incredulously.

Bax shrugged. "It's the only door I know of with your name on it like that."

"Makes sense, I guess," Steve said. "Have you gone in?"

"Locked," Bax said. "I figured you'd have the key."

Steve shook his head. He reached out and grabbed the door handle, which yielded immediately to him, turning easily.

"Okay," Steve said. " 'Thou art that.' "

"What?"

"Nothing."

He pushed open the door, which creaked ominously on cue.

Silence—or *near* silence, at least. The dimly lit room sported metal shelves on which sat random assortments of merchandise—video cassettes, printouts, overstuffed file folders. A heavyset Commodore 64 crouched darkly in the midst of a small wooden desk near the center of the equally small room.

Beyond a door at the other end of the room, some twenty feet away, muffled voices could be heard. It sounded as if a conversation took place, and—

"Canned laughter?" Steve whispered.

Bax nodded. "Sounds like it."

Steve crept closer to the door.

I'd like to say that he opened it, which is basically what happened, but it would be more appropriate to say that it opened him.

"...PLEASE WELCOME OUR *SPECIAL guest*, Mr. Steve Chernowski!"

The applause, gratifying as it was, came with a garnish of that indefinable anxiety which had become the trademark of Life After Mike Flowers. Steve stepped out of the Endless Warehouse and, one blip later, through the blue-sequined veils of the Jack Haines Late-Night CONSPIRATOR Show.

Steve stood, facing a live audience of what appeared to be many species, both Earthly and (very) otherwise. Jack Haines—his iconic bald head and bespectacled face grinning behind a large wooden desk—beckoned him over to the guests' couch.

Steve, unaware of his role in all this, decided to do what he did best: wing it.

He smiled broadly, waved at the audience—earning himself another hooting round of applause—and bowed several times, mouthing "thank you" as he made his flourishing way over to Jack Haines.

"Steve Chernowski!" Jack Haines exclaimed again, shaking Steve's hand before taking his seat again. "We've had a *helluva* time getting you on the show! So glad you could make it!"

Steve, now grinning for real, waved again at the audience before responding. "Well, you know what I always say, Jack, don't you?"

"Lemme guess: *better late than 'ever'*?"

The crowd roared with laughter.

Steve chuckled. "True enough! But seriously, Jack, it's great to be here. Truly amazing show you have. I love it."

Applause thundered through the room.

Jack Haines nodded approvingly. "It's all about guests like you, Steve! Without people like you, we'd still be in Golem Creek, sitting on our asses, drinking beer, and hoping that those lights we keep seeing are UFOs and not just the *cops* again!"

A sting from the drums. Clapping from the audience.

"But seriously, Steve, it's great to have you. Before we get down to it, we'd better do the sponsor bit." Jack lifted up a book from his desk. "Tonight's episode is brought to you by Tower of Koth Books and their latest release from the unbeatable Calder Caine—*Wild Lies II: The Truth is Outta Here!* If you thought Caine's first set of 'wild lies' was something, let me be the one to say it: this new pack *bites*! Our politicians could certainly learn a thing or two from ol' Calder! Pick up a copy wherever long, strange rips in time are sold! Do it *NOW*!"

Jack set the book aside and leaned forward. "Steve! You've recently become something of a legend around Golem Creek for having not only *survived* an encounter with a psychotic occultist, but having made it both into and *out of* Laban Black's 'dream city.' We all want to know: how'd you do it?"

Steve furrowed his brow. "Well, you know, that's a great question Jack. Because the truth is that *no one* has taken the time to explain it to me!"

The audience laughed.

"Do you think it had something to do with this 'Damian Stephens' character?" Jack asked.

"Damian Stephens?" Steve rubbed his chin. "Who's that, again?"

"Aw, come on, Steve!" Jack leaned back in his chair, waving his hand in an attempt to dissipate the nonsense. "You're *in* on it, aren't you? You've got Charley and Julie—"

"Woah, wait a second here! Do you know where they are?"

Jack laid both hands palms down on his desk. "Why...yes. I think I do, actually."

The audience became preternaturally quiet. *A cricket chirped somewhere in their midst.*

Steve glanced at the audience, squinting at the bright lights shining on him, then back at Jack Haines.

It didn't look so much like Jack anymore...there was something...*wrong* with him...

"Hey, y'know, I just remembered," Steve said, standing up, "I've got this audition I've gotta get to—"

"We remember," the Jack Haines impersonator said softly. "*We remember*—"

A crash sounded from the direction of the audience.

Smoke began filling the room as it shook menacingly.

"What the *fuck* is going on?" Steve said, backing to the curtains, hoping the door to the Endless Warehouse was still open.

"*We REMEMBER!*"

The thing was *not*, clearly, Jack Haines, or any other human entity Steve knew of.

Smoke began obscuring "Jack"...the desk...the curtains as Steve bounded through them...

"*Kill me, kill the show...*" The echo of the words sounded through Steve's mind as he landed painfully on a cold marble floor.

He opened his eyes.

A gigantic caterpillar peered down at him, buzzing and tittering with apparent concern.

Steve sat up.

He was in the center of a circle of creatures, all gazing at him.

One of them held a large shopping bag.

A humanoid with pearly, translucent skin asked something, kindly it seemed, in the Galaprian dialect of Middle Kled.

Steve nodded, faking comprehension. "Yep. Yes? Hm. What's—ah, what's this, again?"

"It's Port Mantle," a confident, reassuring voice spoke from somewhere just beyond the crowd. Steve looked up in time to watch the slithering, scampering masses part before a short staircase of seven or eight stone steps leading up to:

"Harvey Lamb," the proprietor of Lamb's Occult said. "Looks like we almost lost you! Come on inside and we'll sort this out."

Steve leapt to his feet and sprinted into the store.

"LEAVE IT TO THAT faery magic to impart *teleportation* alongside luck!" Harvey Lamb said as soon as Steve stepped through the door.

"What in Tartarus was all *that*, my man?" Steve asked immediately, dusting himself off.

Harvey shook his head. "We'll get to that. Follow me."

Turning around briefly, Steve saw a familiar sight.

"That's Golem Creek out there, isn't it?" he asked, pointing.

Harvey nodded. "Indeed it is," he answered. "Main Street. It's always visible from *this* direction, even if the Annex bleeds into other places, occasionally. You might call it an anchor of sorts—much like Laban Black's tomb."

"Hey, I know that place," Steve said. "Been there, done that." He chuckled.

Harvey smiled. "I'm thankful Yassiz didn't *quite* get his claws into you a few moments ago," he said. "Never underestimate the cleverness of the conscientiously non-omniscient."

"Right," Steve said. He picked up a short sword from a basket full of them and waved it tentatively a few times. "Cool merch," he said. He dropped the sword back into the basket with a clang. "So the only thing I'm trying to figure out is what you mean by 'faery magic.' "

"Of course," Harvey said. "Molly Furnival—that's the name you know her by—was kind enough to save your life and call in a favor at the same time. The Queen is always a welcome customer, *especially* when she's in need."

"The Queen?" Steve said. "You mean that—"

Harvey nodded. "Yes. Your Molly Furnival is the present Queen of Faery, much in need of counsel, though not, apparently, lacking in any of the potencies She's wont to demonstrate."

"I should've *known*!" Steve began laughing and clapped his hands. "Bravo, Charley! Gotcha *sweet stuuuuuuff*—"

Steve's impromptu vocals were cut short.

"As lovely as it is to hear spontaneous emissions of joy, we do have a bit of work at hand," Harvey said. "If you'll follow me?"

Steve followed Harvey through the heaps of books and potions and scrolls and magical miscellany.

"So—what was with the evil talk show, again?" he asked.

"Yassiz has set traps among us," Harvey explained, bending low to traverse a narrow arch. "He has nearly *remembered himself*. The chaos in Golem Creek won't keep him at bay for long."

"You mean the high school? All those chicks trying to eat me, and stuff?"

Harvey started up a set of curving wooden stairs that appeared out of nowhere. "Something like that," he said. "Wise's clever Théâtre d'Azif has enabled us—Roland and myself, among others—to transfictionally communicate. There was a bit of fine-tuning involved, which may have caused a few unintended consequences in resonance with Laban's chamber. The only way for us to be free of Laban's magic—for Roland to escape your 'Place of Solace,' and for me to be freed of my contract with the Monolith, or 'PyGoLiRo' as your recent acquaintance Jack Haines would have it—was to destroy your city. The lock on the door, so to speak." Harvey paused in front of a rickety wooden door at the next landing and withdrew a large brass key from his pocket. "Temporarily, of course. If all goes according to plan."

"Woah! So *that's* what that was! With the popcorn—and the reclining seats!" Steve shook his head in amazement. "Never had a chance to get an explanation from Chuckie. Speaking of which: you wouldn't happen to know where I could find that guy? And I kind of promised my girl Julie that I wouldn't ever lose her again—fucked that up quick, I guess."

A ratcheting sound ensued as Harvey, himself silent, twisted his key in the door's lock. He withdrew the key and pushed open the door.

"*Jules*!" Steve shouted as he charged into the room.

Julie couldn't help but smile as he hugged her for dear life.

THERE WERE THE USUAL shouts of joy and cries of elation. There were the usual accusations, finger-pointings, and threats of peril. There was also popcorn, care of Fat Porker's Pig-Out, and Steve Chernowski—despite Julie's completely justified arguments regarding the right-rationing of wishes—was having a ball-and-a-half about it.

"You know what I'd like?" Steve said, shoving yet another handful of popcorn in his mouth and leaning on the back two legs of an antique wooden chair from the time of Henry VIII.

Julie twisted open another of the delicious pumpkin ales sitting on the makeshift lunch table. She tried to ignore the stains of what looked like blood on its intricate surface—there was a good chance that the tag attached to one leg reading "Immol. Surf. / $9,000" stood for "immolation surface," and she still wanted to eat one of the hot pastrami sandwiches resting on it invitingly in their wax paper wrappings.

"I'd like some of that shrimp toast from Mr. Chow's," Steve continued to no one in particular. "Man, yeah. Some of that Mr. Chow's shrimp toast. Incredible." He grabbed a Ringleader's Impeccable Stout from the rapidly emptying six pack sitting in the cooler next to his chair and inserted it into a purple koozie with the words PORT MANTLE MALL: *Seek and ye shall find!* on it in striking neon green.

"You know what else'd be good? Bacon, egg, and cheese," he informed Julie as he twisted off the bottle's cap. "Bacon, egg, and cheese. I always planned on naming my first child 'Baykeneggencheeze Chernowski.' You know? As an act of revenge against a world that wouldn't endow genius with sentience." Steve gulped down half the Ringleader's Impeccable and smiled broadly. "Where'd Harvey Wallbanger get this shit, anyway? It's fantastic."

Julie allowed Steve's stream-of-consciousness meanderings to wash over the silence. She leaned back in the comfortable easy chair in one of the numerous back rooms at Lamb's Occult Annex and closed her eyes. Harvey's explanation of how guys like "Bram" (he'd laughed at the name for some reason) became unwitting agents of magicians or witch-queens like, for example, Molly Furnival, culminated in Julie having a brief panic attack. *Who controlled her actions NOW? Why was she here? And what a waste of a perfectly good wish...*

Finding that Steve had been waiting here for her was a tremendous relief—she hadn't even realized that she'd been feeming for a cigarette since...well, since whatever time it had been back in Laban's chamber in Golem Creek. An unfiltered Gauloise was the very first thing Steve had given her when they'd encountered each other here at Lamb's, having both been—

"—whisked here by that exquisite faery magic in its purest form," Harvey had explained as they wound through hallways of books, scrolls, and magical items to this very room. "Ah, Her enemies are numerous, but there's nothing quite like being in the service of Her Majesty." He'd gone on to explain that the intricacies of faery magic were like the workings of magnificent clocks—what looks like a mass of gears and levers and pulleys is in fact the clever entrainment of "hooks and crooks" (he'd used those words specifically) to lead bits of spacetime to other bits of spacetime.

He'd even referenced a particular book on the subject by the Order of Mages Unkempt: *The Mechanics of Luck; Or, How to Wake Up in No Time*.

"A clock merely tells time," he'd said. "But a spell of Faery tells time *what* to do and *how* to do it!"

Then he'd left them to this feast with promises of returning shortly with a television set—something he typically had so very little use for he had almost forgotten there *was* one somewhere nearby.

And a clattering from just outside the room alerted Steve and Julie to his return.

"Found it!" he exclaimed, rolling an old twenty-four-inch screen CRT television set in on a metal table. Dust puffed from its wood-paneled roof as Harvey bumped it against a back wall covered with an oil painting of someone named "King Billy Cameron of Hilton's Head," a Nordic fellow rearing back on a Clydesdale horse. The chain mail and sword raised menacingly over his head failed to impress a sense of royalty on Julie, who couldn't get past the "king's" thick eyeglasses.

"You have a feast for your bodies," Harvey said after plugging the television set into a sparking wall socket. "Now have a feast to warp your minds!" Harvey stood back from the TV as its vacuum tubes warmed and its screen started focusing images. "Wise Nerds told me to say that. Only one issue, here: your friend Charles is witnessing this from the 'other side,' in the Théâtre d'Azif...before the end of Book Two."

"Book Two? What does that mean?" Steve asked.

"This should explain everything, even if it doesn't satisfy you fully," Harvey answered.

Steve shrugs, gulps down the last of his beer, and reaches for a hot pastrami sandwich. "Now *these* are worth the whole goddamned trip!"

Julie hushes him as the screen reveals a pixelated image of a wizard sitting at a booth in a restaurant, sipping a glass of scotch.

The wizard looks directly at them.

"Okay. Do we have everybody's attention? Harvey? Are they—okay..."

CHARLES

WHEN CHARLEY AWOKE AFTER burning *Fear Club* and (hopefully) helping to save Molly—but not really "awoke," not really, more like he simply blinked rather heavily once or twice—he found himself standing in the midst of a clearing in what could only be described as "an enchanted wood."

Yes, I know, it removes a great deal of the mystery and the magic of it if I simply *tell* you, right off the bat, that, yes, he found himself in "an enchanted wood." And that, therefore, the vending machine in the center of that clearing, and the aluminum box with the glass face on it—within which sat, innocently and none-too-portentously, a GUN—were both there by design, seems precluded by the statement as well.

But it certainly saves on the necessity of deep, long-winded descriptions, e.g.: "Charles Thomas Leland opened his eyes to a new world. A sorcerous radiance emanated from nowhere in particular, casting a yellowish glow over the peculiar objects in the center of the forest clearing. The branches above him ruffled softly in an opium-dream dance..."

Let's proceed to the facts. He shuffled over to the vending machine almost immediately after arriving.

"Fifty cents for a Snickers bar?" he said aloud. "What the hell?" Unconsciously, he patted his pockets, searching for change. While doing so, he glanced at the aluminum box propped up on a metal stand beside the vending machine.

For a Good Time—Break Glass.

The words were embossed on the glass in chipped and fading red paint. A closer look at the contents revealed a—

" 'Samsaric Revolver'?" Charles read the words, dimly visible in ten-point Courier font on a small plaque below the glass proper.

Samsaric Revolver. First used by Mahasiddha Jah-Lee-Zzz in His quest to Unbind Morpheus *and awaken all the Finnegans.*

He didn't like the name. "Samsaric Revolver." It sounded like some clever album title by someone trying to look smarter than they really were.

He turned away from the revolver and the vending machine.

Yep, your basic enchanted forest, glimmering lights in the midst of the trees, a dark purple sky beyond the canopy, and a lightly glowing road leading off from the clearing.

...to?

IT COULD HAVE BEEN hours of walking, the road gave no indication of time's passage, and the trees to either side of him seemed almost to deliberately shield his eyes from much more than the sky directly above him, purple and twinkling.

Where the hell *was* Molly? Steve? Julie? Stek? Had he alone been singled out for some nefarious purpose (as usual)?

He knew something was changing when his footsteps met asphalt instead of the pale dust of the dirt path. Moments later, the forest broke like a fever, and he found himself standing on—

"A *parking lot?*"

It was, indeed, the cracked asphalt and faint yellow lines indicating a parking lot. Before him, stretching higher than he could see, was a Building, and of all buildings One deserving of the Capital Letter.

The parking lot filled a gap of a mere hundred yards or so before meeting with the Building Itself, and stretched to either side, bordered behind Charles by the edges of the great forest through which he'd come and ahead of him by the massive granite and concrete structure, the latter relieved only by a set of opaque glass doors. Words shimmered above the doors, becoming discernible as Charles approached:

PORT MANTLE MALL
Annexes

Without hesitation, Charles crossed the quiet parking lot and entered the building.

He found himself in a small, nearly silent lobby, reminding him of the baggage-claim area of an airport. Muzak ruffled silence's feathers a bit. An elevator squatted before him, a matte-grey monolith promising and revealing nothing.

Charles glanced once toward each fluorescent hallway stretching away on either side of the elevator, then stepped forward and hit the elevator call button.

The doors slid open instantly, revealing a large, wood-paneled room smelling of new carpet.

The expected panel of buttons beside the door gave Charles hardly any indication of what to expect when the doors might reopen. They shimmered, like the letters above the glass doors from the parking lot, and became suddenly legible: short sequences of numbers and letters.

One of the buttons appeared lit from behind, as if an invisible companion waited in the elevator with him. With no better plan, Charles pressed the gleaming button. The doors slid closed.

A moment of panic ensued, following inevitably from placing his fate firmly in the unseen hands of unknown agents.

CHARLES STOOD THERE, DAZED, in the midst of the profusion of species and technologies. Something about his wide-eyed look of naive wonder attracted the attention of a roving "Hare Krishna" type.

"Are you experienced?" It was an oddly soothing voice. The biped, however, looked a lot like a miniature dinosaur wearing a human mask to Charles—plus the expected *shikha*, braided at the back of its head.

"What?"

"Get experienced," the acolyte repeated, and handed Charles a small black-and-white pamphlet with a stapled binding.

Bodhisattva Yeti wants YOU...to Know Yourself! read the title above a pixelated image of—

"The Goblin Gang?" Charles started laughing despite himself. Indeed, it was a candid portrait of the Silent Goblin Gang, Fukkn Drunk, the Monster Squad—many names, one inimitable demeanor—all wearing robes and sashes, heads shorn to the skin, standing two to a side of a creature Charles immediately identified as—

"A fucking *abominable snowman*?" Charles said aloud. Suddenly, Marigold Silverki's prophetic poetry returned to him: *Bodhi-Yeti—Himalayas...*

Charles glanced around himself and spotted a mostly empty bench against one quiet wall.

He sprinted over to it and sat down. At the other end of the bench, three small, octopedal entities, covered in fur, wearing beige trenchcoats and sporting fedoras with multicolored feathers sticking out of them, sat whispering in a huddle.

Apparently, after Charles's last encounter with the Goblin Gang in 1988, Booker Reuchlin skipped out on his contract with the United States government and the four ne'er-do-wells went "on the lam," setting up shop in abandoned areas, living off the land (i.e., robbing and stealing what they needed as they went), learning how to use weapons, and becoming adept at utilizing *portal traversal*, which they had become privy to by way of an "unnamable source." "Bodhi-Yeti" was—according to the pamphlet, published by "Intergalactic Pizza, Inc."—a Fully Awakened Being whom Fukkn Drunk had encountered while on a mission to "hunt and trap a *yeti* for an American businessman."

After several years of living "a mean, *mean* lifestyle," doing "black market business deals" and "rollin' in dough—but not the *good* kind" (this last statement had a small image of a pizza smiley face drawn beside it), they encountered "Bodhi-Yeti" who "took our violence from us."

After which, they quit the monster-hunting, occult-relic-stealing, mayhem-causing business for good and became his disciples, spending two years in Himalayan caves learning and practicing meditation under his guidance.

"With the help of our beloved Guru," the pamphlet explained, "we have made use at last of Portal Technology for the purposes of spreading His Excellent Message: 'Do what you love, and see that no harm befalls any creature by your doing it.' " They started "Intergalactic Pizza"—a not-for-profit organization run alongside continuous meditation retreats on various worlds—at Port Mantle Mall.

The final page of the pamphlet had another grainy image of the Goblin Gang, some of their hair grown back, smiling broadly and kneeling beside several creatures that looked like groundhogs. *Some of our wonderful staff!* the caption read.

CHARLES REALIZED THAT POTENTIALLY his only hope of orientation lay in finding someone, *anyone*, that he knew in this place.

"Excuse me?" he said, deliberately bumping back into the "Hare Krishna" fellow who'd given him the pamphlet.

The entity gazed at him impassively, unperturbed and unspeaking.

"Can you direct me to this place?" Charles said, pointing at the pamphlet. "Intergalactic Pizza?"

The entity nodded slowly and pointed to a bank of escalators at the other side of the gigantic entry hall. "Down several floors to the Warbling Room. There is an express elevator directly to the dining hall. It is gold in color, with an image of Our Lady upon it." He turned swiftly and disappeared into a burst of crowd.

Charles made his way over to the escalators, careful to avoid infringing on the space of even apparently inanimate objects. The central escalator was perhaps thirty feet wide and plummeted a minimum of several floors, disappearing beneath a cantilevered cliff-edge of kiosks.

He stepped onto the first stair, behind a cackling band of black-clad birdmen who seemed absolutely stricken by the essential hilarity of everything they saw, including him. He smiled at them, which they found overwhelmingly brilliant.

SPONTANEOUS UNPLANNED ORDER. STIGMERGY. That and something more.

Charles felt himself taken into the crowd as it became a hive-mind hell-bent on pizza. In the "Warbling Room"—a mystifyingly precise description of the waiting area—the gorgeous golden elevator was impossible to miss: on it, an image of Marigold Silverki, painted to resemble a tasteful pin-up girl.

Once jammed into the elevator, a cheer/roar/buzz went up as the doors closed and carnival lights kicked in, revealing mirrors on every wall. Millions of copies of multifarious enti-ties—Charles standing helplessly in their midst—unfolded to each side as the elevator whizzed off, presumably to Interga-lactic Pizza.

A creature resembling a six-foot-tall, leopard-skinned slug "grinned" pleasantly at Charles and conveyed a completely unintelligible sentiment that somehow "translated" itself in his brain.

Last time I had Intergalactic Pizza, I was high for a month back on Old Batrachia.

"Awesome," Charles said, smiling back at the slug and wondering whether he'd be able to get a basic slice of cheese-and-pepperoni...

The elevator slowed to the accompaniment of more cheers/roars/buzzes and merriment.

The doors opened on the miracle of Intergalactic Pizza.

THERE WAS SOMETHING OF a wait, during which free slices were given to ease one's transition into bliss. Charles had a slice—New York-style, which meant six times the size of a standard rest-of-the-world full pizza—with pepperoni, as planned, although he was clearly informed that the pepperoni (as with all of the animal products at Intergalactic Pizza) was 100% synthetic.

He noticed no difference in the quality of taste. After several bites, his eyes closed in sheer sensual delight. He barely felt the tapping on his arm from a squat figure wearing a cowboy hat staring earnestly at him with blazing green eyes.

"Your name is *Charlez*, yes?" the cowboy managed to say in broken English as he took Charles's empty plate from him.

Charles nodded.

"Then you will come with me, yes?" the cowboy continued, urging him deeper into the restaurant.

Charles followed. "What's this all about? Did Booker or somebody ask for me?"

The cowboy shook his head, then nodded his head, an action Charles was unable to interpret successfully.

They wound around tables and booths, altars with three-foot-high seated Buddhas decked with flowers and pizza coupons, and images, everywhere, in every style, of Marigold Silverki: Marigold as Botticelli's Venus, Marigold as "Mother Mary" holding an ex-crucified Booker Reuchlin, Marigold with a pearl earring—

"Chuckie!"

Steve's voice rang out, hitting Charles full-force only seconds before he was body-slammed with a bear hug by his old friend.

"Holy—Steve!" Charles hugged him back.

"That's what *I* always say, dude! Shit, where the hell ya *been*?"

Steve stopped smothering Charles long enough to indicate the raised mahogany booth from whence he'd ejected. A nearly pornographic image of Marigold as some sort of dakini (the embossed brass label read "Salgye du Dalma") graced the wall behind the table, just above a grinning Julie Evergreen, nearly hidden in a cloud of smoke.

"Charley," Julie said slowly. She waved.

"Don't mind *her*," Steve said, shoving Charles into one end of the semi-circular booth. "She's been smoking complimentary hash." Steve hopped into his seat at the other end of the booth in his classic "I'm about to jump out of this seat again" pose. He immediately grabbed a lit cigarette from an ashtray in the middle of the table with one hand and a half-eaten slice of thick calzone with the other.

"So I got blasted somewhere about a mile out from here,"

Charles explained without being asked. He tapped an image of a slice of pepperoni pizza on a menu and nodded to the mini-cowboy. "I'm sure you're both about to inform me in detail of whatever ridiculous bullshit happened to you. But clearly we're alive—at least, I'm guessing we're alive, even though I've never heard of Port Mantle before. And I'm sure there's a completely unjustifiable explanation for why we all ended up *here* at the fucking *Goblin Gang's* pizza place, which we'll find out whenever Damian Stephens has time for it. So I guess I'll just ask the trillion-dollar question," Charles said. "Where the *holy fuck* is *she*?" He pointed accusingly at the translucently veiled Marigold above Julie.

Steve immediately started laughing. Julie shook her head slowly and took a long drag from the huge joint she'd gotten halfway through.

"Oh, man," Steve said, stubbing out his cigarette and lighting another one. "Oh, *man*. Oh, man."

"Or the Goblin Gang?" Charles continued. "We're here at their restaurant—where the hell are *they*?"

"I'm sure Julie would be saying 'you're welcome' at this point," Steve said, "you know, for saving Molly." Julie grinned and nodded. "But that's beside the point. Molly did some wazoo-shazam stuff on us we just found out about. And the Goblin Gang's on a meditation retreat, supposedly. That's the first thing I asked when we got up here."

"And how precisely did you *know* to come here?" Charles asked.

"Harvey Lamb," Julie said, taking a deep breath. "It was Harvey Lamb."

"Right!" Steve interjected. "Harvey Wallbanger had the nerve to drag us out of our peaceful meditations and into his fucking awesome store, where he shows us a tape that *supposedly* you were seeing at the same time—just way back in time. You know? The fucking Damian Stephens thing where he's getting drunk and telling everyone the story of Yassiz and there's that hot, *hot* chick Pamela there and—"

Charles listened in fascination as a tray of pepperoni pizza was delivered to him. Extra parmesan in place and a Cherry

Coke ordered, he continued to listen. He finished several slices, falling once again into that blissful state which, he decided, the pizza was designed to induce in its consumers.

He gazed at the image of the Dakini Marigold and fell into a half-trance. Steve kept talking, with occasional stoned emendations and additions from Julie.

Eventually, a colorful, somewhat inspired, partially inaccurate version of the events transpiring for each of them unfolded.

"So, yeah, basically Harvey said that 'faery magic' works by activating luck," Steve began to summarize. "Each of us got a wallop or a dollop of Molly's magic and were literally *lucked* out of harm's way. Unfortunately, to pull that off, especially that fast—even for a Faery Queen—takes some skill, and they make use of an element of randomness in the mix. But with enough 'luck' added to ensure that, I guess in our case, we meet back up again." Steve paused and stubbed out yet another cigarette. He followed this with a long chug of pale ale directly from the pitcher, a brief belch, and a smile. "Harvey says: 'Go get yourselves some lunch!' And Julie and I head off here. And I'm guessing Harvey had some notion that you were going to be here. He's got a vested interest, you know."

"What's that?" Charles asked. "And by the way, do you guys have enough money to *pay* for all this shit? I seem to have misplaced my wallet."

"It's on Harvey!" Steve said happily. He dug in his pants pocket and produced a shimmering gold credit card. "What a guy!"

"Harvey's apparently trying to *retire*," Julie said, having sobered up a bit. "But what that actually means, I have no idea. He said we have a lot to thank the Laughing God for. Without him, he never would have gotten the call from Wise Nerds, with a plan to save Golem Creek and free him from his indefinite indentured servitude."

"Well, what do we do now?" Charles asked.

"Harvey's started this divination back at the store," Steve answered. "We're supposed to head back there."

"Yeah, it's a game," Julie added. "Like a boardgame. From *this* dude's store."

Steve smiled and chuckled. "Damn straight! Can you believe that shit, Chuck? My *own* store! Poppa would be proud."

Charles nodded. "Absolutely. If I recall properly, I was the one who first told you about it. Or, at least, the one who told you it was for real."

Steve nodded enthusiastically. "Yes! And I'm going *back* there ASAP, man. Just gotta get this little Yassiz thang taken care of, bitches!"

"I'm happy for you," Charles said. He considered his own prospects briefly and cringed. "I'm not sure, after all this, that I *want* everything going back to normal."

"*Hell* no, man," Steve said. "You can come hang with me, bro. Even my lady-friend can come, if she doesn't mind having an open relationship—*ow!* Damn!"

Julie's intoxication had not, apparently, hindered her striking strength at all. She smiled at Charles and took a drag from her cigarette.

Steve waved the credit card above his head and caught the eye of their green-eyed dwarven cowboy waiter. "I'm about ready to go, y'all," Steve said. "Let's get this party started."

STEVE'S ENERGY WAS UTTERLY undiminished by the two-and-a-half pizzas and three pitchers of nameless beer he'd consumed during Charles's watch. He rattled on and on as they made the trek from Intergalactic Pizza back to Lamb's Occult.

"Charles Leland!" Harvey greeted him at the door. "At last we meet! Something of a legend, in fact. Your book caused quite a stir."

"Yeah," Charles said, shaking the old man's hand and glancing around the foyer of the shop. "I always thought I'd be better at being a chef than a writer."

Harvey chuckled. "You do yourself an injustice, Mr. Leland. We've all got our parts to play."

"Like Damian Stephens?" Charles said snidely as Harvey

began leading them back through the store proper.

"Indeed," Harvey said. "Damian Stephens has discovered that he's as locked into a particular groove as anyone else we'd care to mention."

Charles frowned. "But I thought he's the guy *writing* all this?"

"We'll see," Harvey responded. "Based on my divinations thus far, it seems there's someone else whose work needs to be, shall we say, censored to prevent undue and multiversal repercussions."

From out of nowhere, he produced a paperback book and handed it to Charles.

"*Wild Lies II*," Charles read from the cover. "By Calder C. Caine." He turned the book over in his hands and idly flipped through it. "What the hell is this?"

"I got it in Three Coils," Julie said.

"And we're still not sure who put it there," Harvey said. "It *could* have been one of my part-time employees, which opens up the proverbial can of worms. Or it could be direct interference of sorts from the magicians in the Tower of Koth."

"Tower of Koth... Haven't heard of them. Okay. So what?" Charles said. "You want to burn this one, too? Like *Fear Club*? 'Cause last time we tried that, it didn't seem to do much more than throw a wrench in the gears."

Harvey led them to a large wooden table in the middle of yet another book-bedecked room. Eight gigantic sets of shelves towered over them. Just above, a chandelier made of stag horns sported evaporating beeswax candles, casting an eerie glow over the ensemble.

"Oh, Chuck, this is fucking cool," Steve interjected, grabbing Charles by the shoulder and leading him closer to the table.

Charles stared at the insanely complicated machinery making up—

"A boardgame," he said.

Steve nodded, laughing. "A *Golem Creek* boardgame. Harvey special-ordered it from *my* store weeks ago."

"*Morpheus Unbound*," Julie said, pointing at the box-top. She seated herself in a red tufted sofa at one end of the room.

"A game," Charles repeated lamely. "And we play it to—"

"Encourage chance, a little," Harvey finished. He was collecting some dice from several trays. "Hypnotize the hand of fate." He grinned. "A little. Actions *at every level* are mirroring each other in some form. All the devices of rhetoric are like intuitive apprehensions of how things actually exist, actually occur, on multiple levels of perception simultaneously. *That's* the secret of Trismegistus. That's how magic works, when you really get down to it."

"The secret of..." Charles trailed off, remembering the words of Marigold Silverki. *Laban lies dead but dreaming—the secret of Trismegistus in the reflection of a mirror.*

"Trismegistus, Chuck," Steve said. He snorted, barely able to fake a grimace. "Get with the fucking program, dude."

Charles ignored him. He turned to Harvey. "You said something about the 'Tower of Koth' a minute ago?"

Harvey nodded. "A term used by the High Priest Ech Pi El to describe the last Pylon before the Outer Chaos ensues. It is *chidakasha* of the Dark Lord Koth, where He resides in *satchitananda*. He is Master of the Darkness Between the Stars—and effectively the God of Waking Dreams."

Steve laughed. "And you thought you'd just get fries with that question, Chuck?"

Charles grinned. "At least," he said. He approached the game board. "We're game pieces," he observed, gazing at several pewter figurines with suspicious resemblances to seventy-five percent of the room's occupants.

"Yes, correct," Harvey said, walking over to Charles. "But game pieces that can *roll their own dice.*" He held out the handful of oddly shaped dice to Charles and nodded.

"The gods *must* play dice with their universes!" Steve exclaimed merrily. "They don't have a choice!"

Charles took them. "Okay," he said, grinning. "I can handle this."

"It removes Damian Stephens from the equation, to some extent," Harvey said.

"But what do we ultimately gain from this?" Charles

asked, glancing from the dice to Harvey to Steve to Julie and then back to the gameboard.

Harvey politely took the copy of *Wild Lies II* from Charles and deposited it in a backpack that had been leaning against a table leg.

"The means of escape," Steve said. He clapped Charles on the back.

"What?"

"We discover and invent the means of escape," Harvey Lamb elaborated. He held the backpack out to Charles.

"Okay," Charles said, idly taking it and slipping the straps over his shoulders. "Thanks, I guess. The means of escape *from* what, then?"

"From our externally imposed storylines," Harvey concluded.

"Not sure exactly where that will put us," Steve added. "But when the hell has that ever stopped us before, right?"

Harvey fanned out a deck of cards in front of Charles. "Thus begins the unwritten ending," he said. "Pick a card."

Charles touched one card, withdrew his hand, and immediately touched another.

"I don't know which one to choose," he said.

"That's right," Harvey confirmed. "No one does."

Charles glanced first at Steve, preoccupied with analyzing the game board, then at Julie, who blew a few smoke rings his direction and smiled.

"Why can't one of them do it?" he asked.

"They're going to," Harvey said. "But privilege goes to the one who crossed through first."

"Meaning?"

"The portal in the crawl space during your Death Test," Harvey answered.

Charles nodded. "Right," he said. "Okay."

He grabbed a card and looked at it.

Then he started laughing.

At that moment, a boom and bang and clatter—as of typewriter keys being smacked by some outlandish, authorial force

—shook the room.

"Woah," Steve said as the rattling echoed away. "What does *that* mean?"

Charles thought he knew. In fact, he suddenly felt a wild surge of confidence thrill through him; a knowledge, of sorts, that took him by surprise.

He shook the dice quickly and tossed them on the table.

STEK

THE SENSATION OF DISSOLVING utterly likens more to simply recognizing the *ground of being* than to, say, sugar-dissolving-in-absinthe or salt-dissolving-in-the-ocean. The latter takes one thing and makes it inseparable from another; the former takes two things and makes of them, literally, nothing more than a single reflection in an undiscoverable mirror.

Roland unbecame that way now.

When moments reasserted themselves as conceptual possibilities again, in a context distinguishable from its contents, Roland hovered above Golem Creek, mentally and physically aloof from the crazed chaotic confusion below. Honorius High School, off to his lower right, burned indignantly, arrogantly, like a king stately ascending the gallows. In the surrounding neighborhoods, and downtown, in the other direction, shops and streets writhed with a sentient darkness—the creatures of the Murk crawling like an infestation of ants over everything.

Things that were never to be, suddenly are.

Roland, tentacles restful, perceived with that total vision with which his training had endowed him the etheric shadow of Black's Pyramid cast over the city.

And things that are *flutter and fall like leaves in autumn.*

The clinging madness of his prison break had at last fallen from him. No more identification with random dream-forms in the dream-city of Golem Creek—or any other, for that matter. He *remembered*; a portion of his mind having been stolen by Laban's insidious magic and dragged to the "Place of Solace" (the irony of that name never escaped him);

Laban's many dealings with the many shades of black making up the Magical Underworld, not the least portion of which—the "Monolith," or "PyGoLiRo"—had discovered *how* he'd managed to disappear and remain "dead but dreaming" all these years.

The only way it stays "solid" is by constantly changing...a dream always in the making...

Well, there was work to do, as usual. Duality had its moments, but the very nature of those moments—*always fleeting, always memories*—gave up the show to those who know.

What disturbed him was that Yassiz had been in the crypt beneath St. Bruno's up until just a moment ago.

Where the hell had he gone? And, for that matter, where the hell were Charley and Julie and Steve?

THERE WAS A WAY to find out.

"Stop torturing me," Stek said. He was slurring his speech, preferring intoxication to whole-scale awareness of Golem Creek's decimation.

"It's not *my* fault," Roland answered. "And it's not exactly *torture* either, Stek. Give me a break."

Roland hovered in front of the drunken Faery King behind CJ's, wondering if he'd have to go somewhat martial with his persuasive arts.

Stek took another swig of whatever nameless booze he'd chosen—something that ought to be consumed from a small glass rather than the bottle, presumably—and caught himself just before falling backward off his makeshift throne: an upturned milk crate.

"Tell me something, Roland," he said. "Why're you always hovering instead of just sitting like everyone else?"

Roland's tentacles fluttered briefly. "It's harder for me to 'just sit,' as you say. Most of my physical presence is translucent electromagnetism. If you look very close, you'll literally see right through me."

Stek raised his eyebrows in acceptance of the answer. "Oh," he said, then took another swig from the bottle.

"Look, we've got to get you—"

"You know what? You're right. You're not torturing me. It's *her*."

Here we go again, Roland thought. *If we didn't have to wait for Tom or Nashe to show, I'd do* something *to shut him up...*

"It's *her*," Stek repeated. "Ever since the beginning, you know? Oh, what a lucky break! I'm married to the Queen of Faery! How dasherling—er—" He looked confused for a moment, then remembered the bottle in his hand, took yet another swig, and continued. "You know? This is torture. When she got split by that goddamned Lassie—"

"Yassiz," Roland corrected.

"—it wasn't *my* fault! Blew me to pieces. Next thing I know, I'm just some kid working at FazMart. My biggest worry was whether I'd make it home in time to catch *Next Generation*."

Roland considered Stek's suffering, having heard the spiel before. *We've all become something we're not, for the unfathomable purposes of those whose hierarchies convince us, hypnotize us, help us enslave ourselves...*

Stek had come partway to the realization, once again, that he was, indeed, King of Faery and no mere mortal, stuck in the labyrinth of others' dreams to keep him from aiding his consort. That the Faery Lands—some billions upon billions of Terran miles from where you are sitting now,[*] yet miraculously simultaneous with us, closer than our next breath—housed Royalty that could produce the Vinum Sabbati, the wish-granting elixir composed of the Queen's blood and the King's distress (this latter usually in the form of a musical dirge distilled via esoteric machinery to a liquid form compatible with the Queen's particular effluvia at the time), seemed like a fine, complicated answer to a fine, complicated cosmos. Worlds within worlds; dreams within dreams; and no way to know for sure if the one you're dreaming right now is within reach of your wishes...

Without that Art & Science they teach at places like Three Coils, at least.

Roland followed the train of his thoughts back to their ineffable Source once again.

---

[*] Precisely $e^{10^{68}}$ miles, in fact.

Following the breath, the illusion of inwardness, the illusion of outwardness, the illusion in-between...

"...so *fuck* that demon cocksucker, you know?"

Stek's voice brought Roland back to the bar and environs.

"Where the hell *is* everyone, anyway? I thought we were supposed to meet—"

"I'm *here*! Here am I!" Nashe burst through the back door of The Flying Monkey right as the dimensional shift occurred, drunk as the proverbial skunk, high as the snow-capped peaks of Lêng.

"What took you—so long?" Stek asked between mouthfuls of alcohol. "And where the fuck is Tom?"

" 'Who buzzeth in mine ears I am a spirit?' " Nashe said, quoting something as usual.

"What?" Stek asked. "Do you have *any* original thoughts?"

"Gentlemen, please," Roland said, hovering a bit higher. "Bickering ill behooves us."

Stek snorted, almost made a snide comment, but drowned it in moonshine instead.

"Tom is at task, right on schedule. And 'tis *liquoring* makes our golden trade," Nashe said, grinning, as he produced a flask from his back pocket. He tipped the flask toward Stek. "Try finding that in your Bartlett's, faithless friend."

Roland ignored the exchange. "Nashe, you brought us here to 'fix the mercury,' as you put it. I'm assuming you have a plan to unhinge Yassiz and somehow save Golem Creek?"

"It requires complicity on the part of those reading us, of course," Nashe said, indicating you, "but methinks it can be done, *et dimitte nobis debita nostra*."

"Keep talking like that," Stek said, chuckling. "You'll get this book closed and chucked in the garbage in no time."

"Very good!" Nashe responded. " 'As flies to wanton boys are we to the gods—' "

Stek smashed his empty bottle against the side of a dumpster. "Come over here, you fucker," he said, brandishing the jagged glass of half the bottle as he stood, wobbling.

"Stek!" Roland lowered himself between the two alcoholic player characters. "Please! Nashe, will you be so kind as to show us the next part?"

Nashe reached with his free hand into an inner pocket of his jacket and retrieved a tied scroll.

"Is that...?" Stek trailed off, dropping his weapon and leaning heavily against the dumpster.

Nashe nodded. "'Tis. The end of the story."

"Wise informed me that it was in Damian's home," Roland said. "Why on earth do you have it *here*?"

"We did not count on Yassiz becoming wary of the story told outside the Théâtre," Nashe answered. "Some part of him knew. He managed to shift the timeline slightly surrounding Laban's tomb and now acts as pretender to the authorial throne."

"And it's affecting all the worlds?" Roland surmised.

Nashe nodded, replacing the scroll in his jacket. "Many of them," he said. "Those that matter, at least. Like the fixed-point theorem—dust we are, to dust we return; but lo! What heavy matter stands as impassable boulder in the pulverized world of Lilliputia?" He paused and sniffed. "Something is rotten in Foxend—and it's more than the corpses... *Is he rewriting this as we speak*?"

Stek glanced frantically from Roland to Nashe and back. He pointed an accusatory finger at his potential maker. "Seriously?"

Roland sighed. "I can get us into the liminal state, again," he said. "We can bury it in the Valley of Fear."

Stek massaged his temples. "Yassiz's burial place?"

"Yes," Nashe said. "The Astral Graveyard interpenetrating Foxend." He took another swig from his flask, capped it, and shoved it into his back pocket. "And should Charles Leland rearrive in that Enchanted Wood I've prepared at the outskirts of the story, perhaps this counter-virus will provide him enough of an advantage to see through the Laughing God's truculent survival mechanism."

"Well what the hell are we waiting for?" Stek said. "Roland, do your thing already, so I can get back to investing in my hangover and never see *this* dude again." He folded his arms across his chest.

AND UNFOLDED THEM IN the Astral Graveyard.

"Woah," he said. "That was spooky."

A pitch-black sky arched over them. Stek felt like he was upside-down, as if he was going to fall *upwards*, towards the perfectly circular image of a yellow moon that stared at him banefully.

Nashe had already headed off toward a hill topped by a single grand, ancient tree. Roland floated leisurely beside Stek.

"The tomb, there," Roland said as they began following Nashe. Stek noticed that their voices were muted, and his footsteps left the visual equivalent of an echo in the silvery grass. "That is where the girl uprooted herself from Golem Creek."

"Which girl?" Stek asked. He brushed his hand against a large gravemarker. Millions of softly floating specks of shimmering dust followed him briefly.

"Julie Evergreen," Roland said. "She was bidden to overcome herself by Michael Flowers, during one of his so-called 'ordeals.' Curwen was probably the source of the information."

"What information?" Stek was feeling a bit frustrated with all the lecturing.

"That Julie had witch-blood," he answered. "Enough, presumably, to put the first crack in a key location between the worlds."

Stek sat with the idea for a moment. "Where does this connect?"

"The Snake Den, in Kingsport," Roland said as they began ascending the hill. Nashe had seated himself at the base of the tree, beside the tomb's forbidding entrance. "And Foxend Churchyard, in Golem Creek."

Stek and Roland approached Nashe, who frowned as he tipped the empty flask over. " 'Sit thee down, sorrow,' " he said, then stood up abruptly and burst out laughing.

How the hell is he not falling over? Stek thought.

"Roland! Perhaps one more bit of assistance would not be untoward," Nashe said, rattling the lock on the doors.

Roland seemed to glow with presence while simultaneously becoming more translucent. A beam of etheric energy shot from Roland's brow and penetrated the lock, which disintegrated on impact.

"More uses than a green brick," Nashe said inexplicably, pulling the doors open wide. A draft of cold wind blew forth from it. "Shall we?" Nashe entered, whistling tunelessly.

"You want me to wait out here?" Stek said, his previous drunk being rapidly replaced with a headache.

Roland did the octopoid equivalent of a grin. "Your presence is needed," he said simply, and floated into the chamber.

NASHE'S WILD LOOK MADE them both rather nervous. The scroll he withdrew from an inner pocket of his jacket appeared ancient and expensive; a wax seal bound it together, completing the spectacle.

"What the hell did you write that with?" Stek asked belligerently.

Nashe, standing alongside a raised coffin, dim yellow flames emanating light from two stone urns on either side of him, flashed his crazed smile. "A little gimmicky," he said. "But the wax seal is authentic. Twenty-seventh dynasty."

"He's referring to the Faery Dynasties," Roland explained from his mid-air perch to Stek's left. "Not Egyptian, which only detected the Constellations of Din shortly before the Sphinx's reconstructive surgery."

Stek's mind was addled, but things had begun coming back to him with a vengeance on their entry into the Tomb of Khan-i-Bal, the crux of Yassiz's sorcerous invasion of Golem Creek. In an overlapping shadow of this place, Henrik Shaxplay had built the first version of Mindwarp using displaced protoplasm from the Laughing God...Michael Flowers, under the influence of his uncle Curwen, had sent Julie Evergreen into this very tomb under the assumption that her witch-blood would protect her from the malicious survival mechanism built into Yassiz's *prima materia*—who knew what strange manifestation it took when she approached it, unwittingly or not...?

When confronted with elimination, Yassiz's intelligent substance would attempt to convince its assassin to leave it be, or even kill itself... Part of the Greater Mystery surrounding the Laughing God was how, precisely, he went about the process of "eliminating" bits of himself on his own. But Stek suspected that he had that part figured out: *ars oblivionalis*, of course—the real strength of this particular god was his ingenious use of *imperfection*...

Stek closed his eyes and rubbed his temples under the onslaught of returning memories. He distinctly felt a palliative "fluid" (for lack of a better term) flow into him.

"Thank you," he whispered to Roland, who glowed brighter momentarily as he sought to even out the difference in amalgamating astral matter.

Nashe's grin remained. He lifted the lid of the coffin.

It's happening, Stek thought. Somewhere near/far, Tom Fallow—the unknown shadow-self of Charles Leland, who had split from him the instant he broke through the portal in the crawl space beneath the Flowers residence—held Laban's restless, mummified body as still, as inhibited in its mental movements as possible...Addie Whitfield, the last of the fading line of witches imprisoned in Laban's dreaming, their minds displaced from his sorceries in Candleston, where the Nameless Book still waits, overflowing with magic, desperate to unburden itself on those whose *curiosity* draws them to its pages...*who knew how many worlds it had spawned?*...spinning Cloud-Webs of mind-stuff to catch the rogue god...

Swirling mauve mists surrounded Nashe. He held the scroll—looking more like a human thighbone, now—out before him in both hands, his eyes now closed as the Ecstasy overtook him...

There are no words for this Rite. If the Master of Koth Wills it, it is done.

"*If the Master of Koth Wills it, it is done.* Fiat NOX! *Thisharb! Zod-manas zi-ba!*"

Roland's counter-darkness had become blinding, mingling darkness and light. It was visible and invisible; it was a closed opening and violent gentleness... Stek could barely contain himself. From his very pores shrieked and wailed a chorus of faery voices, drowning out the light, shaking the walls. Tears burst from his eyes; Nashe held on to a mere shred of sanity as an infinite laughter welled up from deep within him; Roland, on cue, unbecame again, echoing the eldritch strains into and through Æons...

STEK OPENED HIS EYES to the fading sound of *a cricket chirping* in some hidden recess of his mind. The room was one he remembered, faintly, yet another among many worldlines.

He gazed down at his hands, at the expensive cufflinks on his tailored dress-shirt; at the wood floor of a room in a pocket world where his Beloved awaited.

He stepped forward confidently and opened the door, beyond which She worked her magic...

There.

She stood in all her glory, a cyclone of mauve magic swirling about Her, disintegrating what once imprisoned them.

He uttered Her True Name.

Their hands met and vanished into each other, spinning and folding the Midsummer Revelry into impossible config-urations...*ah, My Love, ingenious! I should have known! The Pit of Demented Pixies!*

The Faery "Hell"—to adapt a crude term for the sinister backwards world where logic was merely an ever-changing madhouse show—had been cracked open, its agents released.

By the Queen's might and the King's music, the Impossible Place was unsealed... He—even He—felt a twinge of regret... What atrocities would those bedlamite servitors inflict on the Laughing God as he was dragged, netted in their maniac chorus, into the hands of the Monolith...?

Tom

TOM FALLOW WALKED UNTIL he could no longer hear the screams, until he could no longer see the flames, until the bottle he'd purchased from Roland at Bang for Your Buck was utterly, dreadfully empty.

He didn't remember getting here. He remembered the merciless repetition of the same few hours of time, back at The Flying Monkey, over and over and over until, that last time, he simply walked away from the Goblin Gang before Booker could return with the drinks. He remembered somehow making it to Lamb's Occult and taking Harvey's potion.

And finally he remembered seeing Roland inexplicably behind the counter—the signal that freedom was at hand... Then buying the bourbon and drinking it as he headed in the opposite direction of the Monster Ball.

Then something had happened. A mist, a misdirection, a mystification.

He was somewhere in the fields that lay beyond Chicken Hill. A chill wind had arisen; the smell of smoke, carrying faint traces of burning cinders and perhaps of carcasses.

He dropped the bottle. Its empty, sorrowful clink against a large tree root echoed in Tom's sleep-deprived mind. This was the last phase—the last *painful* phase of the contract, and then he was out.

Unhingement.

That's what Harvey Lamb had explained to him when he'd handed over the scroll. *The Ritual of Unhingement...you'll hate it, but you'll be glad that you did it.*

Well, he certainly hated it so far. Hadn't slept in days—the world kept fading in and out. As a final act of (authorized) kindness to himself, he had decided to go ahead and indulge the use of "liquid spirits" to assist him in achieving the appropriate level of trance—really, to bring him down somewhat after the weird orange potion Harvey had provided.

Drink this before you head out there. She will assist you.

He had said that: *she* will assist you. And it had certainly assisted his heart rate—he began to feel both awake and asleep simultaneously...

Before him, a circle of large rocks—like a jagged Stonehenge—appeared suddenly. Ancient trees crouched and bent and angled around the stones; some of the stones seemed almost to merge with the trees, like petrified stumps of lightning-shot wood.

Tom stood at the edge of the stone circle with trepidation.

Entreat the Stones. Call to the Black God, He Whose dreaming sustains us.

Tom walked once widdershins about the circle, testing each of the stones with hand and eye for an entry that was more than physical.

It found him. He placed both hands upon it, and began the enactment of Choronzon's Verse...

...the shapes you must use
in blood drawn
and the abomination of desolation
by great moonlight discover'd...

III.

AUDERE

THERE *IS* NO SUCH book *Morpheus Unbound; Or, Zod-Manas Zi-Ba.* I can assure you of this because I know for a fact that its purported author—referred to as "Damian Stephens" among his imaginary friends—does not, has never, and (if I have anything to do with it) *will never* exist.

The conditions of my release (and perhaps I should title this "The Conditions of Release," in mockery of Stephens's absurd "The Means of Escape"—as if that would attract anyone other than adolescents and dopers to its ragged prose) being made plain to me by Mr. Prescott Mayhew, Esq., in our interview on Bloomsday, 16 June 2021 *era vulgari*, I suppose I have no other choice than to present the facts in the case as clearly and succinctly as possible (which also strikes me as hilarious, since nothing could be considered further from an objective critique of Stephens's *A Good Year for Monsters* than the terms "clear" and "succinct"!).

Did you kill Damian Stephens?

That—*that!*—is the first question on your list! "Did you (meaning me—Calder C. Caine) kill Damian Stephens?" I suppose the simple answer is an emphatic, unequivocal "no." Again, as mentioned *supra*, I didn't kill him because, first of all, I *couldn't.* The bastard doesn't *exist*—hence, his murder would be an impossibility for me, you, or anyone else in this forsaken place!

I say this despite the fact that I have read and re-read the twin calamities you've chosen as part of your vicious attempt to "force confession" out of me. I do not think the ancient alchemists really intended such tripe in their formula—*lege, lege, lege, relege, ora et labora!*—but you never really know with those types, do you? However, given my circumstances—and the fact that *Fear Club* and *A Good Year for Monsters* are the only two pieces of evidence you've provided with which to plead my case—I suppose I'll take some likely advice from these terrible forgeries and "fake it 'til I make it."

As if there's any other way to proceed. I'm tired. I refuse to do any more work before lunch.

THE TURKEY AND LETTUCE sandwich was actually quite good. Perhaps you've laced the salt with a mild tranquilizer, or some percutaneous form of sodium pentathol—I feel noticeably relaxed after eating. And cold apple juice. A nice touch—attempts to induce theta waves and increase suggestibility by way of referencing the classic elementary school sack lunch.

I see what you are doing. But given that my treatment could just as easily be something out of the cesspool of political thrillers, I suppose I can accede a bit, and perhaps try to write this with fewer overt references to my captors' general stupidity.

Ahem! If proof of my innocence in this matter is what you require—and a simple plea of "not guilty" just won't cut it—I'll agree to write out in its entirety the circumstances that dragged me into this mess so that we can all get on with our respective lives as readily as possible. I'll answer your questions if and when they become relevant. You'll have to be satisfied with that.

To begin again: *someone* "died" that bloody night, but it was *not* the imaginary "Damian Stephens." How should I explain this? You know what—to hell with it. I'll indulge the contrarian in me.

YOU ARE ALREADY AWARE of my background. But I didn't start off writing for *Fortean Times* and *UFO Monthly*. There was a progression—in my opinion, a progression from the superficial to the essential, from accident to substance, despite the detractions of friends and family.

An education at the University of Chicago included my first professional mistake: not covering the case of Ioan Culianu when that tragic mess happened, years after I knew him.* We'd crossed paths a couple of times, and I'd attended a few of his lectures. I'd considered doing an exposé on his unique methodology for teaching classes on magic—not, as you know, "sleight of hand" or prestidigitation. Real magic—casting spells and evocation of demons and all that.

Well. In late 1987 I found myself sitting in the back of one of his classes. This was after picking up Margaret Cook's translation of Culianu's *Eros and Magic in the Renaissance*. I was taken with the idea that modern manipulative magic—like the use of various media to engender mass hypnosis in large populations—had one of its earliest codifications in Giordano Bruno's *De vinculis in genere*, his unfinished treatise on "bonds in general." I was particularly enamored (to use the appropriate word) by Bruno's statement: *vinculum quippe vinculorum amor est.*

A beautiful wording of a well-known fact: *love is the bond of bonds.* Or "chain of chains," if you will—the strongest strength of the strong, perhaps, *fortitudinis fortitudo fortis*, to continue the alchemical motif hinted at earlier. This is perhaps what the unfortunate Stek Jarry would use to describe his "attachment" to Molly Furnival—prior to his apotheosis, I mean.

I was beginning to see something very deep in all of this. Professor Culianu went on at length about the natural progression of Bruno's treatise, *De umbris idearum* ("On the Shadows of Ideas"), his earliest known work on the *ars memorativa*, or Art of Memory, and how he demonstrated that the Hermetic Ideal could be attained by way of a complete enchainment of "all and everything"—the microcosm raised in perfect balance with its macrocosmic reflection, one beholding the other, stretching from the misty depths of quanta to the inconceivably vast, extratemporal blacknesses beyond the reaches of any perceivable galaxy.

It—and by "it" I mean *everything*—all started with a

---

* See Ted Anton's *Eros, Magic, and the Murder of Professor Culianu* for the damnably good story.

mistake, mind you. Much like this monological interrogation you've got me engaged in right now. A mistake—the wrong of the beginning, as some of the Gnostics would say, or the shattering of world-stuff that generated the world of shells, of demonic phenomena, and our own world in the process.

I can't remember now what it was precisely that Professor Culianu said to me that sent me off on what looked like a wild goose chase (to those I would now be referring to as "my colleagues" if things had gone differently). All I remember is that it had something to do with his discussion of the story of Actaeon from Ovid's *Metamorphoses*—Actaeon who accidentally witnesses the bathing of the goddess Diana, only to be turned into a stag and subsequently hunted down and torn to pieces by his own dogs.

What was it he said that day? It was peculiar—something about mathematics, about the way computational processes of apparent simplicity can, through iteration, produce wild, unpredictable tangents in many cases. Anyway, he handed me a slip of paper with a symbol on it—a symbol, and parts of words in a foreign language, and a few numbers. Some meditation on the symbols and their possible connections with each other launched me into full research mode. Hints of a connection with, of all things, the strange, dark cult of the Roman god Summanus, a reflex of the more familiar "Jupiter," quickly submerged me in a forest of synchronicities having to do with the Rites of Morpheus, God of Dreams. There were deeper implications—of the existence of a group of Dream Masters associated with the Sorcerers of Lêng, isolated on a plateau in hidden reaches of the Himalayas for tens of thousands of years after reaching this planet from some transplutonic fastness, whose Dreamings spawned places, unknown countries, *worlds* even, that overlapped ours, offering egress from physical reality as we know it.

There were rumors of a vast, black Tower that loomed greatly in the distance of certain dreams, containing dark revelations of the potent magic of the Dream Masters, a fell and heavily diluted form of which had come down to us by way of Milam Yoga, intended to awaken Dreamers to their

Reality as aspects of the Clear Light Mind and freeing them thereby from the vicissitudes of earthly life.

Weeks passed—then months. I pieced together enough of the garbled and (it seemed to me) deliberately occluded technologies of the "Dark Doctrine"—so-called for its functioning as a sort of textbook of the "Scholomance," Night School, a *prayoga* or Yoga of the Shadow—that, with barely a conscious intention on my part, I found myself suddenly a practitioner.

The practices followed logically from my all-encompassing research. I had formulated a thorough subjective synthesis of every bit of data I'd gathered—from obscure "slant" translations of phrases in the *Hypnerotomachia Poliphili* to the "spiral" interpretation of the Hermetic Order of the Golden Dawn's Pentagram Rituals and how the mathematics of conic sections implied and could generate *alien neurological interfaces*, linking our usual brains of blood and grey matter with their ghostly, instantaneous reflections—known as "Boltzmann brains" to the physicists of a later generation—manifesting spontaneously in the Void Space outside the circles of time...

I say "reflections," but perhaps it's the other way around.

A few years later, Professor Culianu was murdered in a bathroom down the hall from his office. I don't know if what happened to him was related in any way to the stuff that happened after I figured out what that slip of paper meant, but nowadays—knowing what I now know—I wouldn't doubt it at all.

I HAVE TAKEN A break because I began noticing that my memory of many of the details of those days are like a complicated dream that you're unsure of how to record. Some of it is nearly perfect, down to the very words I used in conversation; the rest?

I felt that there was something sinister about the relationship between the little slip of paper he had handed me and the sudden appearance during my researches later on of a catalog listing, containing precisely the same sequence of numbers as given in Culianu's helpful little *Zettelkasten*, for a library book that, as far as I could tell (and as I can tell you now for sure) didn't exist.

But I'm getting a little ahead of myself. He had indicated something to me—why me? I lost many nights of sleep thinking about it, puzzling over it, trying to piece things together. I recall that our few conversations had begun friendly and ended in earnest, as if he *knew* something about me, something that I was unaware of about myself, something that could not be gathered simply by gazing into a mirror and studying what I saw.

I barely completed my master's degree, having attempted to return myself to normalcy after a summer's worth of conspiracy theories and late-night drives through harrowing vistas in and around Chicago, fueled by every possible flavor of speculation I could harvest from used bookstores and comic book shops and surreptitious conversation at bus stops with "tin hat"-wearing weirdos. Magazines with wild and invigorating titles—*Cosmic Conspiracies!* and *X-Tra Ordinary Tales* and the indescribably weird ravings of that lunatic "Isaac Asthma"—began piling up in my increasingly filthy one-room apartment. It was to these fringe periodicals that I began to submit codifications of my theses, understanding as I constructed them all of a sudden why *those who know* tended to speak in riddles and hints and half-truths.

The articles were, in general, a "hit," though I never earned from them much more than enough to pay for my meager living arrangements—their only actual purpose. But you know all this—it's part of why you tracked me down in the first place.

Everything boiled down to a simple realization: something was wrong with the world. Something didn't make sense *at all*, and it was being covered up by...well, by *normality*. Normality was a myth being promulgated by...*whom*? Who believed in it? It was a myth—our promised "safety" and the security of school and spouse and social standing...*where was this idea coming from*? The more I researched, the more I became convinced that "normality" was an island in an ocean of *chaos*. I began to see a world *more real* against which this "normality" required nearly constant miracles to save it from utter destruction. In the world I was discovering, monsters of every type and description rubbed shoulders with wizards dark and light; it was the spells of witches and the potions of mad doctors that fueled the apparent movements of sun and moon, of earth and solar system. Wild beasts hid in *every* shadow; constant cover-ups were the stock in trade of the purveyors of this wicked lie of *normalcy*...

So I wrote about it. I dove deep into the myths and legends and alternative histories that generated the very same surface world we all awaken into—usually. Everything eventually linked up with the main thread of my researches. What few friends I had abandoned me after numerous warnings that I was treading territories that had driven more than one honest inquirer "insane."

Then there were the disappearances, of course; the shady informants who were there one day and quite gone the next. I started to make my way from city to city, tracking down leads, following clues, mapping out the intricate webwork that began as chance comments heard in bars and coffee shops and continued in surreptitious conversations by way of public phones, using numbers divined by various Oracles and Psychics who usually looked more like gangsters or common drunks.

I was threading something together. I was finding something out. I was discovering the actual history of the world, and it was scaring the hell out of me.

But I couldn't stop.

HOW PRECISELY DID I end up in my half-rusted Gremlin headed east? Why did I flee the scene without bothering to pack much more than a toothbrush, a single change of clothes, and a briefcase chock-full of a random selection of notes and journals and half-finished articles?

Looking back on it now, my precise engagement with the affairs of Leland & Co. effectively had its origin in that most Lovecraftian of ways. It was the dream I had had the night before I fled Chicago—unbeknownst to me at the time, for good. Despite its completeness, its vividness and wildly precise detail, I did not at first remember it in the slightest. I went about my routine, which usually consisted of immediately diving straight back into whatever research I had fallen asleep over during the night (or, more correctly, late morning) before.

At a certain point in the evening I went downstairs to pick up my mail. Amid the usual garbage was a copy of *Isaac Asthma's Nonstandard Science Magazine*—the latest issue.

Although the cover this month was standard fare—a dark, hulking shape lying in wait for a young couple on a moonlit night—I grinned to see my name listed there among several others, alongside that of a rather famous, if reclusive, "fringe scientist": Otherwise Brainerds, Ph.D. My article on the hallucinogenic properties of certain mauve crystals discovered around the Trinity atomic bomb test site in New Mexico had been published. Next to whatever it was that Dr. Brainerds had written, I felt certain my readership ought to increase substantially, perhaps even overnight.

Feeling the lovely lightness that follows an objective indication of success, I flipped idly through the magazine as I headed back to my apartment. I came upon a unique advertisement tucked neatly away near the back, just before the classified ads. It was almost as if the half-page announcement was *trying* not to be found.

PORT MANTLE

Omniversal Hub of All Worlds

...is just a hop, skip & a jump away!

VISIT

THREE COILS ACADEMY

and learn what makes the universe tick!

Whatever you're looking for, it's a helluva ride!

In a flash, my dream came back to me.

THE OCCASIONAL DIMINISHMENT WAS inevitable. With Jim Buskey's "programming" in place—to clean up after "Weston Gray" as necessary and ensure he was not hindered in his work, and to be sure that at least a handful of the myriad pacts and contracts and deals and agreements in this stupid little game he was playing with PyGoLiRo were either fulfilled or broken in accordance with calculations that would maximize his odds of winning the most space in the least time—Yassiz felt the familiar twinges of excitement, egging him on, the perversity of his self-medication: rebellion, starting with rebellion against his nature—*completion.*

It was the Faery Queen that had him, admittedly, a little on edge.

In *this* Golem Creek, too? Blasted hyper-efficiency of his self-defense mechanisms...

He thought he had her secured neatly away in a "royal scam": keep her occupied as *herself* for a change, the Midsummer Queen, in a tiny little variant of Golem Creek that took only a smidge of energy to maintain. A slight diversion of the irrigation heading this way from Port Mantle...but it was worth it, even if he was caught. If she failed to suspect what was going on, he might have a *continuous* source of the Vinum Sabbati—and PyGoLiRo wouldn't be the only guys in town with a means of escape from any given world. Once she inevitably "did her thing" and generated a new batch of that wonderful "Witches' Wine," Yassiz could simply relieve her of it and head off for new dimensions.

Literally.

He remembered the night he met her—or, at least, the girl she was before she *knew*—quite vividly. The dark cul-de-sac deep in the woods of that hick town: Tulsa, Oklahoma. What had it been that made her do it? He had wondered that. How did she even know it could be done?

She went by a different name then: Marigold. Couldn't have been more than seventeen years old. But such *power*! Even he was impressed. And she had attempted to escape, but without having mastered the Secret of the Cone...ah, well!

The Curse she'd thrown at him when he stepped out of the Triangle was truly a force to be reckoned with. He winced to remember it.

But Yassiz had been around. And he never missed an opportunity to remind Witches and Wizards of that one simple rule: *do not call up that which you cannot put back down.*

He'd been able to repel the Curse with only that mild concussion such entities as he felt when smashed by such things. But Marigold! Poor Marigold. Lovely and powerful and...

Very much broken. Into a thousand of herself, a million, more, perhaps... There was almost no way she could have known. Yassiz, the Laughing God—the *Split One,* Whose Name is Legion...

The Curse had rebounded at her, its *intention* being to cause any harm Yassiz might intend toward *her* to be directed back at *him*. But Yassiz's very *im*perfection had sustained the blow—all the cracks and hollows of his multidimensional psyche had absorbed, enhanced, and thrust it all back at her, splitting her as he himself was split...not to mention her (at the time) unknown consort, whom a severely amnesiac Yassiz had met behind the QuikTrip that same night...

Yes, as he himself was split.

But without the *little benefit* of infinite regeneration.

So.

That was a relief, at first.

But when he found out *why* she'd been able to wield so

much ineffable, raw power...

Well that changed things.

Sure, PyGoLiRo's "deal" with her had made things diffi-cult as usual—the filthy bastards. Eyes everywhere; constantly checking the value of their stock in every possible market across and through each world. Those guys were *impos-sible to beat*, according to everyone who knew of them. They controlled the import and export of most goods, magical and otherwise, through most of the worlds.

And Yassiz had been a thorn in their side since double-crossing them—what was it? Centuries ago, by his own subjective time-sense. Over that Alhazred fellow, wasn't it?

No sense of humor in the lot, that was for sure.

...nor in these *meddling bastards...Pit of Demented Pixies? Are you* kidding *me...?!?*

CALLED THE "ADVERTISERS' Information" line from the number in fine print at the front of the magazine. After ringing endlessly, an irritated (why are they always so irritated?) gentleman answered.

"What?"

His gruff manner put me off my game momentarily. "Uh, hello, my name is Calder Caine?" I said, as if I wasn't sure of it. "You—you're magazine had an ad in it, and I'm wondering—"

"That stuff's for Monday through Friday. Call back then."

"No! Wait! Please. I'm just wondering *who* placed the ad at the back of the last issue? The one that talks about Port Mantle and some place called Three Coils Academy?"

"Huh? Wait."

He set the phone down. I could clearly hear mumbling in the background, followed by laughter. My irascible savior picked up the phone before he finished talking to whomever-it-was at his office.

"...and then she didn't bother to pick up the donuts anyway, goddamnit. Hello? You still there?"

"Yes! Thank you so much for your—"

"Kingsport."

"Kingsport? Is that the company?"

"That's all we got. Kingsport, Massachusetts. It's just 'S.D.' in Kingsport."

"Okay, then. I guess—"

An audible click indicated that he had hung up the phone. I scribbled down the information. "S.D." in Kingsport,

Massachusetts.

I glanced at the clock. Six-thirty. Hadn't had dinner yet, but...I decided to eat on the way.

I was packed and gone thirty minutes later.

I HAD AN OLD road atlas still crammed into a crease between the seats of my car, having learned—from practical experience chasing down threads of stories at the drop of a hat—to *just set out* the instant that gut feeling came over me, the one indicating that something *very important* was about to happen.

I made it to South Bend before noticing the hunger pangs too strongly. Guessing correctly that there would be somewhere cheap to eat near Notre Dame, I followed the inevitable signs and got a couple of cheeseburgers at a McDonald's drive-through.

Sitting in the parking lot of a familiar place in a strange city always induces an eerie feeling. By night, it is the smell, usually—of the trees, the buildings, the denizens to whom you, yourself, are the unfamiliar creature—that generates the aura and the conviction that you have stepped into a dream. I had done this literally hundreds of times before—sat in the parking lot of a McDonald's and felt the uncanny atmosphere seeping into me, making me a part of it, making it more *real* by the very fact of my foreignness within it. For the sustenance of *any* given world is its "fairy food"; it binds you to the laws of that world, though not, perhaps, irrevocably. During my researches, I had begun to suspect that, indeed, there are exorcisms of environments as surely as there are evocations.

It was my expectation, felt certainly now and confirmed moments later, that the strange "hub of the multiverse" known as "Port Mantle" would prove to be exactly the sort of magical space required to answer most, if not all, of my unanswered questions.

In the midst of my meditations, a somewhat haggard-looking kid, probably just out of high school, tapped on my window.

"Excuse me?" he said innocently.

A flood of adrenaline and stimulating chemicals banged

about in my veins. Despite all my dealings with peculiar individuals, I was nevertheless very much unpracticed when it came to matters of hobo etiquette.

I tried stammering out a reply. "Uh—um—I've got to head out! I'm sorry—"

"Wait! I think you're the only one who can help me. Do you recognize the name Calder Caine?"

A *fan*?

Whether or not anyone warns you about the various dangers of being "known"—particularly if what you're known for happens to be everything you'd be loathe to admit you *never want to encounter*—you're almost always met with a paradox when someone recognizes you on the street. It can be summarized thus:

Yes, thank you for your support.

No, I don't want to be your friend.

Given the fact that *no one in the world knew where the hell I was* at that moment, much less the careful lengths I'd gone to in order to avoid any images of me being published anywhere, I felt somewhat more uncomfortable dealing with this exchange than I presumably would have during the daylight hours, back on my home turf.

"I—um—" I continued to stammer, one hand on the keys dangling from the ignition, the other praying that my car—which usually required a number of attempts to get going—might bless me with a singular acquiescence on this night.

"I'm heading to Kingsport," he said flatly. "And I need a ride."

I ceased my purely mental attempts at fleeing the scene for a moment. "Kingsport?" I said. "What makes you think I'm headed there?"

He pressed a battered paperback book against the window and pointed at it with his other hand. The cover showed an artist's rendering of some kind of octopus-headed sorcerer, hovering in full lotus over a cityscape. A black pyramid loomed sinisterly in the mist-filled distance, around which the title emerged: *Wild Lies II: The Truth is Outta Here!*

I didn't recognize it; nonetheless, inescapably, my name

shone clearly at the bottom, hovering ghost-like over the dark background.

I had always felt that of all the elements of which this world is comprised, the *essential* element, the quintessence of experience, was the element of *surprise*. There was a moment, just before the kid told me his name, that I realized something was about to change. Gates to other worlds can open anywhere, at any time—something I know all too well now.

I gazed at the book—one of many dream-gates I would traverse—with the implicit understanding that I was to it as Pandora to her box.

I had to look twice to be sure. But there was a problem.

"I'm sorry—what's your name again?" I asked.

"Charles Leland," he said.

"Yes, Charles, there seems to be a problem with your book," I explained. "I am aware that it has my name on it. But I regret to inform you that—although I am indeed the proud author of the first installment of *Wild Lies*—I must insist that I am in no way responsible for the book you are holding." I paused momentarily. "Er. Despite the name on the cover."

Charles removed it from the window and shoved it into his backpack. "That's exactly right, Mr. Caine. Good for you. We're actually going to try and make sure that this book never happens *at all*."

My senses, to use Rimbaud's beautiful phrase, had been suitably and systematically deranged. It was thus that my unknowing complicity in the matter of Golem Creek—a city I'd never heard of in a world I'd never suspected could exist—sealed both our fates.

And, thus, I became folded into the tale.

THE STORY CHARLES LELAND told me as we headed off that night was totally convincing and utterly insane—precisely the fare I lived on. I couldn't get enough of it.

He had obtained the book from a proprietor of occult goods in some otherworldly location I was suddenly hearing a great deal about—Port Mantle. The notion that some kind of preternatural *boardgame* had been the means of his expulsion from an "externally imposed storyline" basically had me shaking with joy. It was, after all, the logical conclusion of systems of divination, as of systems of enchantment: both had their origin in a set of beliefs about how and why things happened in the first place.

People could "get magic to work" quite readily if they had the courage to divest themselves of everything which implied it could *not*, to untangle themselves from a "world out there" and figure out how something seemingly impossible *might actually happen*, given what they "knew for sure" about things. An intermingling of magical axioms—as, for example, the basic Hermetic notion of "*quod est superius est sicut quod est inferius*," and vice versa (as given by the identification of a person with a game piece, e.g.)—produced the subjectively synthesized world of Golem Creek *along with the capacity to manipulate it at the root*.

Runecasting, shuffling tarot cards, tossing bones or crystals, rolling dice. All suggested an element of randomness *essential* to the world—but with boundaries; stochastic processes, almost (perhaps exactly?) like the motions of gas molecules in an impermeable chamber. And how can we forget the lovely implications of quantum mechanics and nonlinear dynamics, which threaten nothing only when misunderstood...

But our "free will" is a roll of the dice. The fantastic element—that shadow worlds overlap with whatever world one finds oneself within, evoking Machen's fear-inducing line that we dwell only *seemingly* alone "...and with what companions?"—only invigorated me.

"I found myself here," he said as the night sky began lightening to a dull morning greyness. "Or back in South Bend, I mean. Coming out of one of the stalls in that McDonald's, if you can believe it. You showed up shortly after I finished skimming your book." He chuckled. "Like I said, if you can believe it."

I could, and did.

THE ESSENTIAL FORMULA OF the Cone: now, what happens is that you *focus*; round and round you go, whirling into the *center*—but it's a "pointless point."* Nothing happens there, for a change; nothing manifests in any form, and that's exactly what I found out.

As Charles told me his perfect story—answering questions as we went along, taking turns driving when necessary and stopping once in Cleveland for food and fuel, another time after that—the land around us began to alter not-so-subtly.

Something else began to change, but I can't quite tell you about that yet, because I myself am not sure of whether it's just my imagination. I started *noticing* things; things started becoming clearer. Perhaps it was the engaging familiarity with which Charles Leland spoke to me on that drive which did it, or his occasional references to *Wild Lies II*, but I couldn't help feeling as if I *remembered* much of what he was saying.

"And so," Charles began the ending as a massive body of water came into view on our left, "you yourself write *this* piece"—he held up the book before replacing it in his back-pack—"after we make it to the Snake Den."

I was confused.

"But I thought we *were* going to the Snake Den?" I asked.

Charles nodded. "That's correct. But when you wrote *this*, I hadn't accompanied you. You made it to the Snake Den. Then *he* arrived."

---

* قطب

179

By this point, I was relatively certain of which character Charles meant. "The Laughing God?" I said. The name sent chills through me.

Charles nodded again. "It's why I had to come. He's the *one single element* that seems to have swung all the storylines out of their natural arcs and into *his own*. I think it's one way that he keeps things interesting for himself, while at the same time keeping himself 'differentiated' enough to have a few laughs—or whatever he does—before he starts regenerating again."

Yassiz. I heard the name echo through my mind. Visions of strange beasts cavorting through moon-bedazzled woods at night flitted through my mind. A massive, black beast in a graveyard, chomping through the bodies of living and dead alike in the process of *remembering itself*—it was the infernal reanimation of Yassiz in a town called Golem Creek...in a story by the not-so-famous pulp author Nashe St.-Demp: "The Ballad of Cannibal Corpse." Supposedly, there had even been a movie made about it, though I (perhaps luckily) had failed to catch it.

"It's a reasonable theory," I said, shaking my head. I tried to detach myself from the visions, which seemed all-too-real to me. "And if we can escape 'through the Cone' as you say, by way of the primordial portal within the Snake Den, *before* he arrives..."

"Mostly right," Charles said. "There's one slight catch. A *literal* catch, actually, and it's something we've got exactly one chance to get right."

I knew what he was thinking before he said it. "We have to drag him back through that portal with us."

Charles nodded, a sympathetic look on his face. "We must re-fictionalize him if we want to save *any* of our worlds. The Cone is the Key—it takes whatever matter is presented to it and reconstitutes it at some other possible spacetime point. This is the essential aspect of artificial portal construction, according to Dr. Brainerds. But certain 'primordial' portals serve, well, as lynchpins of the laws of physics. The Snake Den is one of them. Lovecraft knew about it. So did Curwen

Flowers." He rubbed his hands together. A sudden chill breeze blew in from over the water. "I figure you can leave most of the heavy-duty stuff to me," he continued. "But, unfortunately, given the presence of the book, which reveals the *whole secret* of Yassiz, describing *everything* that he's been doing for aeons, we're making the assumption that he's coming for *you specifically* in order to make sure it never gets written. He can't risk learning too much about himself—it dampens his chances for delaying deific catatonia."

Deific catatonia—Charles had explained this to me, hadn't he? It was the final end-state of a "god"; their tendency and goal was perfect calculation and "playing out" of all possible storylines in one finite but unbounded loop of spacetime. But something about Yassiz had mutated, like a virus; he manipulated storylines to *avoid his fate*, to extend the possibilities of every "loop" within which he found himself.

No matter what the cost to the worlds he dreamed.

"So I'll be..." I trailed off, forcing Charles to fill in the blank.

"Bait," he said, as I'd expected. "If I can withstand the Laughing God's hypnosis or enchantment or whatever he does to keep himself safe"—Charles glanced at a Thermos he'd been sipping from, considering the bitter "coffee substitute" and the note Harvey had left with it explaining its intended apotropaic effects—"then...well. I guess we'll see. May have to pull a Steve on this one and make do with what happens."

I forced myself to grin at the joke, feeling as if I'd come to know the characters of Charles's story like old friends of my own, despite the undeniably dark air of impending doom that seemed to waft over the conversation. And I couldn't help asking my next question.

"But if he *succeeded* last time—"

"How did *I* get here? Well, it's not like he's *all-powerful* or anything. He only annihilates *your* world, plus Golem Creek and all its variants, and several sub-worlds that apparently only Damian Stephens knows about. I was quite literally lucky to escape Golem Creek before it was consumed. So at least Port Mantle remains to function as an index of the worlds that were. With Wise's technology, we were able to integrate the world-linking capabilities of Port Mantle with his 'Azif Théâtre'—as *Morpheus Unbound*—and do basically what the fairy people do: world-jump."

I kept silent, not wishing to betray the fact that I had every intention of making use of these "portals" at my earliest opportunity.

THE MORNING THAT THE Black God cracked through multiple realities and shattered life on Earth for me forever started out sunny and mild. There was very little traffic; a great hunger—much like the hunger of that Ancient One now hammering at the lid of his coffin—finalized my decision to pull into a diner off the highway.

The imminent arrival of Yog-Sothoth's emissary didn't in any way spoil an exquisite breakfast of scrambled eggs with extra cheese, heavily crisped bacon, and buttered toast.

The coffee at the Wicked Break Diner—originally the Wicker Creek Diner, its name modified by enterprising graffiti artists—was also of mickle might.

"Are you going to let me look at that damned book or not?" I asked Charles Leland after he returned from freshening up in the bathroom.

I had ordered an identical breakfast for him. He lifted a piece of toast, clearly starved (I hadn't seen him eat or drink anything yet), then set it down again before opening his canvas backpack and retrieving his Thermos and *Wild Lies II*.

"Thanks for the breakfast," he said. "But I'm on a very strict diet while I'm here." He poured a tarry substance from the Thermos into the lid-cup and sipped it.

I shrugged. "More for me," I said, and pulled his plate to my side of the table, eyeing *Wild Lies II* as I did so.

"And as for the book," he said, gazing at it as if it were some foreign matter on the diner table, "I will not only *let* you read it. I'm *expecting* you to read it." He took another sip from his Thermos mug, his eyes watering as he watched me scoop scrambled eggs onto toast and take a huge bite. "The sooner the better, I guess. Might as well get it over with." His not-so-hidden reservations regarding this mystified me.

I nodded. "Excellent! I could use a break from all the driving, and I think we're clearly—if you'll forgive the metaphor—on the same page." I grinned at him, a look he returned weakly.

A handful of other patrons sat in booths around the diner, most looking rather tired and focused exclusively on their respective breakfasts. I shoveled the last of the scrambled eggs into my mouth, then turned my attention to Charles's rejected portion.

"Tell me, is it any good?" I asked.

"If you're asking whether the *writing* is any good, I can tell you conclusively 'yes, it does its job perfectly.' If you're asking whether I would consider it *morally okay*, I would have to say— well, I guess I'd say there are some serial killers out there with better chances of pleading their case."

I inadvertently clapped my hands with joy. "And with a title like '*Wild Lies*'? Incredible. I have outdone myself."

The earth shook. I caught a glimpse of something horrifying in the warped reflection of the chrome napkin holder before bracing myself between table and booth.

Charles did the same.

"What the hell was that?" I said, mimicking the wide-eyed looks of consternation among patrons of the Wicked Break Diner.

"We should probably get out of here," Charles said, packing away his Thermos and the book. "I'll meet you in the car."

I nodded, my mouth full, and waved for a doggie bag from the waitress.

MINUTES LATER, CHARLES DRIVING, we fled the scene, deciding on the use of an alternate route of back roads and service roads suggested to us by analysis of my map.

I held the copy of *Wild Lies II* in both hands and gazed at its cover. The figure hovering in the midst of a street at night... *Roland*...a creepy store with a sign reading "Lamb's Occult" to his left...dimly, in the far distance, a black pyramid rising behind and above it all...

I opened it with some trepidation.

WILD LIES II

The Truth is Outta Here!

by

Calder C. Caine

WHEN IN THE COURSE of human events it becomes necessary to rewrite the history of the world, to abolish notions corrupt and corruptible of strange capacities, to disidentify with the whole host of mundane phenomena that one's true heritage might thereby be uncovered, relimned and relimbed, disentangled from the tedious, thorny vines and thick, asphyxiating roots of *the regulating multitude*, I say: *for a good time—break glass!*

Precisely these six words spake uncanny truth in the strange case of Charles Thomas Leland and his several friends, his foes and his fevers. You do not remember it—but you will. This book has come to you by way of every possible fault, mistake merely the obverse of intention, willfulness the loud accomplice of silent chaos.

For a good time—break glass!

And so he did, and so we shall, but first an editing— first, the history of the end of their world. An editing—yes! If we look but close into the word, we shall know, dare, will, keep silent. We shall go in unto our fates secure in the knowledge of the Brains Outside, calculating machines whose devices still are overthrown...

"IT WAS A WELCOME warmth that night, despite the apocalypse." Honorius High lay mostly in ruins. The terrible cackling of unhallowed creatures leaping and cavorting in an orgy of dark joy joined the crackling of fires and shattering of windows and screams of the unfortunate few who had not been hybridized with one of the Creatures from the Murk.

They were there with an express purpose: *to reclaim their world.* After the equivalent of astral grubs and carrion for nearly a century, when the crack in their world appeared, they made for it like moths to starlight—or more like wolves to sheep.

You have heard it or felt it, I am sure: the inexplicable bang or thump or bump in the night. It has awoken you, and you have felt a sensational fear creep into you from the darkness of your rooms, innocuous furniture made malicious by obscurity and that simple, dreadful sound.

I can tell you that I know what that sound is from. I can tell you that I will reveal its source to you soon.

Yassiz, the Laughing God, the Incomplete, from his throne underground in St. Bruno's Church across from Honorius High School, felt it too, and shortly knew what it was.

The Black God returns...

For is this town, Golem Creek, not merely an extension of Laban's dreaming? As the qliphothic creatures from the various hells of Laban's mind swarmed, at last, out of confinement and into the overlap of dream and flesh that is Golem Creek, the Place of Solace below deteriorated. First at its edges...the vast oceans and mountain ranges, as yet uncoordinated into further cities, disintegrated, becoming clouds, mists, mere probabilities, and finally a windy blackness like their very origin.

Simultaneously the forests and roads that led from Forty Winks, to Rookville and beyond, crashed and splintered and shook. Some of those points of Dreaming called their "population" knew, briefly, what became of them—but the brevity was shortly a myth, a distortion in spacetime, as they and their memories were battered and bashed out of existence.

The demons fed—and fed! And fed! Along with blood from torn flesh was let *dreams,* the dreams that sustained the worlds above and below, desires for *other times and other places,* some wilder and some simpler, some fascinating and some tranquil.

At last, the beasts had overrun the place, save One Thing—One Thing that trembled and shook and *woke...*

Their bloodlust temporarily sated—the food of another

dreamworld temporarily sustaining the Reality of that dream—
they themselves slept, in corners, in caves, in groves, in graves,
they slept.

They slept and dreamed. And the One Thing—the
Black God—opened eyes long shut...

Flipping randomly to a page near the end gave an entry in
an informal glossary:

Known to those in the dream-city of "Golem Creek" as "Molly
Furnival," an unassuming—if outlandishly beautiful—girl,
thankfully both older than Dante's Beatrice and younger than
Shakespeare's. All reports indicate that she presently still rules
Faeryland (q.v.) as its Queen along with her consort, Epiktistes
"Stek" Jarry (q.v.)...

THE CAR MADE A screeching swerve off the main road. The
sudden alteration of velocity woke me from a sleep I hadn't
known I'd fallen into.

"Jesus *Christ*!" Charles shouted as we slid to a stop. A brief
silence was exchanged as we gazed out the car windows.

A fault, a fissure, massive and seemingly insurmountable,
functionally ended the two-lane road we'd been traveling.
We had just passed the New York-Pennsylvania border on
what was (perhaps synchronously) called the Portville-Eldred
Road.

Charles and I looked at each other before exiting the car
and making a tentative investigation of the scenery.

"Is this what was meant when they coined the term
'abysmal depths'?" I asked, filling with partial jest my abject
terror.

Charles stood perhaps twenty feet from the fissure, arms
akimbo, shaking his head. "This is—what is this? How does
this happen?"

Creeping forward, we determined that, indeed, the chasm
was insurmountable. It was as if the mile-wide eraser of some
species of giant had been swabbed across the Earth at that
point. As we neared the edge, we saw clearly that the chasm

fell away unfathomably, muting the question of whether the space could be traversed at all.

"This wasn't supposed to happen," Charles said glumly. He turned and headed back to the car.

I stayed gazing out over the deletion a few moments longer. In the distance, the world seemed to continue, though it was too far for me to determine whether that guaranteed any degree of safety on the other side.

"Can we get an airplane?" I suggested, turning around and heading back to the car as well. "Or a hang-glider, maybe? Something that flies?"

Charles groaned quite audibly before getting back into the car, where he sat silently, hands on the steering wheel, car unawakened.

I stood beside the open passenger door and gazed back at the impossible calamity.

"What does this mean?" I asked.

Charles was silent for a moment. "It means that everything's inevitable," he said flatly. "We might as well go back to the diner. I'm starving."

"Wait, wait," I continued. "We can't just *stop*. We set out to get to the Snake Den—"

A blinding flash of white light knocked me to the ground. For several instants, I lost all conscious awareness of my surroundings—an infinite blackness took their place. But in the blackness there was something—something I had forgotten, something I *needed to remember*—

"Are you all right?" Charles knelt at my side in the grass of the low shoulder. "You just fucking conked out. What the hell?"

I felt my face with my hands—*something was not right*—

"I'm—I'm okay, I think," I said. Charles helped me to a standing position, from which I got back into the car. "I probably just need some sleep."

Charles nodded. "We both do. I thought I saw a motel back a few miles. We'll take a break." He waved at the huge crevasse. "The rest of the world should be dealing with this soon, if they aren't already."

IT WAS ON THE news, of course, when we arrived at the motel.

"You guys *seen* this stuff?" Our motel manager, Sven, was ecstatic. "Big crater opened up, clear across the country! Have you *seen* this stuff?"

Charles nodded and forced a smile. "Scared the hell out of us. We just came from that direction. What do they think it is?"

"Scientists are saying it's continental drift," Sven explained as he handed the motel room key over. "That's bullshit, of course. Whatever scientists say is always bullshit, right?" He grinned at us in tacit, presumptuous alliance.

I nodded, as did Charles. "No doubt," I said. We all watched the fifteen-inch Zenith for a few moments as a news journalist quietly explained the catastrophe, her mascara smudged from a recent bout of tears.

"Y'all be careful out there," Sven said as he sat back down. "This probably ain't over. Fuckin' scientists, right?"

Charles and I grinned again, chuckled softly, and left the office.

I WAS ASLEEP ALMOST as soon as my head hit the pillow. Once again, my dreams were vivid, distinct, and inescapably relevant.

THAT UNHALLOWED EVE SWALLOWED *us in its awful jaws... She wouldn't even listen to me anymore. I felt a terrible pull in the wrong direction; my deific anatomy noted the presence of a countering force, and I lost my hold on it all.*

I was furious—but I couldn't help it. I laughed. Hysterically, in fact. I laughed and laughed and laughed—

Pulled through infinity...

And that was when I got a glimpse of their faces—like creatures out of nightmare; not just "demented"! Indefinable... And I knew what a joke was being played on me by Roland and Harvey Lamb and even the kids who had no *idea who they* really *were, or why they were reading* this book right now—

SIX OR SEVEN HOURS later, just after the sun had set, I was awoken by a distinctly felt and heard crash, as if a gigantic tree limb had fallen from a great height onto someone's car.

We had left all the lights on, as well as the television, which had been softly repeating discussions of the incredible land-mass shift interspersed with semi-random interviews of individuals and Sven's confounded "scientists." It was now merely a mass of white noise.

I got out of bed and switched it off, noticing simultaneously that Charles was nowhere in sight.

I glanced around frantically. *Wild Lies II* still sat on the nightstand by my bed. The other bed was ruffled but empty. The bathroom was dark.

I checked out the window. My car was still visible in the otherwise empty parking lot—so Charles had not absconded with it. But where had he gone? His backpack was no longer on the seat by the desk.

Somewhat anxious, but unwilling to allow much discouragement from the issue—I had, after all, never intended to carry on my quest with Charles Leland involved—I freshened up in the bathroom and collected my things, including the copy of *Wild Lies II*.

A second heavy, booming crash sounded from outside, shaking the walls of the motel room. I considered that my cue to leave, and headed first to the motel manager's office to see if he had noticed my companion heading off at any point.

Neither Sven nor anyone else was in the office, which glowed with a low fluorescent light.

I decided not to worry too much about the matter. If Charles had wanted to disappear without a trace, there was very little I could do about it.

Besides, I still had the copy of *Wild Lies II* with me. At worst, all I needed to do was re-type all of it and send it to one of my publishers—it would be the easiest job of my life.

I wandered around the premises for a bit, keeping an eye out for any sign of Charles. The motel parking lot was empty of cars. The motel itself seemed like it had been evacuated—a suspicion that made sense to me, except for my continued presence there. When nothing relevant to Charles's whereabouts—nor the whereabouts of anyone else, for that matter—made itself known, I got back into my car and thought briefly about my situation.

A huge "crack in the world" not twenty miles from where I sat...a copy of a book that I *will* write, in the future, if no one stops me...further progress to the Snake Den—the most likely candidate for migration from this world—blocked off from me for the foreseeable future...*and these godsforsaken, blasted, banging sounds...*

The reflection of a hideous creature in my rear-view mirror sent me into a panic. I had the car started and was halfway out of the parking lot before I realized that I had simply allowed anxiety to overwhelm me. I sat there at the edge of the parking lot, a choice of two possibilities before me: head back—back to Chicago, back home, and see how familiar sights and sounds were dealing with this weird, world-rending catastrophe...

...or return to the "scene of the crime." Go to the edge of the world. See what I could see. Doubtless there would be many others there, similarly investigating...perhaps one of them would have more information about what was happening?

Before I could make my inevitable decision—head back to the chasm and investigate further—the night sky unfolded and in a flash I remembered who I was.

THE CRASH OF REALITIES briefly intermingling, then silence.

Tom stood in the center of a room, a vast stone chamber with tapestried walls, fitfully lit by torches.

Laban's tomb.

The sarcophagus ahead of him glowed with the appropriate level of importance, given the presence of another person on its farther side.

"Who are you?" Addie Whitfield asked reasonably.

Tom took a step closer and blinked several times before answering. "Tom?"

"Hello, Tom," Addie said, feeling suddenly a bit cheered by the presence of another person. "Or should I say 'Tom'?" She made the question mark apparent. "My name's Addie. Don't tell me: you're here to wake up Laban Black and end the world—or whatever that will do."

Tom shook his head. "No, actually, I—wait. Who am *I*? Who are *you*?"

"I told you already," Addie responded. "I'm Addie Whitfield. I guess I'm supposed to help, since everything in Michael's book seemed hell-bent on getting exactly here and doing exactly this."

"I don't—Harvey didn't tell me someone else was coming," Tom said. "I'm sorry. I don't know your role in all this. You know Michael Flowers?"

Addie walked up to the edge of the sarcophagus and leaned over it. "That's deep," she said, gazing in and deliberately ignoring Tom's question. "Where is he?"

Tom felt a sudden pang of terrible fear. The girl seemed relaxed enough—maybe sixteen or seventeen years old; her outfit indicated a typical Honorius High kid. Hell, he'd probably sold her drugs. *Who was this person? A test? A distracting hallucination?* The gods knew he was in exactly the right state for it.

When in doubt, proceed as planned.

"Actually," he said, approaching the sarcophagus with diminished caution, "we're not waking him up. Haven't you noticed?"

"What?"

"*We have to put him back to sleep,*" Tom said urgently. "Before the last shreds of Golem Creek are consumed by the creatures from the Murk."

Addie gazed at him silently, the glow from Laban's grave causing a disorienting entheogenic effect to warp her features. *Well, if she's legitimate, then she'll be game. If not, then...* Tom unconsciously shifted his hand toward the ritual dagger in one of his trenchcoat's inside pockets, wondering somewhere in the back of his mind whether he would have the gall to actually use it if circumstances demanded. The little vial of Vinum Sabbati in the same pocket clinked against it as his hand brushed by.

The pyramid rattled with another raucous pounding from invisible fists on its walls. *What is inside is outside, what is outside is inside...*

Addie turned her gaze back to the depths of the open grave, then stuck her hands into it and pulled out a glowing ball of mauve mist. "I can formulate the Cloud," she said simply. "What are you waiting for?"

WHEN IT CAME TO such stuff as dreams are made on, and the way that same stuff overlapped and interacted, generating world after world, fractally and apparently without end, Tom Fallow couldn't be bothered with details like why and how intention could go out and grab what you needed, could deliver it to your doorstep at just the right time.

But he certainly appreciated such gestures. Especially now.

The room was a haze of mauve mist. Tom sat, weaving in and out of conscious awareness, trying to straddle realms the way Laban's etheric shell did.

Addie was truly out of this world, in several senses. With astonishing accuracy—Tom guessed there were magical prodigies just like there were every other kind, a world he'd always felt rather miffed about not being included in—she gathered *cittam*, top to bottom, side to side, her eyes moving rhythmically, hypnotically, as the obscuring Cloud inspissated.

Tom's part required rather less skill and more sheer endurance. He wondered briefly if that was the sole reason he'd been "chosen" by Harvey Lamb in the first place—that and his general anonymity, which made the drug-dealing aspect of things manageable.

He also wondered—entirely against Harvey Lamb's advice—if this was going to work at all. The Ritual of Unhingement had gotten *him* here; Addie had nonchalantly mentioned arriving by way of Laban's magical chamber, with no explicit preparation whatsoever. It had kind of pissed Tom off, but he was far too out of his head to dwell on the fact for long.

Besides, he was pretty sure that it was *his* work on the Brake Street house portal that had pulled it off.

So there.

The Cloud began to whirl magnificently between them, hovering over the opening to Laban's otherworldly encampment.

Tom held his mind in the center and breathed, gathering more etheric force from deep within his abdomen—where Taoists locate the "lower dan tian"—and issued it into the gap between the worlds. He could never have done this without someone like Addie Whitfield. Nothing in the scrolls that Harvey had supplied, nor the sessions of instruction at Three Coils Annex with "Bram," nor any of his deductions led to the obvious conclusion: to balance the Whirling Force at this particular Source was going to require heavy-duty wizardry. The masculine, ascending gyre *required and evoked* the feminine, descending gyre... It was clearly a set-up from the beginning—lead poor little Tom into thinking he was going to save the day, only to have the glory of the show stolen from him at the last minute by—

He stopped himself again. *No wondering. No thinking. No complaining. Just gather the material and converge. Stay centered.*

It was all happening so quickly, he hardly noticed when the dark shape in the middle of Addie's Cloud appeared, first merely the pupil of an eye, then an obsidian marble, then a large, black egg-shape, the ballooning sides of which seemed to be angering its inhabitant.

Is that—is this supposed to be happening?

Shut up and concentrate.

The second silent voice was not his—it was Addie's. Yet another unexpected tear in the tantra...

He twisted the cap off the vial of Witches' Wine. *Something* was coming through. Harvey had been very explicit on this point: *once the Cone is formulated, Things will be attracted to it—they will come from many angles, and they are usually the hungriest who come through first...*

But what the *hell* was this?

There was a distinct sound, as of a cork popping off a champagne bottle, or the sane lid off a reliable old pot of crazy.

And then *he* was there.

Do it!

Tom could practically feel the "tele" become -kinetic rather than -pathic as the ropes of Addie's silent voice pulled his hands toward the rapidly forming Cone in the midst of the Cloud.

Do it now!

A beaming smile from the dark face in the Cloud almost disarmed him.

"Fancy this," the face said in a pleasant yet sinister voice. "Molly's had a plan *all along*—"

Tom thrust the vial in its entirety at the Cloud. Simultaneously, he saw Addie fling an item of her own into the swirling vortex—a *book*...

A blinding light enveloped the room. A hefty burst of

wind concussed the novice wizards.

TOM AWOKE FIRST TO a calm and silent room. Addie lay slumped over on the other side of the sarcophagus.

The granite bulk of Laban's grave no longer glowed.

"Did we do it?" Addie's voice sounded hoarse and exhausted.

Tom stood and tapped on the solid block of flat rock that now sealed the sarcophagus shut. He ran his hand over the hieroglyphics embedded upon it, the very central image of which was a pitch-black Khephra-beetle in bas-relief, dark as a stain.

"Yeah," Tom said. "But what exactly does that mean?"

A heavy rumbling answered his question.

"That doesn't sound good," Addie said.

Tom shook his head, steadying himself against the sarcophagus. "No it doesn't."

The room shook harder.

Addie crawled over to the other side of the granite slab and slowly pulled herself to a standing position against it.

"Where do we *go*?" she yelled over the threatening roar.

Tom shook his head again. "I don't *know*! There's nowhere *to* go!"

There was a sudden thunderous crack as one wall of the inner chamber split, revealing a grey whirlpool beyond, a vortex of clouds flashing darkly. A sucking wind pulled at both Tom and Addie.

The opening widened, along with Tom's eyes as he watched Addie lose hold of the slab and disappear through the crack.

Shit! I should've known! The goddamned traitorous BASTARDS—

Tom shouted inanely—last act of the lost—as he lifted into the whirling air and followed Addie, wherever it was she'd gone.

THREE THINGS HAPPENED IN rapid succession: Julie made her wish for Molly's safety, Molly lucked everyone else out of harm's way, and something tasted like bad champagne.

Molly realized quickly that it *was*, in fact, bad champagne.

The confluence of wishes and faery magic had done their best, it seemed. Molly gazed out from her palanquin over the campus of Golem Creek University during the Midsummer Festival before closing her eyes in exhaustion and nearly crushing Farmer McNabb.

"Pardon, Your Majesty," his small voice said as she leaned back against him. "I have, of course, obstructed your free movement! Forgive me!"

Molly sat up straight again and shook her head. "Not this again," she said. "Please not this again."

Farmer McNabb removed his miniature tricorn cap, bowed, and swept the cap before him. He stayed bent over.

Well, it was to be expected, after all. *This* was the most likely place—right under the enemy's nose. And there was no better location to ensure that a final blow would do its worst.

She just had to assume that every other piece was in place; that the Monolith, especially, was ready to claim their prize in the way that she was ready to deliver it. Given their new-found wariness of this, Yassiz's little "off the books" skimming of their magical energy redirection system, she felt confident they'd catch it.

And she wanted to see that fucking contract torn to shreds—provided, of course, she survived...which she fully intended to do.

"I'm going to need something," Molly said. "I need a knife. A dagger. A pin. Something sharp."

Farmer McNabb immediately lifted himself and unlatched a nearly hidden recess to one side of her seat. Seconds later he was bowing again, holding a small but wicked-looking jewel-encrusted dagger on both hands before him.

Molly grabbed the knife and banged a fist against the roof of her litter. "Stop at *once*!" she shouted. "Let me off!"

Her bewildered staff of Olympians shuffled to a halt and carefully lowered the palanquin to the ground.

Molly leapt out. A moderate percentage of her wide, flowing gown caught on some obstruction or other hanging from the litter; she grabbed the train of her gown and tore it cleanly off.

"Your Majesty—"

"Not now," she said to Farmer McNabb. "I have something I must do. *Alone.* Cover for me."

Farmer McNabb swept himself low once again as Molly trudged off, between cavorting, carousing college students of all shapes and sizes, toward a familiar-looking banquet hall at the other end of campus.

She was, officially, completely sick of this game. The Monolith—the Laughing God...she was done with it.

What was it about that damned capitalistic mindset infecting witchcraft and wizardry? Even *she* had fallen for it, long, long ago. And Stek, despite all of his failings, could at least be counted on to take the brunt of royal responsibility in all but this case...that is, if he remembered who the hell he was in the first place. But that wasn't entirely *her* fault. Yassiz had just as much to do with it.

There was something here—she *knew* it; she could *feel* it—that could end this absurdity once and for all. She was going to out-Congreve all other "women scorned" if it was the *last goddamned thing she did*—

That the bastard would think he could get away with it forever! Molly's thoughts burned within her skull. *Steal her essence... forever?!?* A literal fire began hovering about her person as she stomped over beer cans and writhing bodies to the brick building that seemed to *heave* with Presence.

PARTY'S THE OTHER DIRECTION, LOVE!

A voice like thunder rang out in her mind. A voice with laughter about its edges. *His* voice.

"Can it, you bastard!" Molly shouted.

There it was. The door in the brick building—the one bearing the Sign.

TRAP.

Molly waved a hand angrily before her. The door shattered into bits, leaving a smoking gap.

WHY DON'T WE TAKE A MOMENT TO THINK ABOUT THIS CALMLY—

Molly entered the building and the Voice—His voice, Yassiz's voice—went silent. She could clearly sense the Presence at the end of the hall.

The lights to either side of her blazed brighter as she passed, then dimly or not at all. In moments, she stood before the plaque from which Charles had taken the Silver Key.

GC YMU AM TFGS G WGJJ SFDTTBQ TFB TGKBJGLBS G WGJJ BQDSB TFB

RMLTBLTS MC KMQNFBUS ULOMULA DS G BQDSB TFBGQ KBKMQGBS

YMUQ SDVGMQS WGJJ CMQEBT WFM TFBY DQB TFBY WGJJ JGVB GL

D WMQJA GL WFGRF TFBY DQB QBDABQS MC TFGS OMMI G RUQSB

TFBK TM CMQEBT CMQBVBQB OY TFB SNBJJGLES GL TFGS OMMI G WGJJ

QBTUQL TM RQDRI MNBL TFB EDTBS G WGJJ DWDIBL TFB AQBDKBQ

MC TFGS AQBDK DLA YMU SFDJJ OB LM KMQB...

GLMW RDKR HKJEKL QRANDALQ KLH RDA IKSCDELC CMH KPA MLA

EL KVTII!

Letting out a frustrated shout, she banged her fist against it and sent the remnants of the cipher message flying.

A lidless wooden box, intricately carved, sat empty and innocent on a small shelf behind it.

Molly grimaced and slit the palm of her left hand with the jewel-encrusted dagger. She lifted it over the box.

"Goodbye, Yassiz, you conniving sonofabitch," she said as her blood leaked copiously into the box's velvet-lined interior.

"Monolith! Are you paying attention now? *Take the bastard!*"

Her mind reeled as a vortex of mauve light began spinning out of the box. The walls of the building she was in were the first to disintegrate back into the raw, magical energy out of which they were created, and wrapped into the brilliant architecture of the spinning Cone...*Oberon stepped through a door at the end of the hall...*

...and the mold of a New Key, silvery with faery blood, took shape as he spoke Her True Name...

NO SENSE OF HUMOR *in the lot, that was for sure...*

...nor in these *meddling bastards...*

Somewhere near/far, Tom Fallow and Addie Whitfield feel the pull of Yassiz on their minds as he is sucked into the vortex they've generated in Laban's tomb.

"There's almost always a time limit on the effects of genius," the Laughing God says, chuckling. "I'd like to thank Port Mantle for supplying the raw materials! I'd like to thank Laban Black for figuring out how to divert the energy sources—and even more so for having the sheer nerve to DO IT! How about a hand for Henrik Shaxplay and that ingenious combination of magic and machines and, well, ME to make it all a thing worth fighting for? Ha! Don't worry, kids! I'll be back! I always end up coming back....!"

Yassiz gave it the old college try, which meant that he exerted as much effort as would have been required to lift a single can of beer to his lips and pour. When that didn't work—because if it *had* worked, well, then where he was going wasn't worth going to—he gave up entirely and relaxed into the flesh-rending tidal forces making up the Arc of Oblivion over the Tower of Koth...

He felt himself pulled, pushed, stuffed, and generally smacked around before a brief wink in the eye of existence functioned to thread him into a wormhole the size of an unpenned period on an invisible page.

And then...

CHARLES FELT AND HEARD the dice clatter away some-where near/far as he landed in the clearing of the Enchanted Wood.

But...but...how many times *are occurring simultaneously? All of them? I cast the dice...I found Calder Caine at the McDonald's in South Bend...I fell asleep at the motel...*

A breeze picked up, spinning leaves lazily around the clearing.

"I did *not* expect that!" Steve said from his position in front of the vending machine. He squinted at the offerings within. "Fifty cents? For a *Snickers* bar?"

"Charley? What the hell did you roll?" Julie asked, glancing nervously up at the twirling tree branches and gathering clouds. She headed off to the edge of the clearing, batting away handfuls of maple leaves. "Jesus. What is *with* this wind?" She stepped out of the clearing proper and leaned up against a tree trunk, where the wind was miraculously nonexistent. "That's better," she said.

"I know this place," Charles said. "Shit. I know where we are."

He stood in front of the glass gun case beside the vending machine.

For a Good Time—Break Glass.

This was it, then. All the players had made their moves...

But where was the Laughing God?

Charles reached into his pocket and withdrew the card he had drawn from Harvey's Deck of Tricks.

This card entitles the bearer to ONE CLEAN SHOT! (And make it a head shot so that it counts.)

He shoved the card back in his pocket.

"I think Jules has the right idea, Chuck," Steve said, jogging around the vending machine. He dodged a tree branch that nearly whipped him in the face. "Woah! Rudeness! Watch it!"

"Charley! What the hell are you doing? Let's go!" Julie yelled over the rising wind.

"No shit, dude!" Steve yelled. "I'm all for the second amendment, but come *on*! Remember the *last* time shit started swirling in a small, enclosed area? I don't think we get two lucky strikes in a row—"

Charles grabbed the gun case tightly as an averse tornado of electromagical energy burst into being directly above him. Steve and Julie anchored themselves against the thick trunk of an oak at the edge of the clearing, clinging to each other unwittingly.

Thunderous laughter echoed from the vortex, striking Charles to his core. He lifted his eyes to the swirling clouds—and saw *it*. Like the pupil of an eye...an obsidian marble...a distended black egg... The Creature from Honorius; the one astonished by its own reflection in a mirror—no longer "Weston Gray" as chaos took hold at the Monster Ball. The one who was—

"Yassiz," Charles said.

The Laughing God chuckled, descending from the center of the cone, holding a comically large purple umbrella over himself like an infernal Mary Poppins. He landed lightly beside the vending machine, a mere two strides away from Charles and—though unruffled by the winds—the torn, scuffed fabric of his tuxedo, the handfuls of scrapes, scratches, and burn marks, the general air that he was, amazingly, *disturbed* by something came across in force.

"My apologies aforehand, Charles, but the villain is obligated to say it," Yassiz announced immediately. "So we meet again!" Unnervingly, the burst of laughter that followed did nothing to diminish the look of reptile hunger in his eyes.

Yassiz let go of his umbrella, which rose into the air and vanished into the cyclone. He lightly brushed his fingernails on his tuxedo's lapel.

Charles made an obvious show of taking in the Laughing God's inelegant condition.

"I see and respect your natural concern for my well being," Yassiz said, his grin widening. "But think nothing of it! Your high-placed friends thought they'd make a show of getting me here. Tell me, Charles, have you ever heard of the Unseelie Court? No? Well, let me tell you: they can be a tough crowd. Not a shred of humor in the lot! Shall I compare it to a cold day in hell? Though less lovely and intemperate!" He burst again into laughter, hammering a fist into the lid of the vending machine.

"*Chuck*!" Steve shouted from the treeline. "Are you insane? Get the hell over here! *That's him*!"

Yassiz's eyebrows lifted dramatically. "Lo! And behold! I have admirers lurking about the story's edge!"

Julie grabbed Steve by the shoulders and shook him. "We have to *do* something!"

Steve nodded. "*Remember me*!" he shouted, and lunged for the Laughing God.

The swirling winds stopped at the same time Steve did—in mid-air. Julie stood equally frozen behind him, paused in mid-shout.

A blanket of silence descended over the clearing. Charles noticed a maple leaf, one of many, still and unmoving, stuck in a single snapshot of time.

"I've still got some tricks up my sleeve," Yassiz said. Again he laughed aloud, his eyes squinting but not shifting their shark-like gaze from Charles.

Charles sensed that Yassiz's overbearing manner hid something he didn't want him to know.

"I know what you're thinking," Yassiz immediately said. Charles inadvertently flinched at the confrontational telepathy. "And you're right! You're right. But what the *world* needs *now*—is the understanding of sympathetic minds! Think of it, Mr. Leland! What hath the gods wrought? In your case, especially—guilty of...what? A bit of a crush? Handcuffed to that fool Flowers and his 'Fear Club'?" Yassiz shook his head, lifting a lit cigar to his lips and puffing on it dramatically. "Ah! Forgive me. Would you like one?"

He pointed at Charles's right hand, where an identical lit cigar was suddenly held between Charles's fingers.

Charles tossed the cigar to the ground beside the gun case. *For a Good Time—Break Glass.*

"A-*ha*! I see now. They've practically ruined you. How about a different sort of trade then? And let's not beat around the bush any longer!" Yassiz continued. The cigar evaporated in a puff of smoke resembling a horned smiley face. "I will let your friends live if you use that gun on yourself."

Charles, bewildered, looked from Yassiz to the Samsaric Revolver and back. "What the *hell* kind of deal is that?"

Yassiz burst into laughter. "Just kidding! Just kidding, of course. We all know that Steve and Julie don't make it out of here *alive*! And I mean, seriously, you *could* use that on yourself, but then what are the *actual* odds of waking up, safe and sound, in a new Golem Creek, happy as could be, a Golem Creek that never even *heard* of Steve Chernowski and Julie Evergreen? Last time we did this—"

"*Last* time?" Charles was incredulous.

"Oh, dear," Yassiz said. He patted his pockets. "Oh, dear, dear. You've forgotten already, have you? I was worried about this..." He reached into an inner pocket of his jacket and pulled out a photograph. "Aha! Excellent. Here it is! Proof."

Yassiz handed the Polaroid photograph over to Charles, who took it from him cautiously. It was, clearly, an image of Charles with his arm around Yassiz. Both of them had gigantic Cuban cigars in their mouths, and both held up glasses half-full of what was probably expensive scotch. A handful of random patrons at whatever bar this was stood frozen in poses of general levity behind and around them.

Someone had scrawled in marker at the base of the image: *Jah-Lee-Zzz & Yassiz, The Flying Monkey, "By gods and men rejected, but friends forever!"*

Charles looked back at Yassiz. "Who the hell do you think I am?"

Yassiz's laughter rang out, clanging like pots and pans in Charles's head.

"Clearly *not* who *you* think you are!" the Laughing God said. "Does that old photo, maybe, jog a memory for you? Tell me, Charles, why Michael Flowers took an interest in you? *You*! Of all people in Golem Creek, he chose *you* and your two hangers-on there"—he waved one demon-black hand over at Steve, still frozen in mid-flight, and Julie, her mouth wide open in a silent shout—"to become his specially chosen disciples? To learn the most eldritch of magical secrets? *Really*?" Yassiz shook his head in awe. "It truly is astonishing what people can convince themselves of, isn't it? Let's forget about this nonsense already and get out of here! Before they catch the *both* of us again—trust me, having just come from yet another reunion with Queen Furnival's 'demented pixies,' I'd like to save us *both* the trouble—"

Charles smashed the glass of the gun case. "You're *lying*! You're a *liar*! This? This *obvious fake*"—Charles threw the Polaroid to the ground and stamped on it—"is supposed to *convince* me that we've been 'best buds' all along? Are you *serious*?" He grabbed the gun and pointed it at the Laughing God.

Yassiz, though his grin had not faltered, stood uncharacteristically humbled before Charles. "Very well. Do it. You've clearly got everything figured out." He sighed dramatically. "Let's get it over with. It's not like we won't meet again. I *told* you—I'm *obligated* to say that. So!" Yassiz dusted off his hands and spread them wide, mimicking a crucified god. "Maybe next time, then?"

What was he supposed to do? Did he shoot Yassiz? Did he shoot himself? Was there something else he was supposed to shoot at?

Charles glanced around frantically. The cyclone above still whirred. He thought he could see vicious-looking, taloned hands and narrow, demonic eyes rising and falling within it...*the 'demented pixies'? Unwilling to let go of their prey...* Steve, in mid-air; Julie, in mid-scream... *What was he supposed to do?* The vending machine, maybe? *Was he supposed to shoot the goddamned vending machine?*

Yassiz cleared his throat. "*Ahem*! Charles, if you're *quite* ready? I'd like to get back to the beginning."

A sudden thought struck Charles. *What did he have to lose?*

He looked from Yassiz to the Samsaric Revolver.

He pulled the barrel away from the Laughing God and pointed it at his own head.

...This card entitles the bearer to ONE CLEAN SHOT. (And make it a head shot so that it counts.)...

Yassiz did the demonic equivalent of a double-take. "Ha! Charles! *My friend*! You've awoken! At last! At last!" He clapped ecstatically. "Bravo, old friend! First round's on me! Carry on!"

What did he have to lose?

Charles cocked the hammer and began the tortoise-and-hare process of pulling the trigger.

What did he have to lose? Really—what did he have to—

"*What the hell is THAT?*" Charles shouted, pointing behind Yassiz.

The Laughing God's grin broke at last as he spun to look—

The gunblast took him by surprise.

Yassiz stood, facing Charles once again.

"Well played," he said, his grin returned in full force. He patted the spot on his brow where the bullet had struck and chuckled. "Nicely done! Who'd've thought you had it in you? But like I said—*I've still got tricks up my sleeve*—"

A blast of violet light engulfed the clearing. The myriad hands of the Demented Pixies shot out in all directions. Charles briefly felt *something* grab hold of him—and terror struck, nightmares upon unending nightmares—before it released him, desperate for its intended quarry.

An instant later—a Planck length of time, really—Yassiz was gone.

...AND REMEMBERING...REMEMBERING...

The leg on this chair.

He laughed when I sat down and almost tipped over.

The damned leg on this chair! Might as well throw it in the fire...

IU.

TACERE

Baron W—:

We removed these papers as of particular interest subsequent to the Creature's most recent theoleucotomy & attempted escape (*vide infra*). Whether the entity secreted the renewed Key in some copy of *Morpheus Unbound* (perhaps in Rookville Mall) remains to be determined. We suggest the implantation of a tracking device, followed by release and recapture.

Pending your approval.

T HERE WAS A TOWN there, once," the old man said before I had even gotten situated.

I finally got the crippled leg of my chair to behave. The old man had just poured two whiskies into two different-sized glasses.

"Out in the woods?" I asked, and took a drink. The whisky was like a dark blaze in my throat.

The old man nodded. "Out in the woods," he repeated, waving his hand around lazily. "It got swallowed up."

"How did you first hear about it?" I asked.

He grinned. The little fire we'd built cast weird shadows against the trees and nameless heaps of junk lining the edge of the clearing. "I lived there," he said simply, and inexplicably pointed to a half-crushed boardgame box awash in shadows at the edge of camp.

"Lived there?" I said, somewhat incredulous. "But if the town got swallowed up—"

"Careful what you wish for," he said, and lifted his glass to me before gulping down its contents.

"I don't know what that means," I responded.

The old man was silent, pensive. It looked like he was trying to remember something.

I faked another sip of the whisky. I was feeling pretty woozy from that first glass.

"Some kids...they're not really built for this world," he said inexplicably. "You know? And they get lucky. Instead of falling for it, for the illusion of this world, eating the fairy

208

food, they wish for a door. A gate. A way out—a means of escape."

I became aware of the crackling of the fire behind the sussuration of night creatures in the surrounding forest. I took another drink. Dangerous—it didn't burn quite as much this time.

"And do they get it?" I asked. "What's the means of escape?"

"The end of the story," he answered simply. "Cheers." He tipped his glass and finished it.

HE TOLD ME WHERE to find the place, or the absence of the place. I followed his simple, clinical directions into the complicated, organic mess of the forest.

I was lost in no time.

But I could see it, I think: the crumbling edge of an asphalt roadway here...the chipped plastic of a grocery store sign there... The remnants of a city.

The pieces of the puzzle began to come together quite rapidly. I followed the fine tracery of the city's outline until, at last, I began to notice my own fatigue couple with the day's fading light.

In the midst of the dark wood, I came upon a Road.

Now, the strange thing about this Road was its basic dysfunctionality. A Road must needs lead those who traverse it from one actual place to another—can we really call something a Road when it simply appears, looking much like a Road, black asphalt embellished with the yellowish stripes of its old rules, and yet seems to lead from Nowhere to Nowhere?

This is what I found. For a thick clump of ancient trees to my left erupted suddenly with modern, well-maintained street. This latter extended perhaps fifty feet before running directly into a wall of rock off to my right.

I stood just beside the Road, mystified by its presence. Perhaps I had fallen asleep?

Too easy. I considered it, this Road, and what the old man had told me about the City that had once been here, where this forest now stood. I sat at the edge of the Road, and pondered.

What had he told me? Memory mixed with drink unprofitably. Something about...*a city...a book...I got out while I still had the chance...*

The sun had nearly set. I had no clear idea of where I was, but I would have to set up camp for the night.

I grabbed my pack. Perhaps at that edge of the Road, off to my right? A lean-to against that smooth rock over there.

It would have to work. Light was in short supply. I would need to build a fire soon.

I stepped onto the Road.

IT WASN'T QUITE A near-death experience, but it did nearly give me a heart attack.

Bad timing, I suppose. The car came out of nowhere, blaring its horn and barreling down upon me at the same time lightning flashed and thunder clapped above. I leapt for the other side of the road; a rush of wind against me whispered of a near-miss.

It was impossible for me to feel it: I had not in any way avoided death. Perhaps my physical form, destined to perish, had brushed against the ultimate companion, but at the moment I sat up on the other side of the road—gasping for breath, a mixture of exhaust smoke from the car whose taillights rapidly diminished in the distant intangibility of this new night, coupled with imminent rain from innocuous skies I'd never seen—I died to impossibilities forever.

It was the beginning of the World.

I patted myself, a quick check for injuries, of which I found none. I stood up and attempted to calm down.

Moments ago, I had stood in the dying light of a forest, investigating the claims of an old drunk. Now, I stood in the living, unfolded night of a new world, unwittingly a part of the old drunk's story.

I was, to say the least, perplexed.

The road stretched out to either side of me into the night. I stood on the shoulder of it, beside a few feet of grass and a wire fence. Beyond the fence stretched a sea of tall grass, and beyond that, more darkness.

The other side of the road, the one I had leapt from, did indeed consist of a thick wall of trees stretching out to either side in the distance.

Another flash of lightning followed by thunder had me grab my pack and choose quickly. I would need shelter before long. As I found myself facing a direction already, I simply began to walk, pacing myself, trying to slow my heart rate, to quell the anxiety that threatened to engulf me between each firm step on solid ground.

RAIN HAD BEGUN TO patter against me perhaps ten minutes later when, at last, I came upon the cracked, weed-strewn parking lot of an old, sprawling set of buildings. Quickly, I sprinted across the clearing, avoiding potholes and the shattered remains of curbs, to a sloping gradient that led down, thankfully, to a trash-strewn clearing beneath an aluminum awning.

The rain began to fall with a vengeance, as it often does once you've "made it," being a mostly considerate kind of weather. By way of the dim light, I took in my surroundings as best I could.

It looked like the loading dock for a large store. A thin sheet of water had begun flowing down the steep gradient of the dock. I discovered a door set into one wall beyond a set of concrete stairs to my right, and tried the knob.

After a bit of shaking and cursing, my luck held. It creaked open; I was able to yank it open far enough to admit myself.

Into blackness.

I paused, mostly for fear of damaging myself in the newfound darkness. The rain continued to hammer furiously against the roof of the building. I rummaged through my backpack and retrieved a flashlight.

I was, indeed, in some sort of abandoned warehouse or loading area. I pulled the door shut behind me, for fear of being seen by a security guard, should one still occasionally roam this presumably forgotten area. Worse to be caught by a policeman than threatened by another bum, most likely. At least another bum wasn't motivated by any sort of self-righteous creeds of convention.

I proceeded into the room.

How long ago had this place been left to rot? There didn't appear to be anything of real value, at least in this room. But the set of buildings I'd seen from the outside were quite extensive; this was hardly any part of them.

That could be good or bad.

I tried to make decent time, occupying my thoughts with finding a hidden corner somewhere of relative safety, rather than allowing myself to be concerned with how or why a Magical Road had transported me to this...City in the midst of a Forest? The first, and perhaps most important, thing I noticed as I made my way across the large, empty storage area to a set of doors in its far end was the fact that the dust and cobwebs thereabouts showed no signs whatsoever of disturbance.

Again, this was something that could be very good or very bad.

Slowly, painstakingly, I gripped one of the knobs on the double doors leading more deeply into the building proper. The rain still hammered wildly against the roof, beset with occasional claps of thunder.

The door opened with a painful screech. And I found myself in a vast, halled chamber, the remains of numerous, empty rooms stretching out to either side.

This place was a memory, or a place of memories.

I proceeded more deeply within. Above, a vast series of glass ceiling panels let in occasional flashes of lightning. The drumming of rain had become a comforting constant, nestling me into this uncompanioned place.

I followed the marble hallway forward, marveling at the peculiar emptiness around me. Occasional sets of silent escalators led up to a second floor, ringed about with glass railing. Of one thing I felt perfectly certain at the moment: judging by the level of disregard, I would be safe here, wherever "here" in fact was—at least for a little while.

I DECIDED TO MAKE "camp," if you will, on the second floor, judging that to be a less likely place of ingress by anyone who might disturb my slumber. My joy at finding the place at all was exquisite; after setting up some temporary lodging behind empty wooden racks in a store with a functional cage-door at its front—I assumed that the rattling of this would awaken me should my position prove compromised—I found myself so energized that I decided to trust my luck and search for the possibility of food.

And I didn't have very far to go. A "food court" presented itself in short order; at the back of some nameless fast-food restaurant I discovered a number of cans and packages still lodged in a vending machine. I was forced to shatter the machine's glass covering—a moment I did not envy, and one I attempted to time with a clap of thunder, though it no less left me shaking with fear of discovery. I filled several paper bags that lay in a cabinet nearby with the entirety of the vending machine's offerings.

In said cabinet, I also discovered further blessings: a large case of bottled water, rolls of paper towels and packages of moist towelettes, and—treasure among treasures in this strange place!—several functional electric lanterns that cast a substantial glow about them (presumably for blackout situations). There was also a thin book of pages stapled together. This latter turned out to be a directory of names and numbers emblazoned at its head with the following bit of priceless data:

ROOKVILLE MALL
CHICKEN SHACK
EMERGENCY CONTACTS

I rushed out of that place, noting the presence of a hallway off to my right bearing the universal symbols of the presence of toilets—perhaps this place still had running water? It had been nearly a month since I'd had a decent wash—and headed back to my camp.

The revelation of this place's name—Rookville Mall—had me racking my brains for references. Rookville... Had I ever heard of such a place?

I had decked out my little camp into something greater: a room that glowed with warm yellow light. I arranged a display table and a chair to provide myself with something akin to a dining area; an old couch in one corner proved clean and free of vermin—I set up my sleeping quarters accordingly. Coupled with the restrooms only ten yards away—which, alas, were not equipped with running water, but at least seemed mostly clean and otherwise acceptable—I had, I felt, for the first time in months, a home of sorts.

I tried not to concern myself with how long it would last. My time thus far on the road had left me—

The thought brought back the strange "reality" of my circumstances. *That Road I took to this place...*

Perhaps the old man had put something in my drink? I didn't know of any hallucinogen that could maintain such a degree of potency after some twelve or more hours in one's system. Perhaps it was something else? My mind finally starting to crumble with the weight of all those years ahead of me, the burden of them at last becoming apparent...?

I shook my head.

I knew exactly what had happened, and wasn't about to fall for any nonsense.

I had traversed a Magical Portal to Another World. The old man had told the truth, and through the haze of our drunken conversation I recalled at least one phrase he'd repeated several times: "That City, that place, is here still, if you know how to find it..."

The most wonderful realization in all the world flooded back into me, a feeling I thought long annihilated by the vicissitudes of growing up: *magic is real...*

First course: Doritos. I ate three small bags of them, and nearly wept. A room-temperature Mountain Dew tasted for all the world like the finest Bordeaux; a package of chocolate mini-donuts was the crème broûlée I'd left unfinished fifteen years ago, at the Château St.-Yves d'Alveydre.

I remembered the meal; I remembered feeling "full." That was why I hadn't finished it. The conversation that night had been the same dull talk of intellectuals I'd grown so used to in my happenstantial career. The publisher had sent me along because I'd written a few books on weird and wonderful things. They felt that they could trust me to impress their latest find: a young prodigy whose latest manuscript had suitably impressed more than a few minds.

That had been the first major mistake I'd made. Presuming that jumping on the bandwagon would further my career, perhaps earn me a greater advance, I ended up bolstering the youth's confidence. The company forgot about me. In a year, I was gently assumed to be no more; after two years, it was as if I had never been.

It took me a further two years to use up the little bit of money I'd saved after my investments tanked. My pride—and what I must now admit was an ignorant and foolish hope!—had kept me from getting another job. I kept writing. Day after day, week after week. Money dwindled; paper and pens suddenly became something I had to "budget for."

Everything went. And here, by the light of these stolen lamps, with the ink of these borrowed pens, I wrote it all down, trying to make a record of what I knew.

Because I had suddenly realized that I *did* recall the name of this place: Rookville. It was a bit of legendry, after all. It was the last case I had been working on before signing off on life and hitting the road. It was a last-ditch effort to resurrect my life, to bring myself back from the grave, if you will.

It was the story of Damian Stephens, which I had, quite suddenly (to my just-now-awakening mind), become a part of.

WEEKS PASSED.

Not a single entity disturbed my new home, though several times I did hear the rumbling of a truck close by, and the passing of a train in the distance. I attempted during this period of tranquillity to mentally reconstruct my research as I scoured the remainder of the old shopping mall for hidden treasure.

It was incredible to me how many useful materials and supplies had been simply abandoned along with the use of this place. Batteries, flashlights, cleaning supplies—including hand and liquid soaps; a large cache of bottled water sat innocently in the back of one shop, and several vending machines supplied me with weeks' worth of food—admittedly, much of it was expired, but of such initially poor quality I felt confident it could be safely consumed, if ideal nutrition remained a low priority.

Imagine my joy when I discovered clean clothes in the form of janitor's coveralls and a reasonably new pair of boots that fit almost perfectly well (with the addition of an extra pair of socks)!

I located a valve in one musty room which functioned to return running water to one of the restroom areas. The ecstasy I felt in finally being able to bathe—using hot water, no less!—was in no way diminished by the fact that I was forced to do so by way of sinks. I was careful to shut off the supply of water as soon as I had finished with it, for fear of alerting some authority to my circumstances.

I made a careful round of the entire place and secured every discernible mode of entry as best I could, using lengths of wire and planks and other objects. I decided this precaution would serve me well, and at least afford me sufficient time to gather a few things before I would be forced to depart.

Many of the shops had doors serving as back exits, but these seemed particularly safe, as they were traversible in only one direction, from the inside, out; these doors, on the exterior side, were a flat surface with no knob or keyhole, even. It seemed an unlikely point of entry for any party.

Glimpsing the world behind these doors was a delicious treat I allowed myself only at night, and only after waiting several moments to ensure that no sound could be heard on the other side. I saw little save for darkened parking lots on one side of the building and, beyond further parking lots on the other side of the building, a dark road: the one I had gained access to the place from.

Glass entryways that had at one time served as main

entrances to the building had long ago been boarded up, and seemed to need no additional reinforcement.

During this time, I began to wonder at the place's decay, and especially at its nearly complete lack of residency. Hardly a stray spider did I discover, and never any vermin larger than that. I did for a few moments begin to fear: had this place suffered from some poisonous radiation, which kept all wise creatures from inhabiting it?

For I couldn't be the only transient seeking shelter here, in Rookville.

I made only a few exceedingly cautious investigations of the exterior of the place beyond my quick, furtive glances out the shop doors. The first occurred one week after I had arrived, in the dead of night. It was cool outside; a soft, fresh breeze felt welcome. I could, unfortunately, discern very little of my surroundings save for what appeared to be the previously identified wealth of forest bordering the parking lot some hundred yards distant.

The second time, a week after that, I decided I would at least peek out during the day. By the light of day, I could easily tell that this place was only part of a group of ramshackle dwellings, all of which appeared to have been abandoned. I did glimpse precisely two vehicles drive quickly by on the road—one appeared to be a garbage truck.

By the time I made my third excursion, also during the day, I felt rather sure of this place's sincere abandonment. My considered opinion was that this area had at one time been a place of reasonable activity, that several of the establishments nearby were almost certainly old restaurants.

But that time was over. Now, it was the outskirts of a town that had been all but forgotten.

NEARLY A MONTH AFTER arriving, I awoke one night from dreams of deep blackness.

It was raining again. Though I felt certain I had slept for something akin to eight or more hours, I could discern no objective indication that it had been much more than a few minutes. Perhaps it was the newly found comfort of my surroundings, their relative safety and security, despite the still-misunderstood means of how I had come to be here.

I sat up on the couch and turned on one of the electric lanterns.

I had Heard Something.

The sound was of something deep within the recesses of the mall, a sound of—crickets chirping?

The sound was notable for its express *absence* from this place during the previous weeks.

I was dressed and ready to investigate in under a minute, a makeshift weapon clutched in my hands.

Silently, I made my way to a vantage point whereby to assess the situation.

I crept up to the edge of the railing on the second story, where I had established my base of operations, and peeked over.

A strange, pink-hued glow emanated from one of the shops.

I watched the area closely, awe and fear combining to generate a sort of magnificent anxiety. I had known my time here was temporary—something about confronting a change in circumstances, at last, seemed to satisfy me while shutting the door on the lovely time I had spent here, safe and untrammeled by the world.

But nothing further seemed to be happening.

I returned to my quarters, sat down, and thought.

If the alteration was due to another vagrant, we would eventually run into each other. What were the rules of transient etiquette in *these* circumstances? I had dealt with a handful of other homeless people, not the least of which was the old man whose Tale of the City in the Forest had ultimately led me here.

Perhaps it was the old man, himself?

I decided, ultimately, that I would at minimum stake out the events occurring down below.

I barely had time to get a quick glimpse of the storefront before your hands were upon me and I remembered... Monolith! I will have the means of escape...!

WHEN THE WIND STARTED up again, briefly, before petering out along with the cyclone and the presence of the Faery Hell's agents, Steve thudded to the ground a meter from Charles. Julie made a brief shout that sounded too loud in the sudden quiet.

"Ouch," Steve said. He gazed up at Charles. "Where is he? Where'd he go?"

Charles glanced at his empty hands, then at the gun case, its glass unshattered, the Samsaric Revolver within seemingly untouched and unused...*in preparation for next time?* The thought made Charles shudder.

"Back to the beginning, I guess?" Charles said.

Julie stepped cautiously out from the treeline and into the clearing. "What happened, again?" she asked.

Steve stood up. "I think Charley saved the day!" he said, patting his old friend on the back. "And I think we just acted like a couple of goddamned *extras*! Jules! Please tell me you've got a *cigarette*!"

Julie extracted a crumpled pack of Camels from her pocket. She held it up inquisitively to Charles.

"Sure," he said. "What the hell."

"SO...I THOUGHT THERE'D BE more fanfare, you know? Like a parade or something?"

Steve's assumption was reasonable, given the hefty gravity of what they'd just been through and accomplished. They sat in a tight circle on the ground before the vending machine as

Charles relayed the story of his encounter with the Laughing God and tried to relax.

"I don't trust it," Julie said. "It's too much like one of those movie endings. You know? Where if you throw enough fireworks and stuff in, the audience will just believe that the monster's been defeated, and all that?"

Charles nodded in agreement. "I'm with you there."

"No shit, right?" Steve added. "All of a sudden, the hero just somehow knows what to do, or whatever? I hate that bull-shit." He imitated the voices in his imagined movie: " 'The monster's here! Ah!' 'Oh! I just realized that the Power of Love will defeat it! Yay!' "

Charles laughed. "Pretty much."

"So are we supposed to just—what? Do we have school in the morning, or whatever?" Julie asked.

"I ain't doin' *shit* tomorrow!" Steve said. "'Cept hanging out at my fucking *store*! Shit! You guys know there's suppos-edly—I mean, Bax told me there's supposedly a *complete* collection of comic books. Not just 'a' comic book—*all* moth-erfucking comic books, dude!"

"We could head back to Port Mantle Mall from here," Charles said, pointing to the road out of the Enchanted Wood that he'd followed the first time he'd arrived there. "Grab some pizza at the Goblin Gang's place? See if they're back from their meditation retreat, or whatever?"

"I wonder if Harvey Lamb's place is closed," Julie said. "I guess if you really stopped the Laughing God, then Harvey's retired. Too bad. I wanted to look around a little more."

"Theoleucotomy," Charles said.

Julie looked confused. "What?"

"That's what it was. It was described in *Wild Lies II.* Yassiz removes parts of himself—usually the frontal lobe of his brain—and his *forgetfulness* thrusts him into another universe where he doesn't have to 'finish' his life. Inevitably, he regen-erates, so he does it over and over again, and the worlds just keep getting jumbled and overlapped while he bounces around, having fun and doing whatever deranged gods do."

"So he's just in another universe?" Julie asked.

"Well, not exactly," Charles said. "This time, Molly and Stek made use of some bad elves—those 'demented pixies,' or whatever—"

"Woah, yeah!" Steve interjected. "That's how Graxx got rid of the Silent Goblin Gang! In Roland's campaign."

"Right!" Charles said. "Right. The plan was embedded in Roland's game! The one you played way back when we were in the Place of Solace—it was just a *suggestion*, built into the game. Something about those fail-safe mechanisms built into these extra or add-on worlds kept Roland from being able to betray his own programming. But if he could get someone *else* to do the stuff—"

"Crack open a magic pipe, for example?" Steve suggested, laughing.

"Exactly," Charles said. "But after that—after everything went down, and Molly tried to escape the loop-world Yassiz stuck her in, well, Jim the Janitor caught her. Only Yassiz really knows how that was pulled off. And you guys remember what happened after. But there's a good chance that if he hadn't gotten greedy, if he'd just let Molly escape, then we'd have gotten eaten up along with everybody else in Golem Creek." Charles paused for a moment to light another cigarette. "After Molly and Stek both remembered who they were, they came up with a plan: the only way to deliver Yassiz to PyGoLiRo and keep him from fucking up everyone's storylines was to have him caught by something *crazier than he is*."

"The Demented Pixies," Steve said. "Groovy."

"Yeah," Charles continued. "And I guess they were able to come up with some agreement that would get Molly out of her contract and fix her and Stek's memory issues."

"Why did she make a deal with them in the first place?" Julie asked.

Charles shrugged. "That's where all the time-loop stuff goes crazy," he said. "Because she *was* Queen of Faery—but she just didn't know it. When she first evoked Yassiz, I mean. That was Marigold Silverki—the Witch Queen of Tulsa."

Steve laughed. "I don't know if that title *quite* has the right ring to it. But if she had amnesia that bad, it was probably like a Jim Buskey thing—you know, powers for favors? And PyGoLiRo realized what a fucking steal it was!"

Charles nodded. "Sure. Probably. Anyway, I guess the rest is, well, history."

"But there wasn't anything in *Wild Lies II* about what we're supposed to do *after* sending Yassiz on his way?" Julie asked.

Charles took a deep drag off his cigarette and shook his head.

"Back to Port Mantle?" Steve suggested. "Seems as good a plan as any. This card I grabbed from Harvey's Trick Deck sure doesn't give any clues." He held it up for them to see.

" 'How many cookies can one man eat?!? As many as he can find, with *this* card!' " Julie read off. "Ha. That's hilarious."

"Yeah," Charles added. "Super weird. Why would anyone even think of that?"

"The most disturbing thing about it is that it makes perfect sense to me," Steve said. "Speaking of which..." He stood up and rattled the knobs on the vending machine. "Does anybody have any change? Like, I don't know, fifty *goddamned* cents, or something?"

Charles shook his head again. "Nope."

"Oh, *wait* a second," Julie said. She stood up and pulled a small velvet bag out of her jeans pocket. "I chose a card from the 'Artifact Deck' before rolling the dice back at Lamb's. This was the magic item I got. Or whatever it is. Check it out."

Charles watched as Julie opened the bag and emptied its contents. Six grimy silver quarters fell into her palm.

"What's this?" Charles asked.

"Vending machine money, obviously!" Steve said, swiping two quarters out of Julie's hand.

"Steve! Seriously, dude?" Charles said.

"Actually," Julie said, handing Charles two of the quarters, "he might actually be on to something."

Steve laughed. He held one of the quarters poised over the coin slot and pored over the contents of the machine.

"I can't believe you're just *going along* with this, Julie," Charles said.

Julie shrugged. "It's because of what was written on the card that went with them."

"What did it say?"

" 'For brain food,' " she answered, and chuckled. "Anyway, I don't know what the hell else it could be for. And Steve's always the best guinea pig for these kinds of things."

"Damn straight," Steve said, at last shoving his quarters into the machine and slamming buttons under the coin slot with unnecessary violence. A whirring sound followed; Steve shouted in triumph.

"What'd you get?" Charles asked.

Steve pulled his hand free of the repository at the bottom of the machine and held aloft a Whatchamacallit bar. "These are probably the best candy bars in the world," he said, tearing open the package. "Especially if you dip them in frosting first." He took a bite, closed his eyes, and chewed quietly. "Just as I remember it. Perfection."

Charles and Julie watched Steve eat the entire bar.

"How do you feel?" Charles asked him.

Steve swallowed the last bite and tossed the wrapper aside. "Like a million bucks," he said. He hopped up and down a few times, dropped and did ten pushups, then shadowboxed brilliantly for a few moments. "Woah. Seriously. Like a million fucking dollars."

Charles looked at Julie. "You want to..."

"Sure," Julie said. "Why not?"

Julie selected Twix; Charles ended up getting a Butterfinger, which Steve attempted to wheedle him out of.

"Hell, no, dude," Charles told him as he tore it open. The bar was, in fact, exquisite.

As Charles and Julie indulged themselves, Steve proceeded to make flying leaps into the tree branches and execute flawless breakdance maneuvers.

"I've *always* wanted to be able to do that!" he admitted. "Electric fucking boogaloo, man!"

Julie's eyes practically bugged out of her head. "I feel—woah," she said. "Holy shit."

Charles made an honest attempt to force the smile off his

face—it was the loveliest failure of his career. "So, let's—ah, what? Let's race back to Port Mantle?"

Steve was off like a shot, followed quickly by a giggling Julie Evergreen.

Charles let them get a head start. He was pretty sure he was going to win.

HANKFULLY, NEITHER ADDIE NOR Tom landed with the expected "thud." There was no extraordinary snapping or cracking of bones; no smashing of internal organs; no unwanted shedding of large quantities of blood or other useful fluids.

Not at all! First of all, consider the *expense* of such an ending. And the cleanup. Not to mention the fact that I happen to *like* Addie Whitfield and Tom Fallow!

So when I tell you Addie blacked out while contemplating her fate—she assumed that she would be eaten by a humongous worm-like creature that became suddenly, terrifyingly visible in the midst of a swarm of clouds...and Tom had a similar scare, though his had more to do with a wild thought that occurred to him after becoming helplessly cast into the seas of probability that reign, temporospatially uncategorizable, between things like thoughts and possible perceptions—that thought being roughly equivalent to the overflowing of a boiling pot, as the incomprehensibility of *eternal flapping around among nothingness* became suddenly a nearly thinkable thing—I must also inform you that there was still some disembodied brain or other suffering from their distress as well, $exp\{10^{68}\}$ miles away.

ADDIE FOUND HERSELF IN a familiar place. A place of solace. Her bedroom at home. Still mostly her own territory, despite being an outsider in her own family. She flopped on her bed and allowed the moonlight from her bedroom window to wash over her. Beneath her pillow, right there within reach of her hand, was the weird little potion she'd conjured up using directions from Michael Flowers's notebook.

She had absolutely no idea if the thing would work at all. But after so many miniature successes since starting to actually use the material in the book, culminating in the manifestation last Halloween—and her mastery of the methods of Dream Control—there was every reason to believe that it would do something *quite miraculous*. Besides, she'd followed the directions *precisely*; she'd thought it was too much of a coincidence that the "appropriate astrological configurations" had occurred only three nights ago—and that tonight was, in fact, Walpurgisnacht, the night of the Monster Ball, the night when, along with the proper starry alignments, the "terrestrial dragon" would be in a receptive enough state to...

Well, that was just it. She didn't know *what* the hell it was supposed to do. But the final ingredient was, apparently, *her.*

...it is something of a test, to be sure; but a radical test, an Ordeal that will break the bonds of the World...it was inspired, so Curwen told me, by a method used by True Witches to avoid the stake, and worse fates...it can only be generated under the proper Constellations, these latter merely the Shadow of Those Other Stars, only a hint of the World to which the Blood-Heirs are Proper...

Yeah, it was typical Mike Flowers, all right. But he was still the only legitimate occultist Addie knew of; all those *Develop Your Psychic Powers!* books weren't worth the $3.95 she'd paid for them.

Flowers, though...

ADDIE FLED BY WAY of her bedroom window. The majority of the town's teenage population safely tucked in to the beginning of tomorrow's hangovers, Addie sprinted across the back lawn, then hopped onto an electrical box and over the fence separating their property from the stretch of forest forming a sort of "back lot" to Golem Creek.

Forty Winks itself was quiet tonight. All the rich kids were at the Monster Ball.

Addie headed for the makeshift log bridge over the

unnamed creek that some kids claimed was the origin of the city's name. Follow this creek on its eastern side through the forest and you'd find yourself in a little clearing which rose steadily to the grounds of the Flowers estate, the first home built to establish Golem Creek, generations ago. A large, misshapen hunk of granite marked the edge of the property—if you looked closely enough at what some people called its "head," you'd see a couple of glyphs:

מת

Supposedly, this "proved" that it had once been a living entity, that the א had been removed when its creator lost control of it, leaving it מת, or "dead." (At least, that's what Mike Flowers claimed. But Addie didn't read Hebrew.)

Back then it was sometimes called "The Black Manse." And there had always been a suspicion of diabolical magic employed here, as Laban was accused on numerous occasions of practicing witchcraft and even of being the infamous "Black Man" of traditional witch lore.

All of this merely fueled Addie's curiosity. When she had finally had the courage to investigate the place after no one seemed likely to return to it, she hadn't been disappointed.

She expected nothing less tonight.

A sort of clubhouse marked a more formal backyard behind the house. She'd glanced in the dirt-clogged windows on several occasions—it looked like a messy hideout for a metalhead. Besides, she determined that she wouldn't be able to get in without breaking a window or forcing the door; and since she'd already been able to jimmy the lock on one of the windows of the house proper, she'd left it alone.

Well, tonight was different. At first, the instructions were maddeningly obscure to her on this point: she was to consume the prepared potion *at the place where the spheres meet.* She had walked around the property as innocently and anonymously as possible dozens of times; had considered for no good reason that the spot referred to might be the Murk on Chicken Hill; and had practically given up before a revelation occurred.

After sitting by the stone "golem" at the edge of the Flowers property one quiet night, letting her mind relax, and *shifting awareness* as per Michael's instructions, she'd heard, quite clearly, a lone cricket chirping somewhere in the woods off to her right. The only thing unusual about the sound was that *she thought it was unusual.* She stood up and walked a distance away—a second cricket could be heard, chirping, this time off to her left...but the first cricket's "voice" was *gone.*

Moving right again, the first cricket's chirp appeared and, suspiciously, the second one's vanished.

The peculiarity became rather marked when she realized that there was a way to *step between the sounds*; there was, indeed, an invisible path marked out by the "spheres" of the respective crickets' chirpings, and it led precisely, exactly, *here*: the Brake Street clubhouse.

Black Sabbath. Mercyful Fate. Venom. The Misfits. Metallica. Slayer...the walls were covered with images torn from magazines. Oh, this one was funny: someone had put devil horns and fangs on Joni Mitchell from the cover of *Blue.* One corner remained immaculate, though: clearly an altar in the shape of a double cube, the Microcosm of Vitruvius inscribed on its top in gold (under several layers of dust, that is). On each of its sides, tables of letters from an alien alphabet, in precise combinations of color: orange and blue, red and green, black and white, purple and yellow.

The floor had a burn mark in it, as if someone had set off a perfectly symmetrical firework in its center. Addie stood there now, uncorked glass vial in one hand, listening, *listening*, and hearing a capitalized Nothing—*the Voice of the Silence.*

All the talk of portals had her—at this instant, when all she'd been thinking about for the last several months was *escape, escape, escape*—literally shaking, anxious with both desire and terror of knowing.

And it was almost too simple: all she had to do was put a few drops of her own blood into the mixture (the notebook had hinted that there were *very specific* types of blood for very specific purposes) and consume it.

Right place. Right time. Right drugs. This has been the formula for adventure throughout the history of the world.

She made a succinct gash in her left thumb using just the barest pressure from an old Red Devil boxknife with a brand-new razor in it. Didn't need tetanus on top of blood loss. Just because she was a powerful magician didn't mean she could afford to act like an idiot.

"Three drops" (very approximately) added to the mixture later, and she started to feel a little dizzy. Like a breeze was picking up...indeed, something was ruffling the torn posters on the walls, whirling about to presage a great reckoning in the little room between Kansas and Oz...

She closed her eyes and cleared her mind.

And right there, right after a last, straggling thought, she quaffed the potion.

THERE WAS A DIFFERENCE, though Tom Fallow didn't know it. He was perfectly happy, in fact. So happy that he'd almost forgotten this was what Harvey Lamb had promised him all along.

It's all right, for some people, he'd said when describing the Work of maintaining enchantments and "Anchor Cities" for places like Port Mantle. *It can be a little boring, maybe. But that takes a while. Maybe a few thousand years, by Earth-reckoning.*

The terror that he had met with on falling into the quantum soup within which Black's Pyramid had once floated dissipated like cotton candy on a tongue or worries after a winning lottery ticket. He hadn't come across the girl who called herself Addie Whitfield since...had that been months ago? Years, perhaps? He'd been so busy occupying himself with the endless novelty of Roland's—*his*, he had to keep reminding himself—newly configured "Dreamkeeper's Emporium" that he couldn't honestly say.

He supposed, if the sense of time had any real value to him, such concerns would return or make themselves obvious. Meanwhile, his job was pretty simple: *watch for leaks*. As given in the note he'd found tacked to the door of this place after shuffling in terror through mists that gradually, bit by bit, began looking and sounding and feeling like *places and things* again:

Dear Tom,

As promised, in thanks for your exceptional conduct throughout this Ordeal X [Tom wasn't quite sure what that meant, but he rolled with it], *you are hereunto granted the Honor and Privilege of Keeping Dreams. Enjoy the place! Learn its "ins and outs"! Find solace in the peace and quiet of the world you'd been wishing and waiting for! Meanwhile, your job in this particular Anchor City (feel free to change names, etc., as you like) is to keep an eye on our old friend, who has returned to his timeless sleep in the Pyramid. That should be easy enough, provided you maintain some degree of vigilance over the place and* watch for leaks!

Yours sincerely,

O.B.

P.S.: Until further notice, DO NOT attempt to unlock any apparent Gates leading Out, lest we undo all that we've done!

So it had worked, after all. Yassiz the Laughing God was (at least temporarily) in the hands of someone or something that could handle him—probably PyGoLiRo. Tom didn't particularly care. They'd saved Golem Creek—and who knew how many *other* worlds in the bargain. If this place—the "Place of Solace," according to graffiti left by "A Finnegan" at some time in its undiggable psychohistory—had returned, constantly creating and re-creating itself as it seemed to, that meant it was anchoring *something*.

That meant it was anchoring, at minimum, Golem Creek & Environs...

And other than that first note, there were no other communications...at least, for a while.

IT CERTAINLY *SEEMED* ACCIDENTAL, of course—he'd only intended to enjoy a movie and a light snack, but right then, right at the part where Ash decides that he's going to "stay and fight it out," the screen blipped and Nashe St.-Demp stared back at him from his usual booth at Rex Dagger's.

Tom was ecstatic. *They figured it out...!* He hadn't noticed the terrible sensation of loneliness creeping into him until its disappearance suddenly made itself plain.

"Are you guys—I mean, can you—"

Nashe squints at the screen, distinguishes quickly between where you are right now and the mini-theatre at the Dream-keeper's Emporium, and smiles.

"A-*ha*! It worked!" he exclaims. "Phase one *complete*! On schedule for full transfictional teleportation!" He rubs his hands together eagerly. "So, Tom, how ya been?"

And Tom, feeling hopeful for the first time in a long while, tells him.

EPILOGUE

SOLVE & COAGULA

IN THE THÉÂTRE D'AZIF, Wise Nerds took a huge bite of his three-cheese-and-avocado sub.

"I don't even *remember* the last time I ate *actual food*," Harvey Lamb said, gazing breathlessly at the spread of french fries, hamburgers, hot dogs, meatball subs, etc., etc., on the huge dining table around which they sat, waiting for the movie to start.

Wise nodded in understanding, chewing happily.

"They've made use of the vending machine," Roland said as he floated into the room, a soft glow of purplish radiance emanating etheric winds of joyous energy. "Doesn't that mean...?"

Wise set down his gigantic sub and fished around in his pockets. He withdrew a small remote control and hit a button on it. "Any minute now," he said as the lights dimmed.

Harvey held a single french fry between his thumb and index finger and gazed at it thoughtfully.

"There's only one way to find out," Roland said to him encouragingly.

Harvey grinned. "It wasn't too late, after all," he said.

Wise held up a bottle of Vanilla Coke. "I'd like to propose a toast," he announced.

Harvey seemed relieved to set the french fry down and lift his glass of Château Lafite. *Start with the small and achieve the great*, he thought, chuckling to himself.

Roland held his hands a few inches apart. A test tube of bright green liquid gradually coalesced between them.

"Andromedan Nectar," he explained to the admiring faces of his friends. "Very clarifying and possibly the only substance in the universe that can briefly intoxicate me."

They held their respective drinks together.

"To fine, complicated solutions in this fine, complicated multiverse," Wise said. "And to artificial intelligences such as our own, and those of our friends—Charles Leland, Stephanos Chernowski, Julie Evergreen, and *you*"—he nods to you—"for assisting this particular world in allowing for more novel computations and fewer dead-end algorithms."

Wise and Harvey clinked glasses; Roland's Nectar glowed slightly brighter for a moment; they all drank to our happily ever afters.

Harvey Lamb reached for a french fry, and the movie started.

"SO IT GOES LIKE this," Nashe St.-Demp starts, sitting in his usual booth at Rex Dagger's Pub & Grill and turning to regard you. "Charles did end up winning the race back to Port Mantle, but only because Steve took a brief detour to investigate Brodley's Retreat Area for Aged Dragons (you know the one—where that crazy red dragon still insists he's the 'Smaug' of Tolkien's story?) and Julie decided at the last minute to be nice and let him. They ended up at Intergalactic Pizza, where an ecstatic group of ex-monster hunters—Booker, Barton, Staley, and Fitz—heaped praise and pizza upon them for successful completion of their quest."

He waves to Rex, using the hand signal that means "*Vieille Provision Saison Dupont* in a Chimay glass."

"That's where Julie Evergreen met Atalanta Whitfield for the first time. Addie, you see, had been teleported via Quark Milk (that's what she drank at the portal site in the Bhairavi Society clubhouse) to her new digs—once known as 'Lamb's Occult Supply Shop,' which has a great ring to it—it's now known as Evergreen & Whitfield's One-Stop Spell Shop."

Harvey's joy at tasting his first meatball sub
is only matched by his relief at the news.

"The two of them are presently having one hell of a time trying to balance their degree plans at Three Coils Academy (where Julie's witch blood would *never* have gone unnoticed for long) and the extraordinary demands of running one of the most famous magical supply stores with an annex in Port Mantle Shopping Mall."

Rex sets a foaming glass of ale in front of Nashe, who nods gratefully.

"Steve Chernowski decided to accept a challenge posed to him by his sole employee, Bax Laird, during one pleasant, snowy night spent drinking and trading stories on the roof of Sector 4F6 at the Endless Warehouse. He has managed to iron out most of the kinks in his current model of 'flying sleigh,' but has yet to find a bright-enough-nosed Rudolph to lead it during a proposed annual tour of several Earths with a holiday tradition of receiving gifts from 'Santa Claus.' Work on his beard and belly has, however, proceeded splendidly.

"And Charles! My old buddy Chuck Leland let Booker convince him to go on one of their Himalayan retreats, where he mastered *shamatha* and *tummo* and all that while learning an alien martial art (called 'Gatha' in its closest human equivalent). At present he practices Gatha and studies the Trapezoid Manuals in preparation for a Grand Quest to the Tower of Koth for instruction in several of the weirder—and definitely more interesting—arts of dreaming.

"None of the members of 'Fear Club' have visited the latest recension of Golem Creek to date. But who knows what will happen? Things change.

"As for Tom Fallow—ah, well, Roland knows damned well how he's doing! In fact—"

Nashe lifts a shapeless sack from the seat beside him and sets it on the table. He rummages about in it.

"Yes! Here." He pulls a copy of the *Multiworld Monitor* from his bag and flips through a few pages. "Here it is!" He holds up an advertisement for—

"*Fallow's Encyclopedic History of Overlap Worlds—With Complete Port Mantle Index*?" Pam "The Rat" Stoyanova reads off as she slides into her usual spot across from Nashe. "Sounds great.

Oh, wait, I chose the wrong word there. I meant: sounds *stupid*."

Nashe crinkles up the paper and tosses it aside. "You'd know, wouldn't you, dear? All about *stupid*, right?" He laughs and takes a long gulp of his ale, all the while maintaining eye contact with her.

"Watch it, old man," she says. "One of these days, I might let them in on a few of your little secrets. Like how hard you cried when Random House rejected *Brain of the Dead Werewolf*."

Nashe slams a fist down on the table.

Pam giggles. "Oops! Did I say that out loud?"

"I swear, Ms. Stoyanova. I will *rewrite* you one day! I will— I'll—*remove all your assets*!"

Pam doubles over with laughter. "Yeah, right! And then who's gonna come have drinks with you? All your *friends*?" She makes a grandiose gesture indicating the viewers in the Théâtre d'Azif.

"Maybe!" Nashe shouts. "Maybe!" He sniffles, then blows his nose into a crumpled napkin.

"What's up, Nashe?" she asks. "You look like you're—"

"Nothing! It's nothing," he responds, wiping tears out of his eyes. "It's just that—you know, I get like this sometimes. When I'm at the end of a story."

Pam holds back a snide comment as she notices how few pages are left in the book you're holding.

"Aw, shucks," she says, and reaches over to pat his hand. "Don't—ah, don't do that."

Nashe looks up at her with tear-filled eyes. "Really?"

"Really," she says. "I mean—ah, how about we just try to be nice for a minute. You know. For them?" She points to you.

Nashe nods and grins. "The usual, then?"

Pam smiles back at him. "The usual."

Nashe signals Rex for Pam's usual—a "Lovely Tourniquet" with a twist of lime.

When he thinks about you—when he really starts to consider that this whole show is nothing but a dream within a dream without end—and starts to get a little skeptical about whether or not you really *did* wake up this morning, he thinks about how you're reading this with the firm conviction that it'll be set aside in a few moments and the story will end.

It makes him wonder about how things really are in the greater scheme of all our interwoven stories; does he continue past this page, past even your thoughts about him? Maybe.

Since all awakenings are false awakenings, I suppose we could say at least that much.

Maybe.

समाहितायां सति चित्तवृत्तौ परात्मनि ब्रह्माणि निर्विकल्पे |
न दृश्यते कश्चिदयं विकल्पः प्रजल्पमात्रः परिशिष्यते ततः ||

— विवेकचूडामणि

DAMIAN STEPHENS is the critically acclaimed author (that is, there are claims that he is critiqued, some-where) of numerous novels, short stories, and works of nonfiction, most written under various assumed names to protect the identities of their informing intelligences. He has died exactly once since beginning the "Means of Escape" series (collect them all!) and found the experi-ence both unnerving and lovely. He would recommend that you yourself try it, but realizes nothing he says could possibly make a difference when the gods have no choice but to play dice with all their universes.

(Even then, it's still just a big question mark, isn't it?)